MAX glanced quickly over the luggage, and then toward the crowd. When he was sure nobody was looking, he unzipped the duffel and wedged himself inside. It was tight, but Max liked tight spaces.

As he began zipping it shut, he peered out at Alex. Her hands were shaking as she lowered the trunk's top over her head. "Are we sure we want to do this?" she hissed.

Max had been asking himself that question the whole trip. Whenever the word *no* popped into his head, he pictured his mom. And the *no* turned to *yes*.

This was their only chance. Grabbing the inner handle of the two-sided zipper, he carefully pulled it shut. "See you on board," he whispered.

"Or in jail," Alex hissed.

FIRE THE DEPTHS

PETER LERANGIS

HARPER

An Imprint of HarperCollinsPublishers

Library of Congress Control Number: 2017943442
ISBN 978-0-06-244101-0

Typography by Andrea Vandergrift
18 19 20 21 22 CG/BRR 10 9 8 7 6 5 4 3 2 1
❖
First paperback edition, 2018

In Memory of George Nicholson
The Colossus of Agents
Whose Influence Is in Everything I Write

"WE ARE ALL, IN ONE WAY OR ANOTHER,
THE CHILDREN OF JULES VERNE."

—RAY BRADBURY

PROLOGUE

BEFORE the day he was abandoned, Max Tilt thought life was pretty much perfect. He had put claws on his drone, had memorized every Cincinnati Reds batting average to 1968, and hadn't smelled fish in thirteen days. Thirteen days ago someone had wedgied him in school, and for some reason unknown to modern science, Max smelled fish when he was scared.

But everything changed on that June morning when Max first tested his drone. His bedroom was perfectly neat, his toilet was perfectly clean, and his parents were perfectly unaware that they were about to be attacked.

All he meant to do was surprise them—make his drone grab a napkin or spoon or cereal box off the breakfast table. The drone in question was named Vulturon, and it had been tricked out with decals to make it look like a deadly tarantula. Using his remote, Max could make the machine swoop, grab and store things up to ten pounds, and scream "cowabunga." This was not something tarantulas normally said—or, for that matter, drones—but that was exactly why he liked it.

As he powered up Vulturon, Max could hear his mom and dad in the kitchen downstairs. Dad was doing most of the talking, as usual. Mom had become very quiet, ever since she'd decided to take a semester off from teaching. She'd been sleeping a lot too. Which was weird, because she had always had so much energy. She and Max had once taken a whole weekend to paint a humongous rainbow across his ceiling. Then they protected it with three flying dinosaurs built from model kits—a red rhamphorhynchus, a feathered archaeopteryx, and a leathery pteranodon. The rainbow was labeled with the words Every Spectrum Is a Rainbow. Max thought of this whenever anyone said he was "on the spectrum." This had something to do with his neatness, his love of facts, and the way he was with people. He used to think "on the spectrum" meant something like "broken," but you couldn't break rainbows. Rainbows were beautiful and perfect. So the painting made him feel good whenever he looked at it.

Which occurred about a thousand times a day now.

He pointed the remote. As Vulturon lifted off his desk, its four rotors whirred quietly, and a stack of homework papers blew onto the floor. Pressing Hover, Max quickly replaced them, making sure to square the corners before he went back to his mission.

The drone left his bedroom, and Max followed it out the door to the second-floor landing. Over the banister he could see the big living room below, where papers were stacked on every chair and sofa. Dad liked to say that he and Mom were on the infrared end of the tidiness spectrum, and Max was on the ultraviolet. This meant, according to Dad, that Max was neat and they were slobs. That was a fact, and Max loved facts. Even though (1) he hated disorder and (2) he was not truly ultraviolet.

Down. Left.

Vulturon swooped under the stairs and out of Max's sight. As it darted into the kitchen, Dad's voice stopped. The toaster dinged. Vulturon said "cowabunga."

And Mom screamed at the top of her lungs.

Max was so shocked he nearly fell down the stairs. Mom never screamed like that. She was a writer. She had written a murder mystery. She *liked* pranks and surprises.

But as Dad stormed into the foyer and looked up the

staircase toward Max, his mother was still in the kitchen, sobbing.

Max realized he'd done something really wrong, but he wasn't sure what. He thought his dad would yell. But he didn't. He said, in a stern but oddly quiet voice, "Maximilian, please come into the kitchen. We have something to discuss."

Dad never called him Maximilian. Even though it was technically his name.

As Max descended, the smell of fish was so strong, he felt like he was walking into the ocean.

1

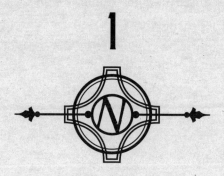

"FIX," said the man behind the desk.

That was it. No hello, no welcome, no offer of a drink or snack or even a hand to shake. Not even the decency to look up.

Spencer Niemand wouldn't dignify that rudeness with an answer. Under most circumstances, people begged him for attention. Under most circumstances, he did not leave his office on his own at the beckoning of a thief. Even a wealthy one like the fat man behind the desk.

But this was not most circumstances.

Dealing with stolen goods in the black market was not for cowards. And Spencer Niemand was no coward.

"What kind of name is that—*Fix*?" the man said after a long pause. He looked up finally. Even in the dark warehouse, he wore sunglasses. He was flanked by two other men, whose scarred faces and enormous shoulders hinted at long hours in the prison exercise yard.

"A fake one," said Spencer Niemand.

"We don't deal in fakes here," the man replied. He pushed a thick, padded envelope across a black table toward Niemand.

As Niemand reached down to the envelope, one of the henchmen grabbed his wrist.

Niemand spun loose, drew a knife from his pocket, and slammed it downward. As the man yanked his hand back, the blade sank into the tabletop. "I only miss on purpose," Niemand said. "Count yourself lucky."

As the two men reached for their guns, their boss held up his hand to stop them. "My men speak in only one language, Fix. It involves action, not words. I will translate. What they mean to say is, you can look inside the envelope, but we need the money first."

Greedy.

Despicable.

Niemand couldn't help but sneer at this creature. He pulled a wad of bills from his pocket and plopped it on the table. "To you, it's all about the money."

"What else is there?" the fat man said as he counted the bills.

"Life," Niemand said. "The survival of the planet."

The fat man threw his head back with laughter. The two henchmen looked at each other uncertainly, then laughed also.

Niemand grabbed the envelope with his right hand. He kept his left in his pocket. No need for anyone to see the missing pinkie finger. It just might give him away. Dear old Kissums, lost in an accident, whose plaster likeness hung from a silver chain around his neck. He wouldn't let them see that either.

Turning the envelope upside-down, he shook out the contents on the table.

A boarding ticket for the *Titanic*, with the name Hetzel. A crumbling sheet of paper with a list of passengers, written in English. A leather-bound copy of a book with the title *Vingt Mille Lieues Sous Les Mers*. And a bunch of notes written in French.

Although Niemand did not like to smile, his lips traced a slight upward angle. This could be what he'd been looking for. He cursed the fact that he'd never learned the language well enough to read this. That would be the domain of his people. His trusted translators.

"The notes," said the fat man, "are very interesting, you'll find."

Niemand felt his heart skip. "You've read them?"

The fat man chuckled. "I'm not as dumb as I look. *Je parle*, you know. That means I speak Fren— "

"I know what it means," Niemand snapped. "But you assured me the material had never been read by anyone."

"Just me," the fat man replied, then gestured to his henchmen. "Not these two. They don't even read English. They were absent the day they did the alphabet in first grade."

"Wrong," said the one on the left. "I had perfect intendance."

Niemand felt his eyes twitch. He gathered the material, nodded as cordially as he could, and turned to leave.

"Don't let the door hit your butt on the way out," the fat man yelled after him.

His henchmen let out a dopey burst of laughter that sounded to Niemand like donkeys braying.

Their ignorance and rudeness had a benefit. It would make it much easier to do what he had to do next.

After all, a secret must remain a secret.

Niemand pushed open the warehouse door with his right hand. Reaching into his pocket with his left, he pulled out a soft green substance with the consistency of Play-Doh. He pressed a tiny sensor into its center until it stuck, then fluffed out the three wires attached to it.

For something so small, it still seemed inconceivable to Niemand that this thing had the power to take out a castle. Of course, it had to be properly activated.

And Niemand was all about proper activation.

He pasted it to the wall under the light switch, his four-fingered hand in full view. No need to worry now.

Stepping out of the warehouse, he locked the door shut behind him.

One . . . two . . . three . . . Niemand counted to himself, now jogging toward his waiting limo. He was beginning to feel hungry.

On *four*, he heard sudden shouting and frantic footsteps from inside the building. They finally realized. Good. Let them know there was no escape.

On *five*, he reached into his pocket and pressed the detonator.

On *six*, as his driver, Rudolph, gunned the limo toward the entrance to the Pacific Coast Highway toward San Francisco, Niemand was already thinking of dinner.

On *seven,* the warehouse exploded.

As he glanced into the rearview mirror, fire plumed upward from where the building once stood. Niemand grinned.

Barbecue, he thought, *might be nice tonight.*

"WE won't be away long, Max," his dad was saying.

"Just a few tests," his mom added.

"Nothing to worry about."

"We'll be back before you know it."

Fish. Fishier. Fishy McFishface.

"I dode believe you," Max said.

"Please, honey, don't hold your nose like that. It's hard to understand you." Mom reached out to touch Max's arm, but he pulled it backward. "We're not lying."

"You bust be," Max said. "Or there would dot be that fish sbell."

"You've noticed that Mom hasn't been feeling well, right?" Dad asked.

"Mbob had cadcer," Max said. "But she was treated.

The cadcer cells were all killed. Killed! They were godd! So she got better. Those are the facts. And facts dote chaidge."

"Yes," Mom said. "But people change. Bodies change. The doctors think there may be something else wrong. Something new."

Max nodded. "I udderstadd. But if it's dothing to worry about, you could have tests here in Savile, right? Dot at the Bayo Clinic in Biddesota. They specialize in serious bedical codditions. So that beads you have subthing serious, and there *is* subthing to worry about. Are you godda die?"

Mom and Dad both cringed. Mom's eyes began to well up with tears. Her hair was dark brown and silky and usually pulled back into a ponytail, but now it was unruly and matted as it fell in front of her face. Dad put his arm around her. His forehead glistened like he'd been sweating a lot, but the thing Max noticed most was that Dad's hair seemed to have turned mostly gray overnight. Even though he'd read that that kind of thing did not happen. That was a fact.

Max immediately felt bad. He unpinched his nose and let his fingers drop to his knees. He would have to get used to the smell, that's all.

"Thank you," his mom said. "The doctors here aren't

equipped. It's something rare. It could be easily treatable." She took a deep breath. "Or not."

"Michele . . ." Max's dad said.

"We owe him the truth," Mom replied. "Look, Max, we don't want you to be upset, that's all—"

"Why can't I come with you to the Mayo Clinic?" Max asked.

"It would be disruptive," Dad said. "Aren't you planning to bring Vulturon to school?"

"I don't care about that," Max said. "There are only a few weeks of school left. Nobody learns anything in the last few weeks. I love you."

Max looked at his mom. She opened her arms, which meant she wanted to hug him. He ran into them and let her do it. She was crying now. He was too.

"I'm not ready to be left without a mom and dad," Max murmured.

"I know . . . it's not fair . . ." she said softly. "George?"

"We can't be sure how long we'll be there," Dad said. "We've already arranged for someone to take care of you. Someone you'll like."

"Ms. Dedrick smells like tangerines," Max said, running down the list of his babysitters. "Jenna won't stop looking at her phone. Sam doesn't get any jokes—"

"It's none of them," Mom said. "It's someone closer

to your age. Your cousin Alex from Canada—"

"Who?" Max said, pulling back from his mom's arms.

Dad looked at Mom awkwardly.

"You remember her, right?" Mom said. "From Quebec City? They lived here in Ohio for three years, and she used to play with you when you were little? She's very patient—"

"No," Max said. "No and no."

"You mean, no, you don't remember her?" Dad asked.

"No, you can't do this," Max said. "You can't leave me. I can't stay with a stranger. You can't do this to me!"

"She's not a stranger!" Dad said.

No no no no no no no.

Max put his hands to his ears. He ran out of the kitchen and across the living room. At the front door, he kicked the huge wicker basket where Mom and Dad put all the mail. Letters went flying across the room.

Mom and Dad were running after him, but he had to get out of there. Run away. Go somewhere.

Smriti.

That's who he needed to talk to. Smriti was his best friend. She always knew what to say.

He could hear himself moaning. Moaning was never

good. He yanked open the front door. It was pouring outside, but he didn't care.

His dad was calling his name.

No no no no no no no.

Max barreled into the street toward Smriti's house. She must have known something was up, because she was on the porch already, looking toward his house. But her eyes were wide, her palms facing him, her voice also screaming "No!"

Max heard a screeching noise to his left. Through the sheet of rain, two car headlights bore down on him like reptile eyes.

3

A HORN blared. A blur of metal glistened silver white. Max's brain blanked, and his legs sprang back. He hurtled through the air, smashing down on the curb and back somersaulting onto the sidewalk.

In the street, a battered Kia sedan screeched to a stop, and the driver's door flew open. A young woman jumped out. She had dark skin and a mass of thick, pulled-back hair. Her eyes were large, green, and angry. *"Are you . . . ?"* she sputtered. *"Are you . . . ?"*

"Don't worry," Max said, catching his breath. "I'm okay."

". . . out of your mind?" she screamed.

Max stood. His back ached. "Are you angry at me or scared?" he asked.

"Why did you jump into the—?" The girl cocked her head. "Wait. What?"

"I have trouble telling the two apart sometimes," Max said. "Angry and scared. They kind of look the same."

He didn't have time to hear the answer. Smriti had run across the street, and now she was jumping on him with a big, squealy hug. His parents were behind him too, asking questions, wrapping him in their arms.

"My baby my baby my baby . . ." Mom was repeating over and over.

"I'm not a baby. I'm going to be fourteen in three months," Max said.

"Max, how many times have we gone over the rules of the road?" Dad chimed in. "You look both ways!"

"I'm just glad you're okay," said Smriti.

This was a lot of hugging. Too much. Max was glad he was okay too. But he was short of breath. And this was a terrible day to begin with. He felt smothered, and smothering smelled to him like . . .

"Sweaty feet!" he said. *"Sweaty feet!"*

Max pushed at them, inhaling the rain-drenched air. *Fresh air. Deep breaths . . .*

Smriti backed away. "Sorry."

"OK, honey," said Mom, letting go.

"Sweaty feet?" said the driver with the thick hair.

"Max has associative smells," Mom said. "A form of something called synesthesia—where one sense substitutes for another?"

"I have it a little too," Smriti quickly chimed in. "Like, the smell of transparent tape gets me in a good mood because it reminds me of the holidays. Right?"

"Uh . . ." the driver said.

Max looked at his watch and realized he would be late for school if he didn't leave immediately. "Can I go now?" he said.

"Don't forget your drone," his dad replied.

"Vulturon!" Smriti exclaimed.

Max smiled. "It is finished."

As he turned to the house, Mom called out, "Wait! Are we forgetting our manners?"

Max turned back. Mom had taken the hand of the driver, who was staring at all of them as if they were strange microscopic specimens.

"This," Mom said with a smile, "is your cousin Alex."

Max's jaw dropped open. The person who had almost killed him was about to become his guardian.

"You guys," Alex said, "are the weirdest family I've ever seen."

* * *

The ride to school would have been better if the Kia hadn't had a hole in the passenger floor, which scared Max. Smriti sat in the back. Max sat in the passenger seat, clutching his knees, with his feet raised up high.

"It's not that big of a hole," Alex said. "You won't fall through. Well, no one has, yet."

She let out a laugh. Max didn't, because in his opinion this was not funny.

"Listen, I'm really sorry," Alex said. "Using the word *weird*. Weird can be good, right? And actually I was kind of referring to our whole family. Including our part of it, the Canadians. The Vernes. We're all weird in our own way."

Max tucked his feet under him on the seat. "We don't look alike," he said.

Alex sighed. "My dad is Caucasian—"

"Mine is Dominican," Max said. "Tilt is short for Trujillo, but my grandfather didn't like that name, so he shortened it. Smriti is Nepalese."

"Nepali," Smriti corrected from the backseat.

"—And my mom is African-American," Alex said. "In case you meant, you know . . ." Her voice drifted off.

"I know what?" Max said.

"In case you meant that we didn't look like each other

because of our skin," Alex said.

"I didn't," Max said. "I was saying we don't look alike because we don't look alike."

Alex smiled. "Fair enough."

"In the spring, yes," Max said. "I'm less fair in the summer."

"Ha!" Alex barked. "I am beginning to sorta like this kid. Almost."

As the car turned onto the school block, Max watched the windshield wipers. Smriti and Alex were both laughing. He wasn't sure why, but it was a friendly laugh, so it made him feel relaxed.

Alex was telling Smriti about herself now. She was supposed to be in college, but she wanted to take time off. Something about wanting to write a novel.

"If you want to write a novel, why are you babysitting me?" Max asked.

"Because I need someone to help me fix the hole in my car," Alex said. "No, just kidding."

"I knew that," Max said. "I have a good sense of humor. I like pranks. But I'm not good with sarcasm. So what's the real answer?"

"I tried to be a waiter to support my writing habit and earn money for college," Alex said. "But I'm too emotional. I'm not that great with people."

"Really? You seem very nice," Smriti said.

"I am supernice," Alex answered, "unless you say things like, 'Didn't you hear me say I wanted another lemon, girl? I don't have all day.' In which case I say, 'Well, I *do* have all day. So get it yourself.' Only with a few four-letter words thrown in. And I get fired—a lot. So . . . when your dad called my mom to tell her what was up, they figured I could use a place to crash and you could use some help, and—voilà! Here I am in Savile, Ohio, helping my aunt and uncle. With this lovable, kooky kid who likes pranks and drones."

"I can give you ideas for your book," Max said. "If it's action adventure, use Vulturon in the plot. He can snatch a secret weapon from the jaws of an evil ichthyosaurus in the Sargasso Sea."

"That's another thing Max likes—prehistoric animals," Smriti explained. "He has a collection."

"I'm more of a sci-fi writer," Alex said, as she slowed down behind a yellow bus that was turning into the school driveway. "It runs in the Verne family."

"Your parents are writers?" Smriti asked. "That is so cool!"

Alex shook her head. "My great-great-great-uncle on my dad's side. Who was also Max's great-great-great-grandfather on his mom's side. He was famous."

"Wait . . . you said your name is what?" Smriti said.

"Alex Verne."

"Verne as in *Jules Verne*?" Smriti nearly screamed.

"You know who that is?" Alex said.

"He wrote *Twenty Thousand Leagues Under the Sea*," Smriti replied. *"Journey to the Center of the Earth . . ."*

"*Oui*, mademoiselle," Alex said. "Max's mom is Michele Verne Tilt."

"Max, you're related to a celebrity writer and you never told me?" Smriti said.

Max shrugged. "He's not a celebrity. He's dead. Celebrities are alive. Anyway, it never came up in conversation."

"Jules Verne . . ." Smriti said. "I think I am going to faint."

"Don't faint," Max said. "The bell's going to ring in two minutes."

As Alex pulled the car to the front of the school, Max gazed out at dozens of kids clustered by the school's front lawn. They included the Fearsome Foursome, a group of boys from gym class. They hadn't been too bad since the wedgie incident thirteen days ago, but even the sight of them gave Max a faint whiff of flounder. "Go as far away from those boys as possible," Smriti said to Alex.

The car sputtered to a stop with a wheezing sound, a

bit farther down the driveway. Max unfolded his legs and let his feet drop on either side of the hole in the floor. "Thanks for the ride."

Alex was looking at him oddly. "Do you always wear shorts to school on a day that's rainy and cold?"

"Sometimes," Max said. "I hate the feeling of long pants."

As he and Smriti stepped out, Max made sure to grab on to Vulturon.

"Where'd you get the limo?" a voice called out from near the lawn.

"Nice legs!" another shouted.

"What the—?" Alex sputtered.

Smriti's expression tightened. "Ignore them."

"Those aren't legs, they're too skinny!" the first voice said. "They're stilts. One . . . two . . . three . . ."

The entire group shouted, *"Tilt the Stilt!"*

Alex was out of the car, walking toward them. "Any of you guys work for Comedy Central? I didn't think so. Because your jokes are brain-dead."

Dugan Dempsey, the tallest and dumbest of the Foursome, bounded over to Max. Ignoring Alex, he swiped Max's lunch bag. "What are we eating today?"

"I smell fish," Max said.

The boys howled. Alex stepped closer to them.

"Don't, Alex . . ." Smriti warned.

Max held out his arm to prevent Alex from getting nearer. He did not want her to get involved. Not while he was forming another plan. "Seriously. Don't."

The guys walked away toward the front door, laughing and giving each other high fives.

Max placed Vulturon on the sidewalk, grabbed his remote, and powered up.

Smriti knew just what he was thinking. With a knowing smile, she took a huge apple from her lunch bag. "I don't need to eat this."

Max grabbed the apple and placed it into a small holding bay on the underside of Vulturon. Then he pressed Lift.

Vulturon rose upward, making a barely audible whirring noise. It swung through the air, about twenty feet off the ground.

As it hovered just over the heads of the Fearsome Four, Max pressed Release.

The apple conked Dugan in the head. As he screamed and jumped aside, Max guided Vulturon downward, where Claw #3 grabbed on to his lunch bag.

The drone lifted upward, his insulated plastic bag swinging freely. Every kid on the lawn was looking at it.

As Vulturon returned the lunch into his hand, Max said, "Thank you, Vulturon."

A wave of cheering went up across the lawn.

"Woo-hoo!" Smriti shouted.

Max tucked Vulturon under his arm and turned to Alex, just as the school bell rang. "See you after school?" he asked.

Alex didn't answer. Her jaw was hanging open.

4

"**THESE** are a lot of words." Alex slapped a pile of papers down onto the living room sofa.

"My mom and dad's caregiver instructions?" Max said. "Don't worry, I memorized them."

"I'm not worried about anything. We are going to have an awesome time!" Alex stood up from the sofa, knocking over a pile of papers propped up on the armrest. The place was kind of a mess. Just to sit, she'd had to move a pile of old magazines. Max was on his knees, leaning over the back of a chair at the other side of the room, looking outside the window. They'd already said good-bye to Mr. and Mrs. Tilt. Max's parents were in their old Toyota Sienna now, still in the driveway, chatting with Smriti's parents in the rain.

One of the living room windowpanes was cracked and patched up with yellowing clear tape. Just below it, a big, dark rainwater stain had grown on the carpet. As Alex stepped on the edge of it, she let out a little gasp.

"Sorry," Max said. "Dad has been meaning to fix that. And clean up the mess."

"I don't mind." Alex stood next to him by the chair. "Messes are refreshing. Real. My parents' house is super-perfect. Superneat. Everything matches. I feel like I can't touch anything."

"I would like that," Max said. "Not the part about not touching anything. But the neatness."

Alex nodded, then grabbed from the coffee table a half-eaten chocolate bar that was starting to turn white. "Almost forgot. I got this out of the fridge. There wasn't much else in there. Do you think it's edible?"

"The white is oxidation," Max said. "It doesn't affect the chocolate taste."

Alex smiled. "What? How do you know that, little guy?"

"I like facts. And I'm not hungry. Or little. I'm in the thirty-ninth percentile in height." His eyes never once moved from his parents.

"Worried, huh?"

Max nodded.

"Yeah, I don't blame you," Alex said.

The minivan made a scraping noise as it rolled over the lip of the driveway. Mom waved to him out of the passenger window, and Max waved back. As the car backed into the street and then straightened out, Max could hear the dull clanking of gears.

With a cloud of gray smoke, the Sienna pulled away down the street, letting out a couple of farewell honks.

"Bye, Mom! Bye, Dad! Bye, Toby!" Max cried out.

"Toby?" Alex said.

"Our car," Max explained. "It has almost two hundred thousand miles."

"Wowzer," Alex said.

"We were going to buy a new one," Max said. "Then Mom got sick the first time. She had to leave her job. Dad kind of stopped working too, to take care of her. He's a lawyer—but the kind that works out of a home office. So he hasn't taken new clients."

"Bummer," Alex said.

"Bummer," Max agreed, slumping down into the seat. Toby was nearly out of sight now. And a new smell was creeping into his nostrils, something acrid and sour and sad, like a skunk.

Alex drummed her fingers on her knees. She looked uncomfortable.

Finally she slapped her hands on her thighs. "Hey, no gloom and doom allowed, right? We have things to do! I'll start tackling the caregiver list, you do your homework, and in a couple of hours we'll break for dinner! You do have homework, right?"

Max nodded. "One hour. I'll be hungry then."

As he stood and began walking out of the living room, Alex began scanning the list. When Max reached the stairs, he heard her crying out: "Whoa . . . May 5 . . . April 23 . . . March 17 . . . what's up with this? Some of this mail goes back to last year!"

He turned and walked back. She was elbow-deep in the wicker basket. The mail, which Max had kicked all over the living room, had been dumped back inside the basket. Normally it was a place Max was not allowed to touch.

"Why are you doing that?" Max said. "It's not your mail. The instructions are all about not touching me, not touching my stuff, letting me have my routine . . ."

"Someone has to do this, cousin."

Alex began spreading the mail on the floor. Her face was nearly white. Many of them had red messages stamped on the front: PAST DUE . . . FINAL NOTICE . . . HAVE YOU FORGOTTEN US? . . . COLLECTION AGENCY . . .

"So . . . I'm sure . . . this is some kind of misunder-standing . . ." Alex said in barely audible voice. She was ripping envelopes open now, pulling sheets out, reading them. "The electric company says they're going to shut off electricity . . . um, yesterday?"

"But they didn't," Max said.

"Right . . . right . . ." Alex nodded. "So maybe it's just a threat . . ."

"Mom and Dad argue about bills a lot."

"They owe money," Alex said. "To a lot of people. Did they never talk about this?"

"They do—but to each other, not to me," Max replied. "Dad is always saying it will all work out. He's always making phone calls. He told Mom not to worry, he was going to start pulling in some big clients."

"He said that before she got sick again?" Alex asked. Max nodded.

"And then things kind of fell apart?"

"Yeah."

Alex let out a big exhalation. She was staring at an envelope now, her eyes wide. Max scrambled around to look at it right-side up.

It was from a company called Savile Bank. And in great big diagonal letters across the front, it said FORECLOSURE NOTICE.

"That's bad, right?" Max said.

Alex ripped open the envelope and read the letter inside. "Oh, boy. Oh, dear Lord . . ."

"We're being kicked out of the house?" Max asked.

"Bingo," his cousin replied. "In three weeks."

5

"THREE *weeks?* Max looked closely at his cousin. It was hard to tell if she was joking. He was hoping this was one of those times. "Ha-ha."

"Look at me," she said. "This is not my joking face."

"But—that's impossible," Max said.

Alex began pacing. "You would think so, right? This is crazy. I'm not—I didn't—*how could they do this?*"

"What do we do?" Max said.

"Call your parents, I guess."

Max imagined himself calling his dad. If he did that, his mom would find out. If she knew the truth, it would upset her. If it upset her, she'd get even more sick. If she got more sick . . .

"No, we can't do that," Max declared.

"We have to," Alex said.

"No." Max shook his head. "No no no no."

Alex pulled her phone out of her pocket. "Sorry, little dude. I didn't think I was signing on for something like this. If I could call my parents to help out, I would. But they have no extra money. That's part of why I'm not in college. We don't have much of a choice."

"No-o-o-o!" Max leaped at her, grabbing the phone out of her hands.

"Give it to me," she said.

"Mom will get all upset!" Max said.

"What about me? *I'm* upset!" Alex moved closer, her palm outstretched. "Okay. Okay. A compromise—we'll tell just your dad. We'll keep your mom out of it."

"She'll find out!"

"Max, I hate to say it, but your mom and dad put us in a very uncomfortable place. Look, I know they've been busy. And distracted. But this is their house, and they should have told us what's up. You like facts? We need some facts. Now."

"No no no no no no no!" Max cried out.

"Be reasonable," Alex said.

"I hate you!"

Alex lunged for the phone. "I don't care what you smell and what kind of mental condition you have, you little spoiled brat, give me that right now!"

Max sprang back, banging his head against the window with the broken glass. As it shattered, he fell to the floor.

"Oh no . . ." Alex said, covering her face with her hands.

Max scrambled to his feet. He was angry now. He hated that smell. It was bitter and sharp like cat pee. "Go," Max growled. "Just go. Now!"

"Your head . . ." Alex said.

"I'll live here alone!" Max said. "I don't need you. *It's my house and my mom is dying and if they kick me out I'll sneak back in and I don't want you here!*"

As he drew his arm back to throw her phone out the window, she ran toward him. His foot slipped on one of the envelopes, and he slid, flipping into the air. His shoulders banged against Alex's torso. They fell to the floor together, and she held him tight. He pushed against her, but she wouldn't let go. Tears sprang into his eyes, which just made him angrier. He began pounding on her shoulders with his fists, screaming words he couldn't control.

"I'm sorry . . . I'm so sorry . . ." Alex said. Max fought against her, but she was bigger and stronger. She wouldn't let go, wrapping him tighter in her arms. "It's okay. I won't call. I promise. I'm impulsive. Everyone says that about me."

"They're right," Max murmured.

"I should have waited. Slept on it," Alex said. "I'm not ready to be a caregiver."

Max's breaths came fast. Being held like this was annoying. But it made him feel less out of control, and a tiny bit less angry at Alex. "That's okay, I guess," he finally said. "I'm not ready to be a kid without a mom and dad. I haven't even read anything about it. I haven't memorized any rules."

Alex smiled. "Sometimes you can't be ready to do the things you really need to do," she said. "You just do them. And that makes you ready."

"Yeah," Max said. "I guess we'll figure something out."

Max's muscles went slack. He closed his eyes. The hugging was uncomfortable, but at that moment, if she let go, Max thought his body would explode into a million pieces. He felt a strange sickening sensation on his face and realized he was crying. Words came racing out of his mouth, and he couldn't control them. "She's . . . sick. Really, really sick."

"I know," Alex said. "I know."

"What happens to her if she——?"

"Don't say it. It won't happen."

"I don't have a mental condition, you know," Max said. "I make jokes, and I'm funny and smart."

"I didn't mean that. I'm so sorry, Max. I'm the one with the problem. I get really emotional and pig-headed . . ."

"What happens to me if I'm kicked out on the street?"

Alex held him tight. For a long time she didn't say anything. Then she grabbed him by the shoulders and turned him around to face her. "We have to think positive."

"Thinking doesn't do anything," Max said.

"We'll see about that. First, I'll bandage that cut and get us something to eat," she went on, touching the side of his face. "Does it hurt?"

"It's just a flesh wound," he said.

"Ha!" Alex grinned. *Monty Python and the Holy Grail?*"

"Ni," Max said.

"So you do have a sense of humor. That's a start. We'll both need that while we roll up our sleeves and figure out how to pay these bills."

"Do you have money?"

"No. I'll get a job."

"But you're a terrible waiter," Max said.

"I'll get better at it," Alex said. "Or I'll find a different job. Work at a shop. Mow lawns. Meanwhile I'll write my novel fast and sell it for a gazillion dollars."

"All that will take time," Max said.

Alex thought a moment. "I can sell my car right now."

"You'll need that."

"True."

"We could sell some stuff from the house," Max suggest. "On eBay. Whatever."

Alex grinned. "I like how you think, my brother!"

"Cousin," Max said.

"Cousin," Alex repeated.

"There's a piano in the basement," Max said. "And lots of stuff in the attic."

"I count three TVs. Need them all?"

"I hate TV," Max said.

Alex thrust a fist in the air. "We are in business!"

"Ni!" Max shouted.

The cat pee smell was gone. It was the best he'd felt all day.

Which wasn't saying much. But it was a start.

The clock ticked to 9:00 p.m. as Max dropped a toaster oven onto the living room carpet. Along with that, the piano, and the TVs, they'd gathered two small tables, three coffeemakers and one grinder, a waffle iron, four bike tires, three bike pumps, seven old but working laptops, two old-model iPods, Max's boxed baby crib, an ugly rolled-up carpet with a tag that said *Happy Graduation, George!*, and stacks of unopened shirts and ties.

Alex was streaming some punk-rock music through the stereo system, and Max began dancing around the pile. "This is awesome," he said.

"You can dance!" Alex cried out.

"You can notice obvious things!" Max replied.

"Ooh, I'll get you for that." Alex was adding up amounts on a sheet of paper. "A few dollars here, a few dollars there . . . okay, we're talking maybe in the high hundreds. What about that stuff in the attic?"

Max stopped dancing. He hated the attic. When he was a kid, he heard ghosts dancing up there. His parents told him it was squirrels, but he didn't believe it.

Fish. Deep, stinky fish.

"I don't go up there," Max said.

"Why?"

"It's dark. And spooky."

Alex laughed. "It's an *attic*!"

"Anyway, there's just junk up there," Max said.

"What kind of junk?" Alex asked.

"Old junk," Max said. "Mom and Dad used to travel a lot, before they had me. They collected things—from other states and countries. Weird stuff. They have weird taste."

"Weird collectibles—perfect!" Alex said. "You never know what you can find. They could have picked up, like, an original Pollock at some anonymous garage sale."

"Nobody sells fish at garage sales," Max said.

"Jackson Pollock," Alex said. "He was a painter."

Alex grabbed a flashlight from the pile of stuff and bounded up the stairs. At the top of the stairs, between Max's and his parents' bedrooms, was a small alcove next to a window. A ladder rested against the wall, and overhead was a trapdoor with a string attached. "That's the attic, isn't it?" Alex asked. "When was the last time you were up there?"

"When I was three," Max said.

"Three? Seriously? You haven't been up there in ten years?"

"It's haunted," Max said.

"You mean, you *thought* it was haunted when you were three," Alex said.

Alex pulled on the string. The hatch was stiff, and it took a few tries—until finally it opened with a low, moaning *scrawwwwk*.

"*Boooo-ah-ah-ah!*" Max screamed.

"Stop it," Alex replied.

Max grinned. "Did I scare you?"

"No."

"Too bad."

The light from the fixture above the stairway wasn't bright enough to illuminate anything inside the black square above them. Max squinted but could only see shadows.

Alex grabbed the ladder and propped the top rung against the opening. "After you."

"I want you to face the monsters first," Max said.

"Promise to save me if I meet someone with a hockey mask?" Alex asked.

"Maybe."

"I'll go up and find the light switch. There must be a light switch." Alex scampered up the ladder and into the darkness. Max expected her flashlight to switch on, but it didn't. Maybe the batteries were dead. He could hear her footsteps overhead and some muffled mumbling as she bumped into things.

And then the sound stopped.

Max waited for a light to go on in the attic, but it remained dark. "Alex?" he called out. "Are you finding the switch?"

No answer.

Max began climbing the ladder himself. "Alex?"

Halfway up, the light at the top of the stairs behind him flickered off. He shuddered, nearly falling off the ladder. Now the alcove was in darkness.

He turned to look over his shoulder. The entire house was pitch-black. Every light was off.

"I waaaarned you not to mess with the de-e-e-ead!"

It was Alex's voice. Obviously. She wasn't even trying to disguise it. "Not funny," Max said. "All the lights are out. Did you do that?"

His eyes were adjusting now. The moon shining through the alcove window gave the tiniest bit of light, and he could see a vague movement in the attic above. A dark shape began to move into the opening, silhouetted in the blackness.

"Alex?" Max squeaked.

The form was human. Max's mouth opened into a scream that stayed silent.

Out of the black hole, his arms reaching downward, a man hurtled directly toward him.

6

AS Max hit the floor, the body landed on him. It was cold and heavy and smelled of dust and mildew. *"Get off me!"* he pleaded, struggling against the tangle of legs and arms, pushing hard against the dead weight.

Finally the body rolled to the side. An arm ripped out of its side, and Max held it aloft. He felt like he was about to pass out.

"What did you do to Melvin?" Alex cried out from above him.

She was laughing. *Laughing.*

Max forced himself to stare at the arm. That's when he noticed the sawdust and cotton sticking out of the shoulder joint. He threw it aside, and it landed with a thump next to the rest of the figure. The moonlight cast a dull amber glow on a waxy, expressionless face.

Of a department store mannequin.

"I can't believe you did that," Max cried out.

"I—I couldn't help it!" Alex said, practically hiccuping. "It was a perfect horror film setup. The dark attic, the ladder, the mannequin . . ."

"You could have killed me!" Max said.

"I thought you liked pranks," Alex replied.

"Not that kind of prank! What if I hit my head when I landed?"

Alex was climbing down the ladder now. "Why'd you turn the lights off?"

"I didn't."

"Then who did? Freddy Krueger?"

"I thought maybe you did."

"From up in the attic? How could I possibly have done that?" Alex glanced around in the darkness as she reached the bottom of the ladder. "Ugh. Just what we need, a power failure . . ."

"Is that sarcasm?"

"Yes. Do you know where the circuit breakers are—a box of little switches that shut off if there's a power surge—"

"I know what circuit breakers are," Max said. "I could draw you the electrical plan of the whole house. They're in the kitchen."

She pulled the flashlight from her belt. Together she and Max made their way carefully down the stairs and into the kitchen. Max found the small, square metal panel on the wall at the back of the pantry. He pulled it open, revealing two columns of light switches. At the top was a switch bigger than all the rest. "This is the master," he said. "Here's something else I know. The way you get the lights back on is to flick this off and then back on again, like this—"

He pulled the switch to the left and then back to the right again. Nothing happened, so he tried it again.

Still dark.

"It's supposed to work," Max said.

Alex sighed. "Not if there's no electricity coming into the house."

Max knew exactly what she meant. "The letter from the power company . . ." he said. "It said they were going to shut off the electricity yesterday."

"They lied," Alex said. "It was today."

The kitchen was dimly lit only by the reflection of the neighbor's rear floodlight, and Max sank into a chair by the fridge. Usually it hummed, but not now. "So, no lights, no fridge, no TV, no computers, no Wi-Fi . . ."

He stared at the fading photos of him and his parents, near the Golden Gate Bridge in San Francisco, at the Purple People Bridge in Cincinnati, in front of the Statue of Liberty. In two of the photos, his dad was wearing his favorite T-shirt that said LIVE LARGE. Everyone looked so happy in all those places. And that just made him want to cry.

"Positive—remember, positive thinking!" Alex said, pacing back and forth.

Max nodded numbly. "Live large. That's what my dad always says."

"Hm," Alex said. "Well, we'll work on living medium. I can call the electric company on my cell tomorrow and explain everything. Maybe they'll cut us a break."

"And if they don't?" Max asked.

"We'll do what the pioneers did—work hard during the day and go to bed at night! We'll charge our phones at a diner."

Max nodded. "Or at Smriti's."

"Exactly! One way or another, we'll survive until the money starts coming in from the stuff we sell."

"So . . . we'll go to sleep now and look in the attic tomorrow?" Max asked hopefully.

"Why wait? I'm wide awake now," Alex said. "And the

attic will be just as dark during the daytime as it is at night."

Before Max could protest, Alex was heading for the stairs. With the flashlight.

He had no choice but to follow her. In minutes he was climbing the steps to the attic.

"Fish fish fish fish . . ." he murmured.

"Seriously, if you're going to do that, you might as well wait downstairs," Alex said, raising her eyebrows. "All alo-o-o-one . . ."

"Don't scare me."

"Woooooooooo . . . ah-ha-ha-ha . . ."

Max took a deep breath and imagined the fish swimming away, downstream. As he stepped into the attic, Alex shone her flashlight beam at a battery-operated lantern that hung from the ceiling. "Bingo."

"Why do you say 'Bingo'?" Max asked.

Alex shrugged. "My dad says it. It's like voilà."

"I like voilà better."

"That's because you have French blood." Alex flicked the switch on the lantern, and the attic was awash in a dull orange light.

The space was directly beneath the back part of the house, and the roof was slanted sharply downward. Max could walk upright to the left and right, but going deeper into the attic required ducking low.

Not that they could travel far anyway—the place was jammed full. The flashlight beam passed over at least two old typewriters, a sewing machine, two more mannequins dressed in seventies-era clothes, two steamer trunks plastered with stickers from foreign countries, and piles of old books and vinyl records. Resting on the back wall were framed paintings, shrouded by white sheets. One of the sheets had fallen off, revealing a scowling white-haired man in a black suit.

The man's dark eyes peered out over a bulbous nose. They seemed surprised and angry, as if Max and Alex had interrupted a very important business meeting.

Max let out a gasp. He stepped backward, tripping over an open toolbox. A hammer, a screwdriver, and a small crowbar fell out onto the floor.

"Clumsy," Alex called over her shoulder. She was crouched down before a collection of small stuffed rodents sitting on a pile of boxes. "Awesome! I love these. Your parents are cool."

Max looked away from the painting. "What? Those things aren't cool. They're disgusting. They're rats."

"Some museum of natural history might want these critters—wild guess, two hundred dollars." Alex moved toward the typewriters and record player. "Antiques! People love this stuff—movie companies too. You know, props for old-timey films. Maybe one hundred bucks. The old mannequins? Say another two hundred . . . just a ballpark estimate."

Max followed close behind her. He hated being there. What made it worse was that the old man's eyes seemed to be following him, growing angrier. Quickly Max reached down and tossed the white sheet back over the painting. A cloud of dust puffed upward, and Max began to cough.

"What did you just do?" Alex asked.

"Sorry," Max replied. "But that guy . . ."

Alex turned, shining the flashlight on the painting. The sheet slid off again, setting off more dust, as if the guy had steam coming from his ears.

"Relative of yours?" Alex asked.

"Can we turn him around?" Max said.

She shone the light on a plaque bolted into the frame. "Whoa. Max, do you know who that is?"

Max leaned closer and read the inscription:

JULES VERNE
1828–1905

"He doesn't look like either of us," Max said.

Alex shrugged. "Well, wait till you grow a beard."

"He definitely seems . . . smart," Max remarked.

"To write like he did—I think so," Alex said. "You've read his stuff, right?"

"I'm thirteen."

"The perfect age! *Twenty Thousand Leagues Under the Sea?* Three guys captured by a madman in a submarine. A kick-butt underwater adventure from Antarctica practically to the North Pole. You feel like you're there. Only when he wrote it, the submarine hadn't been invented yet!"

"Cool," Max said.

"*Around the World in 80 Days?* A chase around the entire world for a cash prize, in a race against time by this guy who never breaks a sweat, pursued by a cop who can't wait to throw him in jail for stealing. I could go on. *Smart* isn't the word. Genius, maybe. I've read each book about five times."

"So how much could we get for the painting?" Max said.

Alex shone the light in his face. "You, Max Tilt, are directly descended from a god. Wouldn't you want to keep this as a reminder?"

"His eyes are creeping me out," Max said.

With a weary sigh, Alex yanked open a drawer in a chest near the far-right side of the attic, revealing a stack of yellowing newspapers. The top one read: "Astronaut Neil Armstrong Is First Man to Walk on Moon!" "Ten bucks," she said.

Max pulled a funky-looking veiled women's hat out of a drawer. He lifted it over Alex's head. "This would look nice on you."

"Don't put that thing anywhere near my face!" Alex jerked away.

Max wasn't sure if she was joking or not. It was hard to tell with her. And it really was a beautiful hat.

So he moved closer.

As she backed away again, her foot clipped the fallen crowbar, and she lost her balance. Max dropped the hat and clutched her left arm. Her momentum pulled Max with her. Flailing, his fingers clasped a large brass hook bolted into the wall at the far-left side. As they both crashed to the floor, Max heard a hollow *clonk*.

"Sorry," he said.

But Alex wasn't looking at him. She was sitting up and reaching for her flashlight. "Did you see that?"

"What?"

"The wall. Where you grabbed." Alex rolled to a sitting position and shone her flashlight toward the hook. A big rectangular section of wall had swung out toward them. A hidden door.

She crept closer. "You've never seen this before?"

Swim away, fish. Go. Away.

"N-N-No!" Max exclaimed. "Like I said, I don't come up here. Ever."

"Do your parents know about it?"

"How should I know?"

Alex wrapped her fingers around the hook. "Should we open it?"

"No!" he said.

Alex pulled. With a deep, loud croak, the rusty hinges swung open wide enough to let a person through. A musty, sweetish smell wafted out of the opening. It tickled Max's nose, and he began coughing. So did Alex. Covering her mouth, she trained the flashlight into the space and then stepped inside.

Max tried to protest, but his vocal cords were frozen. He stepped back and turned to go, only to come face-to-painted-face with Jules Verne.

Follow her, my lad.

Max stood there, stunned.

Did Verne say that? No. He couldn't have, because he was French. Max had to have imagined it. Paintings couldn't speak. It was not possible!

Then why did it seem like Verne was waiting for an answer?

Max gulped. He thought about all the roller-coaster changes over the last few hours. In the life of Max Tilt, impossible was the new possible. He had heard Verne speak, and he was too afraid to say no. Or whatever *no* was in French.

"Voilà," he whispered in reply. "It's the only French word I know, sir."

"Come in, it's beautiful!" Alex called out.

Maybe it was the slight shock of Alex's voice breaking the silence. Maybe Max was just rattled. But he could have sworn that the beard on the old man's face moved, as the lips underneath curved upward into a tiny smile.

Max turned away and caught his breath. Swallowing hard, he stepped through the door.

He gazed around, taking in a room that seemed to be about six feet by eight feet. On the long side to the left, the attic ceiling slanted downward. But Max's eyes were drawn to the artwork on the walls—a vibrant, colorful mural that wrapped around the entire room. At the far left, where the ceiling was lowest, a giant squid seemed to be emerging from beneath an inky sea. As he looked around clockwise, he saw a submarine approaching the squid. A bearded man was staring at it from inside the sub, through a porthole. Above the sea, a massive balloon hovered among the fluffy clouds, and to their right a stiff-looking guy in nineteenth-century clothes was riding on a fancy sidecar attached to an elephant, while a befuddled, round man was lying flat on the animal's back, trying not to fall off. Behind Max, a team of explorers burrowed under the ground, toward a civilization of people who looked like rodents.

Alex was right, it was beautiful. Crazy beautiful. Or maybe just crazy. Max couldn't decide. It was like a fantasy-novel artist was let loose with paints and no rules. Max tried to appreciate it. But there was also something in the middle of the room that took most of his attention—a huge wooden chest.

"Pinch me, I'm dreaming . . ." Alex said, her jaw hanging open.

Max pinched her.

"Ow! It's an expression," she said, jumping away. "These paintings . . . they're amazing."

"The word I was thinking was *wack,*" Max said, heading toward the chest.

Alex shook her head. "These are scenes from Jules Verne stories, Max. This is like a shrine!"

"Or maybe a crypt." Max's knees began to shake. The wooden chest was creepy. It reminded him of a sarcophagus he'd seen in a museum in New York. "What if someone's in here—you know, like in the pyramids?

They would bury the Pharaohs in these death rooms, with paintings and jewels and stuff, to make them feel at home when their dead spirits rose? I can draw you a cross-section of the pyramid paths, if you want. Like now. So we don't have to spend another minute in this room."

Alex ignored him, moving toward the chest. It was a little more than knee-high, but it looked like it could survive a nuclear blast, with bands of thick metal surrounding it, and a massive padlock on a hasp. "We have to find the key and open it," Alex said, shining her light around the small room.

Max summoned up all the courage he had. Standing over the chest, he gripped the padlock and swung it out to examine the words stenciled into it. "It's in code," he said.

"It's in French," Alex replied.

"How do you know?"

"I'm from Quebec. I'm fluent in English and French. I've read all Verne's books in their original versions. They're much better that way."

Max nodded. "All I know is voilà."

Alex looked carefully around the room. "I don't see a key, do you?"

Max shook his head no. "Maybe we could just sell the trunk, locked," Max said. "Like a mystery package—one hundred dollars for an ancient chest and anything you can find within it!"

"What if there's a treasure inside?" Alex offered.

"What if there's a body inside?" Max replied.

"Jules Verne was not a murderer," Alex said. "He was a very rich author. If he left money or gold, it would be ours, Max. Our problems might be solved."

Max pulled the padlock down as hard as he could, once, twice, three times . . .

"That'll never work," Alex said with a chuckle.

With a hollow-sounding *clack*, it fell open. "Whoa . . ." Max gasped.

Alex's eyes widened. "Guess I lied."

"It rusted out, that's all. We are in luck!" Max yanked up on the leather handle, but it ripped clear off the chest.

"Some luck," Alex said. "Now it's totally stuck shut."

"Think positive," Max said. He backed out of the room and went into the main part of the attic. In the dim light of the hanging lantern, he grabbed the old crowbar from the floor. Quickly he ran back into the hidden room and thrust the bar into the gap between the lid and the rest of the trunk. "Help me out."

Alex was at his side instantly, and they both pulled. The top juddered upward. Dropping the bar, Alex and Max grabbed the metal edge and lifted.

The lid let out a deep, cranky noise as it opened.

Alex and Max gazed inside at a thick muslin sheet covering a bulge underneath. "Let it be gold pieces . . ." Alex chanted under her breath. "Let it be gold pieces . . ."

She gripped the sheet and pulled upward.

Max screamed. His legs sprang back as if they had a life of their own. He hurtled through the door and landed on his rear in the attic.

He didn't care what Jules Verne thought. He didn't care if they were thrown out of the house tonight. He could never unsee what was in there.

He had joked about finding a body.

He hadn't expected to see one in there.

7

ALEX held on to Max's arm as tightly as she could. The whole attic smelled like a rotten, stinking fish market.

"Let go of me!" Max shouted. *"I was right. There's a person in there—"*

"Dude, stop this!" Alex said. "It's not a person, it's a skeleton."

"It *was* a person!" Max snapped. "How do we know it's not Jules Verne? Someone murdered him, hid him in a chest, and now here we are! We'll be arrested!"

Alex turned him around and sat on him. "You will not move until we talk. Jules Verne is buried in a cemetery in France. Think about it, Max—your parents have collected stuffed squirrels and glass eyeballs in here. It doesn't mean they killed the squirrel or poked someone's eye out. My biology teacher had a skeleton in the class-room and no one arrested him for murder. Stop thinking 'yuck' and start thinking 'ka-ching.' Some medical school might want to buy it."

"But why is it here? In our attic in the middle of Ohio?"

Alex thought for a moment. "It might be a warning. Like a skull and crossbones on a jar of poison. I don't know—to keep us from something underneath."

"So what's underneath?" Max asked.

Now Alex was yanking him back into the room, shining the flashlight into the chest. Into the hollow eyes of the skull.

"I think I'm going to be sick," Max said.

Alex let go of Max's hand and pulled the skull out of the chest. It was bright white, with a seam running up the middle of the forehead. She held it there for a long moment, examining it with a serious expression.

Then she set it on the floor and pounded the fore-head with the butt of her flashlight. The skull collapsed, the center pulverized into a pile of dust.

"It's fake. Plaster of Paris." Alex reached in and pulled out a collarbone, arm bones, a rib cage. "Which means it is a scare tactic. There's got to be something else in here, Max."

Max took a deep breath. He shook away the last dregs of his fear and began pulling out bones too. They *felt* fake. They weren't even scary. But as he grabbed the last group of foot bones, his fingers brushed the bottom of the chest.

A flat, empty, wooden bottom. The chest was completely empty.

"Nada." Max sat back with a deflated sigh.

"Sorry, Max," Alex said. "But all's not lost. We'll get something for the antique chest. Come on, let's bring it out and do a final inventory with the rest of the stuff."

As Max gripped the edge of the chest, he paused to look at the murals. The submarine, the balloon, the tunnel . . . they were growing on him. Everything else in the attic was so dark and weird, but these had a sense of adventure and energy. He was glad Alex hadn't suggested somehow trying to sell them.

He looked back out into the attic. The painting of Verne still seemed to be smiling.

"Someday, sir," Max whispered, "I'll tell you about Vulturon."

"What?" Alex said.

"Nothing," Max replied.

He knew it couldn't possibly be true, but the guy seemed to wink at him.

* * *

It was almost midnight when Max heard a rustling at the front door. He and Alex had found candles in the pantry and arranged them in a circle in the living room. There, Alex had spent the past few hours listing objects on craigslist and eBay while Max worked on Vulturon.

Alex sighed. "I'm figuring we'll need about five thousand but we're not even close—"

"Shh!" Max said quietly. "Did you hear that?"

"Hear what?" Alex looked up. For a moment nothing happened, and then they both saw it—a movement of shadows under the door. "Someone's there," Alex whispered.

"Maybe the police are coming to kick us out," Max said. "We're too late to raise money."

"At midnight?" Alex whispered. "I don't think it's police. Or anybody else that's good."

Max grabbed a baseball bat from a corner of the room. Alex tiptoed over the squishy carpet to the front door and placed her hand on the knob.

A sudden sharp rapping at the door made them both stiffen. Max raised the baseball bat as Alex pulled the door open.

A small figure in a baseball cap let out a choked squeal and jumped back. "Whoa. What is going on here?"

Max dropped the bat. "Smriti?"

"You scared us," Alex said. "It's late."

"Your doorbell isn't working. I pressed and pressed . . ." Smriti said, walking inside. "I couldn't sleep. I was worried about you. Then I looked out my window and saw the flickering lights."

"We lost our electricity," Max said. "It's a long story."

As Smriti sat on the carpet, Alex returned to the listings. Max carefully gave Smriti all the details of what had happened. She listened closely, her eyes moistening at the bad news. "Why don't you come live with us?"

"You have two sisters and a baby brother," Max said.

"There's always room somewhere," Smriti said.

Alex nodded, looking up from the screen. "That's really nice of you, but I don't want to wake up your whole family. We'll stay here tonight and see if we can get the lights back on tomorrow. We do need to stick around and sell this stuff."

"If we lose our house and have to move in," Max said, "can I have my own desk?"

Smriti smiled. But before she could answer, Alex jumped back from the laptop. "Hit. Me. Over. The head.

Someone's asking about buying the chest!"

"What?" Max said, looking over her shoulder.

"At midnight?" Smriti added.

Alex leaped up and hugged them both. *"We're going to do this, cuz! No stopping us now!"*

8

NIEMAND stared at the message on the screen—the translation of the document he'd bought from the fat man.

1 kilo flour . . . 1 bunch red grapes . . . rack of lamb . . .

It was a shopping list.

A blasted shopping list! All that effort at the warehouse for a piece of utterly worthless junk.

Sophia had translated it in seconds. Niemand could practically feel her mocking laughter over the email message. He sipped from a double shot of espresso in a black cup and nearly choked. Slamming the cup down, he said, "Heat this up for me, Rudolph. I want it scalding."

A man dressed in black took the cup. He had wispy brownish hair and shoulders the size of a desk. "Any good news?" he asked, lumbering toward the microwave.

Niemand swept the laptop off the table, and it crashed onto the floor.

"Guess not," Rudolph said.

As the espresso heated, Rudolph walked across the carpeted office. All windows were frosted to prevent snooping, and the front door was emblazoned Private: Authorized Personnel Only. Rudolph liked being authorized. Mr. Niemand was the only person who had ever given him that honor. Special Envoy to the President and Founder of Niemand Enterprises was a long way from Cell Block 11, Prisoner 9.

On the opposite wall was a countertop with all kinds of electronic equipment, along with a stainless-steel supply cupboard. Rudolph opened the left-hand door, took a fresh laptop from the top of a tall stack, and brought it to his boss. "Hey, cheer up," he said. "We got reports from Iceland that a big, fat greenberg fell into the sea."

Niemand turned to him slowly. His eyes seemed to jump out of their sockets and stab his face. The stub where his left pinkie used to be was bright red, which was always the sign of a bad mood. "Greenland . . . and iceberg, you nincompoop!"

"Sorry, Mr. Niemand." Rudolph hated when his boss got like this. It made him so nervous, he always said the wrong thing. As he opened the laptop and placed it on the desk, he spotted an alert at the top of the screen.

NEW ITEM: #4215, 19th-century chest belonging to famed author JULES VERNE. Starting price, $250

"Did you see this, Mr. N?" Rudolph asked. "On craigslist?"

But Niemand was ignoring him, checking his phone.

The microwave let out a *ding*. As Rudolph turned toward it, Niemand slammed down his phone and let out a small barrage of curses. "More disgraceful news. It's the lab. They're telling me the SWATO tanks have a structural flaw and won't be ready for weeks."

"SWATO?" Rudolph said.

"Seawater-to-Oxygen!" Niemand snapped. "Great waves of Neptune, am I paying you to forget your training?"

"Here you go, boss," Rudolph said, carrying the coffee cup with a hot mitt and trying to sound upbeat. He smiled, which for him was a lopsided grimace that looked like he was being stabbed. "Hot enough to burn steel, just the way you like it."

As he set it down, Niemand smacked the cup angrily with his left hand, sending the liquid into Rudolph's face.

The big man yowled, but Niemand's eyes were fixed on the alert at the top of his laptop. His pulse quickened as he clicked on it. Quickly he sent an inquiry to the seller. To his surprise the seller responded instantly.

With an address.

Niemand leaped from his seat. *"Rudolph, we've done it!"* he shouted.

But his henchman was squirming in pain on the work-shop floor. With an exasperated sigh, Niemand picked up his phone. "Medical? Would you bandage up Rudolph, relieve his pain, and get him ready to leave, stat?"

"Th-Th-Thanks," Rudolph said, his hands covering his burned face.

"Only the best for my people," Niemand said. "Make it quick. We leave in half an hour."

THE phone woke Max up Saturday morning at 6:09. Half asleep, he grabbed it off his night table. "Heechhhurrr . . ."

"I'll take that as a hello," said his father's voice on the other end.

"Dad!" Max sat up instantly in bed. "How's Mom doing?"

"Fine!" his father replied cheerily.

"Can I talk to her?" Max asked.

"She's sleeping. But . . . later maybe. I was calling to ask how *you* were. Things are working out with Alex?"

"Ahhhh, crrrap!" came Alex's voice from downstairs. *"I hate this!"*

"Excuse me?" Dad said.

"She's great!" Max quickly shot back. "Fun. And smart. And she's going to be a famous writer someday. Like Jules Verne."

"Glad you get along," Dad said, "because we may be here a little while longer than we'd hoped."

Max felt his stomach sinking. "How much longer?"

"It's unclear," his dad said with a sigh.

"Wait. That sounds really bad, Dad."

His brain was screaming at him to urge his dad to come home now, no matter what else was going on. *We're going to be kicked out of our house! Come home now, and fix everything!* But he couldn't. Or at least he wouldn't. Not with Mom so sick.

Max held the words back. He knew Alex was on her phone now with the electric company. She'd made him promise he'd give their plan some time to work. He had to have faith. Mom's condition had deteriorated, and stress would only make it get worse. Sometimes the truth had to be . . . delayed.

"You know your mom, she's a fighter," Dad said.

"Right," Max said, nodding, as if his dad could see him.

"Once Mom and I get back, we're going to have to deal with this hospital bill. And a lot of other bills, I imagine. I can't even imagine how much the treatment will cost and how we'll pay for it. But hey, you know the Tilt family motto—"

"Live large, because there are no extra days," Max recited.

"Attaboy," his dad said. "Keep those flames burning for your mother. And say hi to Alex for us."

"You bet, Dad. Love you."

When his dad responded, his voice was soft and crackly. "Love you too, buddy boy."

Max listened to the phone go silent, then hit the Off icon. He had two bars of power left and no electricity in the room. As he glanced around, his eyes landed on his old desktop. And his plastic-coated ten-pound dumbbells. And his basketball and football that he'd hardly ever used. All of them could be sold for money. He had to think of the whole world that way now. Except maybe his flying dinos and rainbow banner.

He exhaled sharply and jumped out of bed. In minutes he was washed, dressed, and running downstairs.

"Sleeping Beauty rises," said Alex in the kitchen. She was wearing a jacket and hunched over her laptop. Next to her was a napkin with the remains of a mostly eaten blueberry muffin.

"It's not that cold in here," Max said.

"I was outside," Alex snapped, "a couple of hours

ago, when it was dark and freezing. I walked to the Angler's Diner, which has an exquisite pancake breakfast and even more exquisite wall plugs for charging electronics. For use by hardworking, responsible citizens while their lazy little cousins stay home and enjoy their beauty sleep."

"You must have had the pancakes *à la* nasty with cranky syrup," Max said.

Alex let out a snort and gave him an astonished glance. "You *can* be sarcastic!"

"I'm learning from you," Max said. "How'd we do with sales? And did you call the electric company?"

Alex angled the laptop so Max could see it. On the screen was a big spreadsheet with three columns: Item Name, Asking Price, Price Offered. But Max's eyes went right to the bottom, to the line marked Total.

$104.93

"It's only been a few hours," Max said. "It'll get better."

Alex nodded. "Of course it will. We don't have to do it all online either. We may want to have a tag sale on the front lawn."

"No," Max said. "The neighbors will notice. They might call Dad."

"Good point. Anyway, so far people have bought cheapo things. Bargains. I may have to relist most of these things at reduced prices. I recalculated my estimation of what we can expect on the low end. About a thousand."

"Ugh."

"I was going to throw in money from my savings, because that's the kind of person I am." Alex turned to him with a grin. "But I can't. Because I spent it on something else."

"Pancakes?" Max asked.

Alex reached out and messed up his hair, which was extremely annoying. "No, doofus. I contacted the electric company through their twenty-four-hour chat, and the amount due on the bill was just about exactly what I'd saved up. So I did it, I paid the whole thing."

"Really?" Max felt stunned. "Thanks, Alex. That was nice."

"You're welcome," she said. "Anyway, the good news is we'll be getting power any minute. But the bad news is . . . well, everything else."

"Like, we're not going to raise enough," Max said.

"Nowhere near," Alex replied. "This stuff is quirky and fun. But the internet is full of that."

Max thought hard. "We need to sell something that no one else has. That no one has seen before."

"The Jules Verne chest is unique," Alex said. "We did have interest in it. I gave them our address. They haven't bid yet, but maybe they'll come over and see it. I told them they could come any time, any hour, twenty-four seven."

Max played back last night in his head. The painting . . . the stuffed animals . . . the newspapers . . . He imagined walking into the secret room and seeing the chest, looking around at all the . . .

"Hand-painted murals!" he blurted.

"Whaaat?" Alex said.

"They're amazing—beautiful," Max insisted. "They seemed to move."

"I think they're painted onto the walls," Alex said.

"Thin walls," Max replied. "You can tell. They're nailed onto the studs. Someone could pull them off. Use them in a kid's room. Or exhibit them."

Alex shrugged. "I don't know much about art, but I guess it's worth a try. Let's get some pictures of them to upload."

In the dim light, Max thought the paintings seemed to be emerging from a fog. The balloon, the submarine . . . one seemed to be moving, the other sinking deeper into the sea. "Let's get the chest out of the room," Alex said. "A clean view of the murals will be breathtaking."

As they dragged the chest back toward the door, something inside thumped.

Alex and Max froze.

"Did you hear that?" Max said. "A kind of sliding noise . . . like *ssss*, and then a thump?"

"Let's see." Alex opened the chest and shone the flashlight inside. A flat metallic floor stared back. "Nope."

"Something's in there, I swear," Max said. He shut the top and lifted one end of the trunk high.

Sssss . . . thump.

Now Alex was paying attention. She set the chest down and rapped on the base with her knuckles. The sound was deeper than Max had expected. "Hollow," she said.

"It's a trick floor!" Max tilted the chest upward again. Keeping it in place with his knees, he knocked on the bottom and on the inside of the chest floor. "Yes. Two sheets of metal, with space between them."

Alex brightened. "Awesome!"

"The skeleton *was* scaring intruders away," Max said. "From . . . whatever was inside."

"Or *is* inside," Alex said.

Max gulped. There was no latch, no way at all to open

the metal bottom. "We could drop it from the window. The metal doesn't seem too thick."

Alex shook her head. "If I were the hider of something valuable, I would want to be able to get to it again. Which means I would have built into the chest some method to open it."

Max grabbed the flashlight and began examining every inch of the chest, beginning with the top, the edges, the molding . . .

Alex ran her fingers along all of it, tugging, pulling . . .

"Max, shine it here!" she said, her fingers around the old hasp. It hung from the side of the chest where the lock had broken off—a rectangular brass hinged plate that was wobbly and loose.

With a strong yank, Alex pulled the entire hasp off the chest and threw it on the floor. In the rectangle where it had been was a rusted metal dial with numbers. In the center of the dial were the initials *JV.*

"It's a combo lock," Alex said. "Under the hasp that held the key lock."

Max narrowed his eyes. "Wait. The chest opened after the other lock broke. Which means that lock was keeping the chest closed. So . . . what's the point of this one?"

He glanced up at his cousin. She seemed deep in thought. "Unless . . ." she murmured, "this one unlocks something else. Like the false floor!"

Together they stared at the big *JV*. Jules Verne, obviously. Around that, the numbers went from one to twenty-six.

"OK, that's weird . . ." Max said. "Usually these things go from zero to fifty."

"Does it matter?" Alex asked.

"I'm thinking . . ." Max drummed his fingers on the chest. "Why twenty-six? It's a weird number."

"There are twenty-six letters in the alphabet . . ." Alex said.

"That's what I was thinking," Max said.

"You were not."

"I was! I'm looking at the *JV*. *J* is the . . ." He began counting on his fingers. "Tenth letter. And *V* is the . . ."

"Twenty-second!" Alex said. "So you think the *JV* is giving us the hint for the combo—which is ten, twenty-two?"

Max struggled to turn the dial of the rusted lock, but it was stuck. Alex darted to the toolbox and got a can of WD-40. With a few sprays, he was able to spin it easily.

Ten . . . twenty-two . . .

Nada.

Nothing happened at all.

"Maybe dropping it out the window wasn't such a bad idea after all," Alex said.

"Maybe . . ." Max murmured. "But let's not give up yet. I mean, *JV* is just an abbreviation, right? Maybe it's not those two letters, but the whole name?"

Alex grabbed a clipboard and pen and began scribbling:

$$JULESVERNE$$
$$10\ 21\ 12\ 5\ 19\ 22\ 5\ 18\ 14\ 5$$

"Like this?" she asked.

"Let's try it." Patiently Max spun out the combination 10-21-12-5-19-22-5-18-14-5.

He and Alex stared into the chest. "No click," Max whispered.

"No trumpets either," Alex remarked. "I was hoping for trumpets."

Max let out a sigh. "OK, here's a Plan B: we get a big drill that goes through metal . . ."

Before he could finish the word, there was a soft groan. The bottom of the chest snapped upward on a hinge. It hit the back part with a loud *whack*.

Max and Alex recoiled. Then, leaning forward, they

shone the flashlight into the chest.

Max held his breath. He wasn't expecting a pile of gold. Not from the sound of things. But a rare book would have been nice. Or valuable art.

Not this.

He reached down and pulled out a burlap sack. Inside was a thin booklet—three sheets of crinkly yellow paper held together by a leather coverlet, secured by string.

"The pages are all blank," Max said, leafing through them.

Alex held them up to the light. "No," she said. "There's one word."

Max squinted.

Citron.

"It means *lemon*," Alex said.

"All that for one word?" Max asked.

Alex dropped the booklet onto the floor in disgust. "Well, that was seventeen kinds of fun. Guess someone in our family had a sick sense of humor. Let's take those pictures and get back to work."

She stepped away, pulled out her phone, and began clicking away.

But Max didn't move. He was smelling ammonia. He didn't smell that often. Only when someone was trying to trick him.

Lemon.

He knew some facts about lemons. They could be sour or sweet. People could eat the skins of Meyer lemons, which were grown in the South and the West and named after Frank Nicholas Meyer, who originally brought them to the United States from China. Lemon juice was used for many things. It removed stains. When heated, its properties changed . . .

Max stood up so fast he was momentarily dizzy. "I need a match," he said.

"A match?" Alex said. "Like, a match you strike and make fire with?"

"Yes."

"Why?"

"To read the rest of the message," Max declared.

"What message?" Alex asked.

Max held up the little booklet. "*Lemon* isn't a random word. It's an instruction. The words were written in lemon juice. It's an old method of invisible ink. If we gently heat these pages, we will be able to read them."

Alex reached into her pocket and pulled out a book of matches labeled Olympian Diner. Max gave her a look. "You smoke?"

"None of your business," Alex said. "I took them from the last place I worked."

Max lit one of the matches and held it to the sheet of paper, just far enough so the flame didn't singe it. A message in French appeared.

"'Remove me from my wooden box,'" Alex translated. "'There, at my back, your instructions await.'"

Max narrowed his eyes. "Are you sure that's what it says—remove him from his wooden box?"

"Totally," Alex replied.

"What do you think it means?"

"It means his coffin, Max," Alex said, letting the note drop to the floor. "It means we're supposed to dig up his body in France and . . . I don't know, search his back pockets or something. And don't tell me you think that's cool. Just don't. Because it's disgusting."

Max picked up the note. "It doesn't make sense, Alex. How could Jules Verne arrange to leave a note on his own corpse?"

"Bribe the undertakers?" Alex asked.

"Maybe he's talking about a different kind of box, not a coffin," Max said. "A Jules Verne jack-in-the-box."

Alex rolled her eyes. "Pop goes the author."

"Or . . . a gift box!" Max said. "With a Jules Verne action figure."

As his eyes swept the room, the portrait of Jules Verne seemed to be staring at him. Inviting him into a conversation. Max exhaled. He wasn't sure an after-life really existed, but if it did, maybe it had translators. "Dude," he said softly, "please. Tell us what you mean."

Alex looked for a moment like she wanted to laugh, but she was staring at the painting too.

Maybe she was seeing what he was seeing.

"My wooden box . . ." Max murmured.

Alex nodded. "The frame!"

"Yes."

"Max, we need to take that painting apart!"

Max was already reaching for the portrait. Alex managed to find a screwdriver, and as he set the painting on the floor she began separating the backing.

As crazy as it sounded, Max could swear Jules Verne was grinning.

THE LOST TREASURES
A MEMOIR
By Jules Verne

— PART ONE —

(Translated from the French by the Amazing Alexandra Verne,
from a pamphlet found in a framed portrait of the author)

Dear reader, if you have found this, I am profoundly grateful. For it means, I trust, that the world still exists. That the aims of my nemesis have not borne fruit.

I write this in a pen using ink based in iron, in the hopes that it will last and not fade. This writing unburdens my soul of secrets so dark that they will not be heard, let alone believed, in my time.

For the truth must be heard by ears that are ready to receive it. This time, I believe, shall come soon. But for now I fear I shall take these secrets to my grave.

Read on. Take heed. If you do, you will prevent a destruction so deep and complete as to end life as we know it.

I will not fault you, dear reader, for scoffing at these words. You know Jules Verne as a teller of fanciful tales and fantastical stories. If you have not read them, then you know someone who has. But here is what you do not know: these works are not fiction. Yes, some names have been changed. But every detail, every scrap of dialogue, has been transcribed from life.

And here, for the first time, I present the truth without the filters of style and novelistic technique. Here I guide you to follow my path. If you do, you will soon find riches unimaginable by the greatest of kings. But this will not be the final aim. Because by following the journey to the end, you will earn the gratitude of every soul on earth. Those riches, may it go without saying, will do no good on an empty planet.

I call my memoir *The Lost Treasures*. O how I wish I could leave all of it here, for you to devour in its entirety. But my enemy is wise to my aims. I must tell the story in sections. This, then, is merely an introduction.

A blueprint.

You will find the pieces of the greater whole. Each will lead you farther in your journey. Which was my journey.

You must not be faint of heart or weak of body. You must possess the cunning of a wolf, the strength of an ox, the intelligence of a scholar.

Only with these will you find the hidden fortune.

The gains were ill-gotten, the plunder of my nemesis. They are in a place his followers will never discover. You will need funding to continue the journey.

You shall embark from the land of Bartholdi's lady and begin the portion of the voyage as traced out by Srem Sel Suos Seueil Ellim Tgniv. Upon reaching the great unruined chamber at the prime locations of the fifteenth, third, and second to the Pole Star and eleventh, seventeenth, and fourteenth to the sunrise, be guided by the camptodactyl of the king.

Godspeed and good reading.

J. Verne

Paris, France
July 1904

11

"FORTUNE?" Max read the word from Alex's laptop screen on the kitchen table.

Until the moment he read that word, he had been annoyed at Alex. She'd pulled him away from working on his drone, and now it was nearly bedtime.

But *fortune* . . . well, that changed everything.

"I just wanna be rich . . ." She was dancing across the kitchen, singing way off-key. "We did it, Max!"

Max could see her turning toward him with a gigantic grin. He knew what that meant. "Don't hug me," he said. "Are you sure about this?"

"I checked every word," Alex said. "I mean, everything except the nonsense stuff at the end—"

"I don't mean is it accurate," Max said. "I mean, is it true?"

Alex stopped dancing. "Of course it is!"

"You said he wrote *Twenty Thousand Leagues Under the Sea* before submarines were invented," Max said. "If submarines didn't exist, he couldn't have really taken a trip on one."

"Well . . ." Alex flung up her arms. "Maybe he secretly had access to one that no one knew about."

"If he lived through *Journey to the Center of the Earth*," Max continued, "he'd be burned to a crisp."

"Okay, so maybe it wasn't the *center* center," Alex said. "Maybe it was just deep. You know, artistic license."

Max sat. "I used to think all the *Dear America* books were true. They were fake diaries written by novelists pretending to be real people. Who were made-up."

"Wait. You think he didn't write this?" Alex sat back down and began toggling through webpage tabs. "Here's a sample of his handwriting . . . matches the note exactly. It's him, Max. He's communicating to us through the centuries! Why would Jules Verne send people on a wild goose chase? This guy was an adventurer, a traveler, a banker. He had a thick gray beard. He was Mr. Turn-of-the-Century Serious French Guy.

He's the dude who hates pranks.'"

Max could not get his eyes off the word *fortune*. So far the most expensive thing they'd listed was the chest, and they hadn't even sold that. They'd probably make enough for a few small bills, but that was about it.

"Think about this, Max," Alex said. "What if it's all true, and instead of following the path, we just sit home? Will we regret it? We could be passing up the possibility of saving your parents' house and getting your mom the best health care money can buy!"

Max nodded. He scanned the translation again. "I'm okay until the stuff at the end."

"I looked up *camptodactyl*," Alex said. "It has something to do with bones. The part at the end that looks like nonsense words—that's probably some other language. First things first. He's sending us a clue about where to start the journey: 'the land of Bartholdi's lady.'"

"That name sounds familiar to me," Max said.

"Some friend of his, I'm guessing—but who? And where did she live?"

"How do you know it was a friend of his?"

Alex shrugged. "He doesn't say Bartholdi Johnson or Bartholdi Schwartz. So they were clearly on a first-name basis."

"Verne was a famous guy," Max said, his fingers

reaching for the keyboard. "So his friends were probably famous too."

As he searched the name Bartholdi, Alex leaned over his shoulder, waiting to see the search hits.

"'Bartholdi, Frédéric-Auguste, architect/sculptor,'" Max read. "It's a last name!"

He clicked on Images, and Alex let out a deafening whoop.

Max stared at a giant image of Bartholdi's factory from the late eighteen hundreds. Where he was building the Statue of Liberty.

"His lady lived on the water," Alex said with a smile. "In New York Harbor."

"I should have known this—we visited there!" He pointed to the refrigerator photo of his family at the giant statue.

"Well, buddy, looks like we're going back!" Alex said.

"We can't. I have school."

"We'll only be gone for a few days. A week at most. How much can you miss?" Alex turned and pulled the photo off the fridge. Max was a couple of years younger, grinning from ear to ear and proudly showing off a T-shirt with the words NEW YORK CITY. "Look how happy you are here. New York is cool. It'll be an adventure." She drew a big star over the words "New York

City" and a flurry of exclamation points.

"What are we supposed to do when we get there—ask around for a treasure?"

Alex glanced at the translation again. "'. . . the portion of the voyage as traced out by Srem Sel Suos Seueil Ellim Tgniv.' That's the part in the other language. I don't know . . . use Google Translate?"

Max typed the words quickly into the Detect Language box. "Just spits back the same thing."

"On the way, we'll figure out what the rest means. We'll have nine or ten hours."

"I feel very uncomfortable about this," Max said.

"First thing tomorrow," Alex said, "we head for the Big Apple!"

Before he could protest, she wrapped him in her arms. He couldn't say much, even think of much, when he was overwhelmed by the scent of sweaty feet.

When the doorbell rang, Max was asleep in his bedroom with his head in his backpack. He hadn't meant to doze off, but the change of clothes was so soft and comfy. He jolted awake and checked his watch. 10:15 p.m.

"I'll get it!" he cried out to Alex, who was somewhere in the house gathering some supplies for their trip. "It's probably Smriti! I texted her we were going. She said she'd come say good-bye!"

Max quickly checked his pack to make sure Vulturon was tucked in there. He'd designed it to fold up to the size of a thick book. Hooking the pack over his shoulder, he raced down to the door and yanked it open.

It wasn't Smriti. This was, in fact, the un-Smritiest person he had ever seen. In an instant the fish smell was back, big time. Tinged with a little ammonia.

A tall, smiling white guy stood on the porch, wearing a black jacket, gray pants, and extremely shiny shoes. His face was tanned to a deep bronze, his fingernails shone, and his teeth were as even and white as piano keys. A streak of silver ran down the middle of his shoe-polish black hair, and he gave a small bow. "I am looking for the chest belonging to Jules Verne," he said.

"Hi!" Alex called out, pushing Max aside. "Come in! Come in! You caught us just in time. We're going away tomorrow morning!"

The man stepped inside. Behind him, a black Mercedes van idled by the curb. Max knew by the shape of the tail-lights that it was brand-new.

Inside, a man whose face was bandaged like a mummy sat at the steering wheel. His two small eyes peered out from within the bandages, and Max felt a shiver run up his spine.

"Bring in your partner!" Alex said cheerily.

Max could see the man stiffen. He turned to the car, made eye contact, and snapped his fingers.

The bandaged man pushed open the car door and nearly fell out in his eagerness.

"His name is Rudolph," the skunk-haired man said. "And he guides my sleigh."

12

MAX watched the man peer inside the old chest, and for some weird reason he saw himself slamming the top down on his head.

He had to get a hold of himself. They were just . . . people.

The man was taking his time, as if inspecting every grain of wood. "Pretty cool, isn't it?" Alex called out from the kitchen.

"Pretty empty, isn't it?" the man growled.

"There's a trapdoor," Max piped up. "You can put stuff in the bottom."

Skunky stood up instantly. "Oh?"

"Here we go!" Alex walked into the living room holding two glasses of water. She set them down on the coffee table in front of the men. "Let me know if it tastes funky. It was nearly black after the electricity came back on, but I think most of the microbes are gone."

Rudolph grabbed the glass of grayish-brown water and slugged it down, but Fix waved it aside with a sneer. "May I ask if you happened to have found anything beneath this . . . er, trapdoor?"

"Y— " Max began.

"No!" Alex elbowed him in the side. "Nothing. But just imagine the possibilities. You could have secure storage of your treasured valuables, Mr. . . ."

"Fix," he said, training his eyes on Max. "So which is it, yes or no?"

The man reached out and patted him on the head as if he were a pet. Max recoiled, gasping. He felt himself sliding down out of his chair. He didn't stop until he was on the floor, hiding under the coffee table.

Max knew he was supposed to be polite to visitors and respectful to all adults. But there was something about this guy.

"What's with Junior?" Rudolph mumbled.

"He doesn't like to be touched," Alex said cheerily.

"Of course," Fix said. "And neither do I."

"We take cash and money orders, no credit cards,"

Alex said. "Sorry to be in a hurry, but we have to go. On . . . vacation."

Max pulled himself into a tiny ball under the table, small as he could get, invisible to the adults. All he could see were feet now. He couldn't help but notice that for all of Fix's neatness, his shoelaces were loose. In fact, one of them was nearly untied.

Max smiled. Growing up, he had spent a lot of dinners under the table like this. And he'd gotten really good at pranks.

He reached toward Fix's shoelace.

"I propose an even better deal," Fix said, taking a tightly rolled wad of twenty-dollar bills out of his pocket. "Now, I admit I may be asking for the impossible. And I don't mean to be rude. But if—just if—anything were inside this hidden compartment, I would certainly offer a great deal of money for it. Say, a thousand dollars."

"*Really?*" Alex exclaimed, taking the money to examine.

"Two thousand," Fix said. "There's another thousand waiting once we get it in the car."

"Two grand is a lot for a kid," Rudolph mumbled.

Fix turned his foot and jabbed Rudolph with the point of his shoe. As the bandaged man squealed in pain, Max pulled his hand away.

"I—I—" Alex stammered. "That's very generous!"

"I know," Fix said. "I have a weakness for children."

"But like I said, there was nothing in the chest at all. So thank you for the generous offer . . ."

"Nothing? Really?" Fix purred.

"R-R-Really," Alex replied.

"Do I detect nervousness, little lady?" Fix leaned back in his chair, idly crossing his ankles. "Because if you are keeping anything from us, we may have to take action."

Rudolph snorted. "Right. Action."

"Did you just call me 'little lady'?" Alex said.

The feet were still again. The men were inches away from each other.

Perfect.

Quickly Max untied Fix's shoes and then tied them to each other. Rudolph's shoelaces were a little tighter, but he managed to loosen them and tied his feet together too. Leaving one lace free, he tied Rudolph to Fix.

Stifling a giggle, he slid back to his chair and emerged from below the table. "I feel better now."

Fix stared at him. His features softened. "Good lad," he said. "Your cousin and I have reached a bit of an impasse."

"I didn't know imps had them," Max said.

"I beg your pardon?" Fix replied.

"Asses," Max said. "Which is what you're about to feel like."

"Max?" Alex said.

Max pushed back his chair and began running to the door. *"Let's go, Alex! Now!"*

The two men jumped up from the table. As Rudolph turned toward the door, his foot pulled on the tied laces. Fix let out a scream. He fell straight back onto the sofa, upsetting a pile of papers. Both men tumbled to the carpet, cursing at the top of their lungs. *"My Italian silk shirt is ripped!"* Fix shrieked.

As Alex bolted out of her seat, Rudolph stood and lunged for her. Max ran to her side, but Alex snatched her backpack off the floor. "And the little lady takes a big swing!" she announced, whapping the big man in his bandaged face.

Rudolph recoiled with a howl of pain. But his reflexes were quick enough to wrap one beefy hand around Max's throat. "One of you will suffer for this."

"Rudolph, what are you doing—this is a child!" Fix shouted.

The skunk-haired man yanked on Rudolph's foot. The big man released Max and lost his balance, falling to the floor. His head smacked against the solid-steel edge of the Tilts' coffee table.

Max was free. Alex pulled him toward the door.

"Hasta la vista!" he called over his shoulder.

On his way Max stooped to grab his backpack too, then he followed Alex out the door and into the night. A few paces ahead of him, she was headed for the Kia with her key in one hand.

With the other hand, she stuffed Fix's money in her pocket.

13

HUMILIATED wasn't the word for it.

In fact, there was no word for this wretched and wretchedly beautiful feeling that had overcome Spencer Niemand.

Shoelaces! It was so simple as to be brilliant. He let out a soft, barking laugh as he paced the living room. On the sofa, Rudolph lay splayed among the papers, out cold after knocking his thick head against a coffee table.

Did the boy know that the shoelace material was from the secretions of a rare silk moth from Uzbekistan? That by toppling the two men, he had ruined a shirt that cost more than the yearly paycheck of dear old Rudolph?

Of course not. Max was a child.

And Spencer Niemand had a soft spot for children.

So innocent. So impulsive. So many dreams.

He knew about dreams.

Niemand held up his left hand to the ceiling light. He'd lost the pinkie finger when he was the age of the Tilt boy. It happened in the office of Oliver Niemand, his father, because little Spencer had been operating equipment he'd had no business touching. But touch he did. Go ahead, the elder Niemand had said. You think you're so smart? At the memory, Spencer Niemand winced. He could see his father's mocking face later that day as Spencer lay in a hospital bed. Why so sad? You still got nine more, don'tcha, boy? That's what you get for playing with things you're too stupid to operate.

Dear Mum had wrapped the severed finger in tissue and brought it home. She'd had a plaster cast made in the finger's shape, which Niemand now wore around his neck on a sterling-silver chain. It became his best friend. His reminder of the past. His muse.

Dear little Kissums.

Spencer Niemand lifted Kissums to his lips. The old man was gone now, and Niemand Enterprises was his. In his world, he would make sure children could dream and dream big.

But, of course, they could not stand in his way.

Passing by the cheap, ratty sofa, he kicked Rudolph's

legs back up onto the cushions. He checked his phone but there were no messages from the office. Tracking a decrepit, old red Kia should not be too hard with the resources of his company. But it would be a lot easier if he had some idea—some clue—of their direction.

He would give Rudolph five more minutes. The old soldier had coffee burns on his face and a head injury—a rough day.

Walking into the kitchen, Niemand stopped short. Leaning down, he picked something up off the table.

A photograph. The boy and two attractive adults, who must have been his parents. They were standing in front of the Statue of Liberty. Circled in red were the words "New York City."

The red marker lay next to the photo. The circle, apparently, had just been drawn.

A grin grew slowly across Niemand's face. He whipped out his phone and called headquarters. "Yes, Mr. Niemand," a voice chirped.

"Alert every station, position every satellite on major roads between this location and New York City. Red Kia, at least ten years old, driver a dark-skinned female approximately eighteen, passenger a Caucasian or Latino boy of around thirteen, left these premises forty-five minutes ago."

"On it," the voice replied.

Spencer Niemand hung up the phone, grabbed a glass from a cupboard, and yanked open the freezer. A foul, rotten smell blasted outward, and he grabbed a few yellowish lumps of ice. Dumping the ice in the glass, he filled it with water.

The thought of drinking it turned his stomach. But this glass was not intended for him.

"Rise and shine—time to go!" he called out, walking into the living room.

He emptied the glass onto Rudolph's head and headed for the front door.

14

MAX was in no mood to die that day. Or to be stopped by the police. Both of which seemed equally likely given the way Alex was driving.

"Slow down!" Max said, managing to crane his neck to look out the back window. "Those guys are nowhere near us."

"This is always how I drive when two strangers have just viciously attacked me for a note about a secret treasure!" Alex snapped.

Max rolled down the window and tried to gulp in fresh air. Alex yanked the steering wheel onto the entrance to the State Highway. At this hour of the night, traffic was pretty sparse. Alex's eyes darted toward the rearview mirror, and she began taking deep, slow breaths. "Sorry.

I should slow down—and I should say thank you. You saved us, Max."

"Did you see the way they fell down?" Max said.

"'*My Italian silk shirt!*'" Alex shouted.

Max snorted, which made Alex cackle. And then they were both laughing so hard, she nearly drove off the road. "How much did he give you?" Max asked.

"Count it," she said, pulling a stack of twenties out of her pocket.

Max quickly tallied up the total. "Two hundred sixty. He lied to us. He said it was a thousand."

"So he's a cheapskate too—on top of being a liar and a thief." Alex groaned. "Anyway, we have all night. Literally. I am too wired to go to sleep. My tablet's in my backpack. Read that message again."

Max loosened his seatbelt, spun around, and grabbed the tablet from her pack. As he swung back to his seat, he glanced at the message:

the portion of voyage as traced out by Srem Sel Suos Seueil Ellim Tgniv

"Okay, we're ruling out another language," Max said. "So I'm thinking it's a code."

Alex nodded. "A substitution thing? Like *a* is really *b* and *b* is really *c* . . ."

"Maybe," Max said. "Or a word scramble?"

"What does it say backward?" Alex asked.

"Vingt . . . mille . . ." Max said, sounding it out. "Nothing."

Alex jammed on the brakes, drove onto the shoulder, and stopped the car. "That's not nothing! Give me that."

As she took the tablet, Max looked nervously at the passing traffic. *"Vingt Mille Lieues Sous Les Mers . . ."* she said. "That's it, Max! That's the title of *Twenty Thousand Leagues Under the Sea* in French!"

"Okay, so what does it tell us?" Max said. "We trace out the route he took in the book?"

"Exactly!" Alex agreed.

"Where did the voyage start?" Max asked.

Alex's face fell. "Japan, I think. Or close to it. The hero is shipwrecked, and that's where he's captured and forced into the submarine."

"That doesn't make sense. All that stuff about the Statue of Liberty. He's telling us New York, not Japan." Max stared at the words. He imagined a world map. Then imagined a line tracing their route—starting in

Japan, streaming across the ocean . . . "Alex, where did the voyage end?"

"I'm thinking . . ." she said. "The captain of the *Nautilus* was this show-offy egomaniac. He takes this crazy route from the Pacific to the Atlantic, up through the Mediterranean, veering west, south, north . . ."

"Was New York City anywhere on that path?" Max asked.

"Yup. I think so. Toward the end."

Max nodded. "He's giving us two clues. The starting point, and the map of the journey. He means for us to take the voyage in the book—but only after it passed New York City. We get to skip the first part!"

Alex jumped in her seat, nearly smashing her head against the ceiling. *"Max, you are awesome, and I love you!"*

As she jammed the car into drive and pulled back onto the highway, Max let out a sigh. "Thank you," he said, "for not hugging me."

The morning sun glared into their eyes as the Manhattan skyline emerged over the entrance ramp to the Lincoln Tunnel. Max could barely sit still. "The one with the pointy, shiny top is the Chrysler Building," he said. "Its crown was assembled in secret and hoisted to the top at the last minute—in order to win a contest for tallest building in the world! The runner-up was Forty Wall Street, which I bet you never heard of, right?"

Alex shook her head and let out a yawn. "History is written by the victors."

"Victor who?"

"Never mind."

"I love facts like that," Max said. "Did you know Jules Verne was a stockbroker? Or that he would disappear for months to travel? Or that Manhattan has so many skyscrapers because the island is made of granite? Or that a plane once crashed into the Empire State Building? New York is factoid heaven. I just memorized about a hundred of them."

Alex yawned. "Do you know anything about Harlem? The Apollo Theater? Striver's Row? Duke Ellington?"

"Give me a minute."

"Or maybe the location of Verne's treasure?" Alex pleaded. "We haven't figured that out."

"True . . ."

Alex eased on the brake as the car headed for the tunnel. Max's GPS app chimed: "After the tunnel stay to the left and take the exit for Forty-Second Street."

Alex exhaled. "You know, suddenly I have the strong

feeling we should turn back . . ."

Max nodded. "No way. I looked up Jules Verne's route in *Twenty Thousand Leagues* and matched its path to a cruise liner that's leaving this morning. The SS *Sibelius*. All we have to do is get on board."

"With what money?" Alex asked

Max frowned. "We have two hundred sixty dollars."

"There's no way that's enough for two cruise tickets!"

"Oh." He picked up his phone, went back to the Port Authority of New York and New Jersey site, and clicked on rates. His heart thumped. "Tickets for today's cruise start at seven thousand. Each."

"What?" Alex swerved out of the tunnel lane, nearly side-swiping another car. Car horns blared, and people shouted every nasty word Max had ever heard, and about three new ones. "How are we going to do this?"

"Ask them if they need waiters?" Max asked.

"Think again, and think fast!"

Max put down the phone and tried to think fast. But the only fast things were the cars emerging from the tunnel and into the snarl of city traffic. An enormous Greyhound bus veered from the left lane to the right, cutting them off.

Alex slammed the brakes and pressed her horn. *"Watch*

where you're going, idiot!" she shouted.

The luggage bay passed by Max's eyes, about six inches away. And Max realized he didn't have to think fast anymore.

He had his idea.

15

LEAVING the Kia in a New York City parking lot, they strapped on their backpacks and marched along the docks of the Hudson River. Water lapped onto the wood pilings, seagulls cawed and swooped, and across the water in New Jersey, glass apartment towers blazed in the morning sun. Max checked his phone for the location and led Alex onto a wide dock, where a towering luxury liner was moored. He couldn't help but crane his neck upward. The thing was the size of a skyscraper turned on its side. Already people were starting to line up to board—hundreds of them.

On the side of the keel, in big gold letters, were the words "SS *Sibelius*."

"You're out of your mind if you think this is going to work," Alex hissed.

"I think there's enough room for us," Max said.

He looked left and right. Opposite the ship was a stocky, tan-brick building with offices and shops. The place teemed with passengers preparing to board and tourists taking in the sights. Families kissed and cried, couples hugged, and ice-cream-cone-eating kids clung to their parents' hands. A man pushing an elderly woman in a wheelchair shouted angrily at a kid who rode by on a skateboard. Bikers sped along a narrow path, inches away from idling buses lined up at the curb.

"Come on," Max said, pulling Alex toward the bus line.

He eyed one bus discharging its last passengers. Its luggage bay was open, and one of the porters was pulling out the last piece. The passengers were crowding the sidewalk, standing still, taking selfies, moving slowly toward the ship. Max eyed the luggage, which had been pushed against the brick wall. These people did not travel light. Steamer trunks, enormous rolling suitcases, duffels the size of human beings, golf bags teeming with clubs—it was like a city skyline itself. At some point, all of this would have to be loaded onto the ship.

Two or three bus lengths farther down, a team of dockworkers was tagging the luggage. "Good. They haven't gotten to this bus yet," Max whispered.

He crouched low behind the skyline of luggage and grabbed two items—a huge trunk decorated in pink and a giant, blue rolling duffel. With a pocketknife from his backpack, Max poked two holes in the sides of the trunk. Just enough to let in air. He opened it and pushed aside piles of clothing. "You hop inside this one," he whispered. "Plenty of room."

"*Pink?*" she said, horrified.

Max unhooked his own bulging backpack. "And can you take this with you?"

"What's in it?" Alex asked.

"Vulturon," he said.

"You couldn't have left it behind?"

"We'll need something to do in our spare time."

Grumbling, Alex stuffed both packs into the trunk. Max glanced quickly over the luggage, and then toward the crowd. When he was sure nobody was looking, he unzipped the duffel and wedged himself inside. It was tight, but Max liked tight spaces.

As he began zipping it shut, he peered out at Alex. Her hands were shaking as she lowered the trunk's top over her head. "Are we sure we want to do this?" she hissed.

Max had been asking himself that question the whole trip. Whenever the word *no* popped into his head, he pictured his mom. And the *no* turned to *yes*.

This was their only chance. Grabbing the inner handle of the two-sided zipper, he carefully pulled it shut. "See you on board," he whispered.

"Or in jail," Alex hissed.

16

ALEX didn't know which was worse—the darkness, the smell of someone else's underwear, the hum of the engine, the scritching of little animal feet, or the suffocating warmth.

"There are rats down here!" she whispered.

"Ssshh!" came Max's voice in the darkness.

"I'm sweating like a pig."

"Maybe that's why the rats are attracted to you! They love pigs."

"Stop it!"

For a moment Alex heard nothing. Then a soft rhythmic tapping on the floor of the cargo hold.

She held her breath. Whatever it was, it was coming nearer.

Squeeeeek . . . squeeek-eek-eek . . .

Alex tried to block out the noise. Rodents were small. And the trunk was thick. Solid. She glanced at the holes in the side. Rats were known for fitting into small spaces. Could they . . . ?

Tiny paws skittered up the side of the trunk. Alex felt her throat tighten.

The trunk's latch clicked. Alex froze.

"Max . . . ?" she whispered.

The lid seemed to move. And then the trunk slowly opened.

Alex screamed. She lurched backward. The trunk toppled over and the lid fell open.

Max was standing over her, grinning. "Got any cheese?"

"Is that supposed to be a joke?" Alex shouted.

"You're like a ghost!" Max said with a howl of laughter.

"And you're toast," Alex said, storming toward a door at the back of the hold.

Max couldn't understand why Alex was so mad at him. He had thought she liked pranks. And he thought she'd be grateful for getting them on the ship.

But she hadn't said a word to him up a flight of grimy stairs, down a hallway, and in a short elevator ride.

"I promise I'll never do that again," Max said as the elevator door opened. "But I did get us aboard. I solved our problem."

Alex didn't answer as she stepped out.

The deck of the SS *Sibelius* was jammed with people waving to friends and family. Behind the crowd, Max and Alex walked carefully, breathing in the fresh air. Two enormous smokestacks towered overhead, and the ship cabins rose up behind them like a giant gaudy hotel.

Max didn't like it up here. People were staring at him. Which made sense, because he and Alex didn't have tickets. It was one thing to solve a problem. It was a whole other thing to know what to do afterward.

"Next time, we buy tickets," Alex grumbled. "Or steal them. Or pretend we're the lounge singers. Anything but what we just did."

Max nodded. "OK, OK. But I miss my duffel. It was cozy in the cargo hold. There are too many people up here."

Alex looked up to the sky. "Am I truly related to him?"

"I belong . . . I belong . . ." Max murmured.

"What are you doing now?" Alex said.

"Pretending I belong," Max replied. "People are looking at us. I think they know what we did."

"Max, they don't." Alex squeezed his hand. "Everyone's just being friendly. It's like a big summer camp."

"I'm scared. And you hate me."

"No, I don't," Alex said. "OK, I admit, there would have been no other way to get on board. I didn't like the prank, but your plan was pretty awesome."

"Thanks," Max replied. "But now what? I've been trying to think what to do next. And all that happens is I smell ham."

"What's that?" Alex said.

"Confusion."

"I have to write these down."

"Here are the facts. We don't have a place to stay. We don't really know what to do. We don't know how to find this fortune. Do we stand on deck humming to ourselves and wait for a monster-size seagull to swoop down with a treasure chest?" Max let out a deep breath.

"We're a team, cuz," Alex said, taking his hand. "We need an emergency meeting. Let's find a private place where we can brainstorm quietly."

To their left was a bank of plate-glass windows containing a minimall of shops and cafés. Max and Alex headed for the door. Just to one side of it, a man with a straw hat and Hawaiian shirt was going face-to-face with a woman crew member who was dressed in crisp whites. "The room is tiny!" the man bellowed. "I can hear the engine. It sounds like a moose! No flowers, no chandeliers, terrible views—nothing like the picture in the brochure. My wife and I were expecting that room."

"Is that room available?" said his wife with an expectant smile. She looked about half her husband's age and one-third his weight. "We had our dreams set on that."

"Ah, the Dolphin Penthouse," the officer said with a polite chuckle. "That room has been closed for repairs, but come with me and I'll see if we can find better accommodations for you."

Alex pulled Max past them. "People are so picky," she murmured.

As she grabbed the door to the café, a deafening hoot blasted from the smokestacks. People on the dock let out excited squeals. Max could feel the ship moving out of the dock and into the Hudson River.

Even the complaining couple had paused to wave to someone on shore. The ship's engines sent up a wake behind them as the jagged skyscrapers began to recede into the distance.

Max gulped.

There was no turning back now.

* * *

Alex grabbed a seat at a small table. As Max pulled his chair close, she displayed the image of the translated note on her phone. "I'll be right back."

Max stared at the message on the screen.

Upon reaching the great unruined chamber at the prime locations of the fifteenth, third, and second to the Pole Star and eleventh, seventeenth, and fourteenth to the sunrise, be guided by the camptodactyl of the king.

It was gobbledygook. Max stared and stared. Finally he closed his eyes.

"Sleeping already?" Alex slapped down two orangey-pink drinks, each with an umbrella on a long toothpick skewering a stack of fruit chunks.

Max took a sip and gagged. "It's too sweet."

Alex set down her drink and unfolded the map on the table. It showed the route of the SS *Sibelius*—up the northern coast of New England and Canada and then off into the Atlantic Ocean. "You were right. It's superclose to the same route as the *Nautilus*."

But Max was staring at the note again. "'Pole Star' . . . 'sunrise' . . ."

"Say what?" Alex replied.

"I am trying to break down the message," Max said.

"Into parts. Like a math equation."

Alex nodded and peered at the phone. "The Pole Star is the same thing as the North Star, right?"

"Exactly," Max said. "And the sun rises in the east. So we have two directions."

"How does that affect the message?" Alex said. "Fifteenth, third, and second to the north . . . eleventh, seventeenth, and fourteenth to the east!"

"Sounds like geo coordinates to me," Max said. He scribbled the numbers on a napkin, then accessed Google Maps and tapped them in: 15°3′2″N 11°17′14″E

They watched in excitement as the map moved.

"Drumroll please," Alex said. "Ladies and gentleman, we are going to . . ."

The map sharpened, dropping a pin on the final location.

"Southern Niger?" Max said.

"That's Africa," Alex said. "Niger is landlocked."

"We're doing something wrong . . ." Max pocketed the napkin and tapped his fingers on the table. "It's got to be on some coast. Or some remote island."

"Or buried out to sea," Alex pointed out. "Verne was traveling in a sub!"

Max sighed. "That does complicate things."

"OK, first things first," Alex replied. "Let's find our room."

"We don't have one," Max reminded her.

Alex swigged down her drink in one long gulp, then leaped up from the table. "You're not the only one with bright ideas. Follow me."

The sign on the door of the Dolphin Penthouse was in black and white with enormous letters: Please Excuse Our Appearance During Renovations.

"That's a pretty clear no," Max said, his eyes darting up and down the empty hall. "Can we go back now? I want to finish my awful-tasting drink."

But Alex was squinting at a collection of small-printed notices taped to the door beneath it. "The work doesn't begin until next week. It says so on the permit."

She pushed down on the latch and the door swung open. "Well, well . . ."

"What are you doing?" Max said, standing agape.

"Welcome to my boudoir . . ."

"Does that mean *gigantic mistake* in French? We can't go in there!"

But she was already inside.

Swallowing hard, Max followed her in. The room was

lined with glass windows overlooking the water, with a vaulted ceiling and a chandelier of hundreds of tiny lights. Two plush sofas faced a humongous flat-screen TV, and a doorway led into two other bedrooms. As he headed for them, Alex cried out, "Max, this is perfect!"

"This is criminal," Max replied.

She headed into the biggest bedroom and gestured to the peeling paint on one of the walls. "There's the problem. Water's coming in through the wall. Can't very well charge some rich people top dollar for a leaky room, so that's why they have to keep it empty." She jumped on the bed and stretched out. "Their loss, our gain."

"This makes me very nervous," Max said. "Couldn't we just sleep on the deck in one of those lounge chairs?"

"Uncle Jules would want us to do this in style!" Alex sat up and threw her head back dramatically. "Could you ring room service for some tea sandwiches and foie gras, my dahling?"

She shut her eyes and fell back in a flounce. To Alex, the gentle rocking of the boat was soothing and peaceful. The last sea voyage she'd taken with her parents was a ferry ride from Cape Cod to Martha's Vineyard. They had had a fried-clam dinner and ice-cream cones. It was nothing like this.

In her mind's eye she saw the cover of a book with a

romantic image of this room. She imagined her name—Alexandra Verne—splashed across the bottom. Along with quotes: "A masterpiece of adventure!" and "No one does it better!"

This—*this* was why she'd taken a year off. Saving a life . . . living an adventure . . . making a fortune . . . cooking up a bestseller.

Alex smiled and drifted off.

She was in the middle of a dream about meeting J. K. Rowling when she heard a knock on the door.

"What the—?" she said, bolting up in bed.

Max was sitting on an armchair near the room door, looking at his phone. "I was reading. You're right. *Twenty Thousand Leagues Under the Sea* is awesome. I'm at the part where they find the underwater city, and it's all destroyed—"

"Max, there was a knock at the door," Alex said.

"Sorry," Max replied, setting down the phone. "Must be room service."

"Room service?" Alex said.

Max stood. "You're in luck. They had both those things on the menu."

"What things?"

"Tea sandwiches and foie gras."

Alex leaped off the bed and held Max back. "That

was a joke, Max! I didn't mean for you to actually call room service!"

"Now you tell me."

The room door opened with a click so loud it seemed to echo in the living room. A moment later, a man and a woman in security uniforms walked in, giving Max and Alex baffled looks.

"I'd like to cancel the order," Max squeaked.

The woman gestured to the door. "Come with us, please."

"NO parents. No tickets. No passports . . ."

The ship's captain paced his office as he spoke. Behind him was a plate-glass window with a view of a rocky coastline, dotted with nice wood-shingled houses and small beaches. The man had a strong Australian accent and a deep red-brown tan. His thinning hair was plastered across his head like guitar strings. He patted it down while he paced, as if he were afraid it might fly off.

All Max wanted to do was disappear, fly through the window, and swim away.

"No, sir," Alex said softly. "We have none of those things."

"Quite a feat," the captain said. "Do you know what

the penalties are for stowing away on a commercial vessel?"

Max shook. "F-F-Firing squad?"

"Not quite so drastic," the captain said with a laugh. "But we will have to drop you at the next port. I would advise you to call someone and have them meet you in Newfoundland."

"Newfoundland?" Alex said.

"We don't know anyone there," Max said. "My parents are in Minnesota."

"Can't we just stay on?" Alex said, digging in her pockets. "We'll pay what we have. And we'll work for the rest. Dish washing, waitering, singing—"

"Not singing," Max said.

"I'm afraid I can't do that." The captain gestured to one of the security guards. "You will be under the guardianship of Mr. Robles until we dock. If you cannot be met by a family member in Newfoundland, we will need to leave you in the custody of the local police. They will help you further, and your parents will be billed for your time on the ship and our administrative costs. Mr. Robles?"

Before they could protest, the captain picked up his phone and turned away.

Mr. Robles had a thick mustache and a stony face

locked into a permafrown. He held the door open, and Alex and Max slumped out of the captain's office.

They emerged at the end of a corridor and onto a deck. To their left was a wide-open space with a huge pool, where kids were laughing and zooming down long slides. "Go toward the stern," Mr. Robles said in a gravelly monotone.

"Is that the front of the boat?" Max asked hopefully, looking toward the pool. "A swim would be great."

"Stern is back, bow is front." Mr. Robles gestured to the right, away from the pool. "And by the way, this is a ship, not a boat. If you're facing the stern, port is to the right, starboard to the left."

"Thank you," Max said.

"Facts always make him feel better," Alex drawled.

"Loud bad music makes her feel better," Max piped up. "Can you sing anything by the Ramones?"

Mr. Robles silently led them into an elevator, where they rode grimly up to the penthouse floor. As they emerged and began following Robles toward the penthouse, Alex pulled Max back. When the guard was a safe distance ahead, she whispered into Max's ear, "We have to ditch this guy. After we get our stuff."

"We have no place to go," Max pointed out. "A ship like this is a closed system."

"There are a gazillion people on board," Alex said. "We get lost as best we can. We sneak back down into the cargo hold. Then we find the luggage that we came in, and we zip ourselves back inside."

"Good," Max said. "That's good. But we need to have a secret signal. Something we can say aloud. A code word that means 'Time to escape.'"

"How about *Go*?" Alex said.

"That's not secret. I was thinking . . . *Aronnax*! You know, the hero of *Twenty Thousand Leagues*?"

"Fine," Alex said. "Till then, just act normal."

Mr. Robles had disappeared around a corner, but now he stuck his stonelike head back in the hallway. "Come!"

"Yes, sir," Max said.

He and Alex scurried after him. When they reached the corner, he gestured toward the Dolphin Penthouse at the end of a short corridor. "You will retrieve your belongings, and then I will take you to our back offices. There will be water and food, but you will not be able to mix with the regular paying guests. If anything is missing, you will be billed."

"Thank you, Mr. Bubbles," Alex muttered.

As Robles waited in the hallway, Max followed Alex inside.

She quickly disappeared into the inner bedroom.

Max took one last look at the view outside the window. He would miss that.

"Hey, Max?" Alex called out. "Is the note from you-know-who in your backpack?"

Ducking into the bedroom himself, Max lifted his pack off the floor and opened it to look inside. That's when he noticed Vulturon sitting on the floor by the wall.

He moved closer. "I didn't take that out," he murmured.

"I don't have the booklet, do you?" When Max didn't answer, Alex spun toward him. "Don't tell me. You smell fish."

Max nodded. "My stuff. Someone touched it. It's not the way I packed it."

"But the note's in there, right?" Alex asked.

"No," Max replied.

"That's impossible," Alex said. "Look again."

"Come, come!" Mr. Robles yelled from the living room.

Alex and Max quickly dumped out their packs, sorted the stuff, and repacked. They looked everywhere in the bedroom. In the living room. In the rooms they'd never entered. The note was nowhere.

"We're missing something, Mr. Robles!" Alex protested. "Someone stole it from us!"

"Nobody was here," Mr. Robles said.

"How can you be sure of that?" Alex asked.

"You may file a claim with the lost and found," Mr. Robles replied. "Now come. I have a schedule."

He stood and gestured out the door. Alex gave Max a look. They were stuck.

Max stuffed Vulturon back into his backpack, hooked it onto his shoulder, and trudged through the door. Alex followed behind him.

Mr. Robles locked the room behind him. "A lot of good that does now," Alex said.

"She's being sarcastic," Max explained.

Without a reply, Mr. Robles began walking back down the hallway toward the elevator. Alex took Max's hand and walked slowly. She eyed a door at the end of the hallway marked Emergency Exit.

The moment Robles turned the corner, Alex whispered, "Aronnax."

She leaned into the door's horizontal latch, pushed it open, and pulled Max along with her. An alarm echoed in the stairwell. *"Hey!"* Mr. Robles shouted. *"Stop!"*

But Alex and Max were already racing down the metal steps. At the first landing, Max burst through another door. He emerged into a corridor that was longer and wider than the first. He and Alex sprinted down a hall full of stateroom doors. They scurried around a group of three old men making their way slowly with walkers. "Excuse me . . . excuse . . ." Max said.

As they disappeared around a corner, Max could hear a crash behind them. And then Mr. Robles's voice yelling at the three elderly passengers.

Alex and Max made it past the elevator bank when one of the doors dinged. Even before it opened, Max could hear the crackle of walkie-talkies from within.

Security.

Max's eyes focused on a closet near the soda machines. He yanked on the door. It opened into a boxy closet full of shelves containing sheets, pillows, and cleaning supplies. "Come on," he said, pulling Alex inside and shutting the door as quickly and quietly as he could.

Their breaths sounded like buzz saws in the small room. Max hoped they couldn't be heard outside. Footsteps clattered by—then Mr. Robles's voice barked out a report, telling the others something in a language Max didn't know.

Then nothing.

One . . . two . . . three . . .

Max counted to thirteen, his age, in total silence. Then he slowly pushed the door open. The hinges creaked mournfully like lost sheep.

Halfway down the hall, the three old men were

waiting for the elevator. At the sound of the closet door they turned toward Max and Alex and gave them a long look. "We told them you went to Section C," one of them said. "You're good for a few minutes at least."

"You lied?" Max said.

The old guy smiled. "We're on your side. That fella with the mustache was very rude to us."

Alex ran to him and planted a kiss on his cheek. "Thanks!"

"I will not kiss you," Max said. "But yes, thanks."

The elevator door opened, and they both stepped inside. The three men waved to them as Max pressed B1. "Where are we going?" Alex asked.

"After we stowed away in the cargo hold, we climbed the stairs to level B1, remember?" Max said. "Then we took an elevator up."

"Yeah, but it didn't look like *this* elevator," Alex said.

"Must have been a different part of the ship," Max said. "But when we get down there, I think I'll be able to retrace our steps."

Max held his breath as the door opened. The hallway was empty. It did not look familiar to Max at all. As they stepped out, he tried to adjust his bearings. "I think we need the starboard bow."

"What does that mean?" Alex said.

"Follow me." He ran to the left. The engine noise was loud down here, and Max felt as if the floors were vibrating. They stopped at a *T* intersection. To the left was an empty hallway. To the right, Max saw a sign that said Lifeboats.

"I think we go right," Alex said. "Right?"

Max was losing his sense of direction now. "This looks wrong to me," he said. "I'm pretty sure we need to go the other way."

Alex was already halfway down the right-hand corridor. As she turned toward Max, she stopped halfway. Her eyes were fixed on a porthole at about eye level. "Come here . . ." she said. "Now. Look at this."

Max ran to her side. Outside was a narrow deck, and beyond it a lifeboat suspended on a winch. To the right of the hanging lifeboat, two men were looking over the railing down into the sea. They were wearing floppy hats, their backs to Max and Alex, and the bigger of the two men had a small string bag slung over his shoulders.

"So?" Max said.

"Look closely," Alex whispered.

Max squinted. The thinner man was waving at someone down below with his left hand.

Which was very clearly missing a pinkie.

18

"**ALEX**, *don't!*" Max shouted.

But his cousin had pounded through the door and was lunging for Rudolph. As the big guy turned, Alex caught him off-balance, and he fell.

With a quick, graceful move, Fix managed to slide the string bag off the bigger man's beefy shoulders. He clutched the bag tight to his chest. "Don't you think dear Rudolph has had enough physical trauma?"

"*You* haven't," Alex said, balling her fists. "But we can change that. Give us the bag. I know what's in it."

"I quiver with fear," Fix replied.

"*That's a lie!*" Max shouted. "Unless you're being sarcastic."

Fix gave him an odd look. "Yes, you're right, dear

boy. I'm not quivering, because I'm quite happy to see you. And very grateful to receive such a precious gift to humanity. You will benefit someday, I promise."

Rudolph stood and grabbed Alex by the front of her shirt collar. "I would love to heave-ho both of these pains in the—"

"Manners, Rudolph, manners," Fix said. "These are children, and children are the planet's great hope."

Alex swatted aside Rudolph's arm. "Brush your teeth, Hagrid, your breath is like day-old roadkill," Alex said. "As for you, Mr. Fix-It, I don't know how you guys found us, or how you got on this ship—"

"Fix is the name," the silver-haired man said. "A nickname, I should say. To the world I am known as Spencer Niemand. Yes, I am head of Niemand Enterprises, the number-one global company forging a dynamic synergy between telecommunications, exploration, shipping, and environmental innovation. In person."

Alex and Max stared at him blankly. "Never heard of you," Max said.

"Suffice it to say we have eyes and ears," Niemand snapped. "Plus ample private aircraft and ground transport—and more than enough financial resources for a last-minute cruise ticket. Although I admit we almost lost you after the parking garage." He chuckled.

"Kudos on a very clever move with that luggage. Don't you agree, Rudolph?"

Rudolph scowled at Alex. "I did brush my teeth."

Max could see her coiling to lunge at him again. That, he knew, would not work. He held her back with one hand and reached out the other to Niemand. "You can keep the string bag, but give us what's inside. It belongs to us, and you're stealing."

"And what will you do if we don't return it—report us to security?" Niemand smiled. "How do you suppose that will work for you?"

Alex's teeth were gritted, her eyes intense. "Give. Us. That. Booklet."

"Maybe you can tell us what it says," Niemand replied. "That would save us a lot of time and expense. Neither Rudolph nor I read French. We could all form a big, happy team."

"As if," Alex said, shaking her head.

"I take that as a no," Niemand said.

He held the string bag over his head, swung it out over the side of the ship, and dropped it.

Max screamed and ran to the railing. But Alex stood there, staring at Niemand in disbelief. "Th-that made no sense! You just shot yourself in the foot, fool."

"Alex—" Max said.

Alex laughed. "Let it sink, Max," she said. "We already know what it says. But they—"

"Alex!"

Max pulled her to the railing and made her look over. Below them was a sleek silver-and-black cigarette boat. On it, a man dressed in a black uniform was placing the string bag into a chest. He revved the engine and glanced behind him.

Alex spun around. "Max, Niemand and Rudolph are gone!"

Over Max's shoulder, he saw the door swinging slowly shut. He could hear the clatter of footfalls in a nearby stairwell.

"We can't catch them," Max said.

"We'll have to jump," Alex replied, putting one leg on the railing. Below them, Niemand and Rudolph burst through a door exactly one level down, ran to the railing and leaped over, one after the other.

Niemand landed smoothly with help from the uniformed man. Rudolph missed entirely and had to be quickly helped into the cigarette boat.

"It's too dangerous," Max said, pulling her back.

"They have the message!" Alex pleaded. "They'll figure it out. You read what Jules Verne said. He hid the fortune to keep it away from bad guys."

"Bad guys from the eighteen hundreds," Max said.

"Niemand and his BFF have been looking for this forever," Alex said. "They smoked out my craigslist post and came all the way to your house. They nearly killed us and chased us to New York City. And they bought at least fourteen thousand dollars of cruise tickets and hired a speedboat just to steal it. Do you think it's just possible that they're somehow connected to Verne's bad guys?"

"When you put it that way . . ."

Max was eyeing the lifeboat that hung overhead. It was attached by two strong ropes to a winch. The winch had two pulleys that were operated by a crank at the level below, where Niemand had just been. But that crank was protected by a thick padlock.

The cigarette boat was turning away from the ship now, picking up speed. Max knew they had to get down there. Now.

He bolted for the door behind them.

"Where are you going?" Alex cried out.

"Follow me."

Max darted down the hallway, pushed through the exit door, and rushed down to the level below. The cigarette boat was headed for the horizon as Max unhooked his backpack from his shoulders, opened it, and dug his hands in.

Alex stared mutely as he pulled out a pocketknife and began cutting through the rope that held the lifeboat above them.

As the rope severed, the port side of the boat abruptly fell. Minutes later Max worked through the starboard rope, and the boat crashed into the water, barely missing the keel of the cruise ship.

"Jump," Max said, throwing his backpack over his shoulder again. "And don't say no. I need you. I don't know how to work one of these boats."

"Wait—neither do I!"

Max climbed over the railing and fell onto the deck of the lifeboat. He stood and reached up for Alex.

As she jumped in beside him, Max cried out, *"Hurry!"*

"Me hurry?" She glanced with panic at the outboard engine and pointed to a wooden knob at the top. "OK. OK. We can do this. I—I think that's a cord. And you pull it. Like a lawn mower."

Max yanked on the cord once . . . twice . . . but the engine groaned and sputtered.

"Let me try." Alex took the knob, gritted her teeth, and yanked it as hard as she could.

The motor sputtered to life. Alex jumped back. With a solid *thunk*, the boat crashed into the side of the SS *Sibelius*, leaving an ugly dent.

"Can you straighten it out?" Max said.

"I'm trying!" Alex yanked the tiller to the left and eased up on the throttle. The boat spun slowly and soon faced out to sea.

Up on the deck, Mr. Robles burst from the exit. His face reddened at the sight of Alex and Max, and he began screaming into a walkie-talkie.

"Now what?" Max demanded.

Alex held tight and pointed them in the direction of the cigarette boat, which was now a dot on the horizon. "Sit down, cousin. And pray."

19

"CAN'T *you go any faster?"* Max shouted.

The engine was roaring like a trombone with indigestion as the boat bounced on the choppy water. "We're at full throttle!" Alex said.

Max stared straight ahead at the dot. Saltwater sprayed up from the sea on both sides, cold and nasty, but he didn't care.

In a moment, he realized the little black dot of the cigarette boat was actually beginning to grow. They were gaining. "I don't believe this . . . they stopped."

Alex saw it too. "Why would they stop in the middle of the ocean?"

"Out of gas?"

"I don't trust them. We may have to defend ourselves."

Alex gestured toward a wooden chest with a slanted top marked Equipment. "Check in that thing."

"You think there might be weapons in there?"

"Spears, harpoons, flares, crowbars, nunchucks, whatever we can use!"

Tentatively Max pulled open the chest and rooted around inside. Life vests . . . extra rope . . . GPS device . . . hooks and tools . . .

At the bottom was a small, black leather box. Max lifted it out and unlatched the top.

It wasn't a weapon, but it was a pair of binoculars. Lifting them to his eyes, Max found the cigarette boat. Three figures were standing on the deck, but even with the magnification he couldn't recognize faces. "They're just standing still—not even looking our way!" he called out.

But now Alex's eyes were trained on another black dot behind them—another boat with a whining engine. *"Max—the other direction—back toward the cruise ship!"* she shouted. *"What's that?"*

Max swung the binoculars around. A lifeboat sped toward them, with the words SS *Sibelius* emblazoned on the hull. On deck were two people in white uniforms. "It's security! They're after us."

Alex cringed. "Oh, great. What do we do now?"

"That boat is the same design as ours, the same engine," Max replied. "Which means they can't gain on us. We can do this. We can get to Niemand!"

Alex stared straight ahead as they neared the cigarette boat. Through the binoculars, Max could make out the two very clear, very shocked, faces of Niemand and Rudolph. "They've spotted us!" Max cried out.

"I want to see their expressions," Alex said, "when I split their fancy little boat in two."

Max watched the men carefully, expecting the boat to start speeding off. But the two men were turning away. They were facing the other direction now, like they had been moments before. And in a moment, Max saw why.

Just beyond Niemand's boat, a black shape broke the surface of the water. From this distance it looked like some kind of sea monster. Max felt his fingers tense on the binoculars. But the monster was glinting in the sun. Which meant it was made of metal, not flesh. "I don't believe this . . ." Max said.

"What?" Alex demanded.

The monster had a gyrating dish. And a periscope. And a steel hull emblazoned with these words:

THE CONCH
A PROPERTY OF
NIEMAND ENTERPRISES

"It's a submarine," Max said. "They were waiting for it to break the surface—that's why they weren't moving!"

"They're using it to escape, Max!" Alex said. "We don't stand a chance."

Max put the binoculars down. They were maybe two hundred yards away now, not going nearly fast enough to reach Niemand.

But maybe something else would.

"Air travel is faster than ocean travel, Alex," Max said.

"Thank you, Mr. Factoid!" Alex said. "But I can't fly and neither can you."

Quickly he slid his backpack off his shoulders, reached inside, and pulled out Vulturon. "We can't. But *this* can . . ."

"This is a joke, right?" Alex said. "What do you plan to do, Max, drop an apple on their heads?"

"We don't need one. Trust me." Unfolding the drone, Max placed it on the deck and held his remote. "Do your job, Big V."

He powered on and pressed Lift. The drone rose slowly, teetering in the strong wind. Using the controls, Max guided it forward. It tilted and hovered for a moment.

Then it shot toward the cigarette boat.

With one hand Max held the binoculars to his eyes, and with the other he guided Vulturon. A bearded guy had emerged from the hatch of the submarine, and he was laying out a ladder connecting the two vessels. Niemand stepped up onto the ladder, but he looked scared. Neither of them seemed to be noticing the drone.

"What do you see?" Alex said.

"Rudolph has the bag . . ." Max replied.

Now Vulturon was in the field of vision of the binoculars, dropping from above. Rudolph was still holding the ladder steady for Niemand. The string of the bag lay diagonally across Rudolph's massive shoulder.

Rudolph's arm kept the string tightly in place. Stealing the bag away would be impossible.

Unless . . .

Max brought Vulturon down . . . slowly . . . until it just grazed Rudolph's head. The big guy looked up with a start.

Up . . . up!

Vulturon rose, but not too far. Just barely out of Rudolph's reach. The big guy jumped, trying to grab the drone from the air. Now his arm was pointed straight skyward.

Perfect.

Max would have to move fast. He'd have only one chance. He let Vulturon drop quickly—maybe five feet—at the same time activating all four claws. Before Rudolph could react, Claw #4 clasped the bag's string, and Max yanked Vulturon upward again. The bag moved with it.

Instead of slamming his arm down, Rudolph tried even harder to grab Vulturon. Which meant he kept reaching upward . . . grasping . . .

Yes!

The drone lifted the string up the length of Rudolph's straightened arm until it was free. In a moment the string bag—and the booklet—were flying high over the Atlantic, back to Alex and Max.

"Woo-hoo!" Alex screamed. *"Remind me never to doubt you again!"*

"Okay. Alex, never doubt me again." Max put down the binoculars. In the last couple of minutes, their boat had sped much closer to the cigarette boat. They were maybe thirty yards away.

As Max angled the drone toward him, a gunshot rang out.

Max nearly dropped the remote in shock. Rudolph was pointing a pistol at Vulturon. On the ladder, Niemand lifted a megaphone to his mouth. *"Keep the bag in the air!"* he bellowed.

"Listen to him, Max," Alex said.

Max pressed Hover. Vulturon stopped in midair, about halfway between the two boats. The bag swung back and forth with the momentum.

"Now cut your engine and bring the bag back to us, or Rudolph shoots the drone to smithereens!" Niemand said.

"Fine!" Alex shouted. *"Go ahead and shoot it! You'll never see the booklet again!"*

"Alex, I spent weeks working on that drone!" Max snapped.

Rudolph swung the gun toward Max.

"Duck, Max!" Alex pushed Max off his seat. As he fell to the deck, she let go of the throttle. The engine sputtered and died. "Now listen to me, cousin. Do as they say. We won't do any good by dying."

Before Max could react, he heard Niemand's voice from the cigarette boat. "Rudolph, what has twisted your feeble mind? He's a child. We do not shoot children!"

As Max peered over the gunwale, Rudolph pointed his gun at Alex, who gulped back a shriek. "I think the girl is a grown-up," the big man said.

Max leaped up and stood in front of his cousin. He held the controller in the air for them to see. *"Stop! You can have the booklet!"*

"Thank you," Alex whispered.

"But you have to put the gun down first!" Max insisted.

Rudolph hesitated, then slowly lowered the gun. Max glanced quickly over his shoulder. The rescue boat was coming nearer by the second. In a few minutes they'd be here. And Max and Alex would be headed back to the SS *Sibelius*—without the booklet, without Vulturon, and in big, big trouble for stealing a boat.

While Niemand would be on his way to the greatest treasure known to humankind.

Max carefully moved Vulturon closer to the cigarette boat. The string bag swung lightly. Niemand and Rudolph were there looking up, mouths open, like baby chicks in a nest. Behind Max, Alex was silent but he could feel her frustration like a heat wave.

When the bag was close, the two men reached up. "I got it, boss," Rudolph said.

"No, this time *I* shall do it, thank you," Niemand replied, shoving the big man in the chest with both arms.

Off-balance, Rudolph windmilled his arms and slipped off the boat. As he splashed into the sea, Max released Vulturon's claws. Niemand pulled the bag close to his chest. He didn't smile, didn't say thanks, didn't look Max's way at all. Instead, he crossed over the ladder and disappeared into the submarine.

Alex let out a groan of disappointment.

Rudolph floundered in the sea, the current taking him past their lifeboat. "I can't swim!" he bellowed.

The other boat was only a few yards behind Max and Alex. Alerted by Rudolph's screams, one of the cruise ship guards was tossing him a life preserver.

Max turned back toward the sub, keeping a careful eye on the hatch. He heard a thick rope thump down onto the stern of his boat.

"Hold on to that towline, kids!" shouted a familiar voice through a megaphone from behind them. "We're pulling you all in!"

"Great, it's Bubbles," Alex murmured.

Ignoring Robles, Max guided the drone over the sub. "Alex, get ready to move," he said softly.

"What?"

"When I say Aronnax, we go full throttle." Slowly he guided Vulturon until it was hovering directly over the sub's open hatch. Inside, the bearded man was pulling in the ladder.

Max waited until the last inch of the ladder was

sinking into the hatch. Then he jammed the controller hard. Dive.

Vulturon free-dropped. Max could feel sweat pouring down his face. The bearded guy's hand was pulling the hatch shut. *Go . . . GO . . .*

With a sickening metallic crunch, Vulturon smashed into the hatch door's opening. The rotor blades whined and spun, stuck in, keeping the hatch from shutting.

"Aronnax!" Max shouted.

Alex pulled the throttle so hard, Max fell back. As they sped toward the sub, Max kept his eye on Vulturon. It was mangled and broken beyond repair, but Max couldn't be happier. As long as the hatch was kept open, the sub would have to stay above water. And if it was at the surface, the bad guys weren't getting away.

Now the SS *Sibelius* lifeboat was close behind them. Mr. Robles was shouting through the megaphone, but Max's eyes were fixed on metal handholds attached to the hull of the sub. *"Pull up to the hatch!"* Max shouted.

Alex steered the boat alongside the sub and cut the engine. Grabbing the handholds, Max hoisted himself up to the hatch. He looked down through an inches-wide gap to see Niemand, the bearded guy, and two other strangers staring back up, their jaws hanging open. One of them had climbed the ladder and was trying to dislodge Vulturon. But the blades were spinning too fast and he couldn't see how to get his hand in without losing a finger or two or three.

"The SS *Sibelius* security will be boarding in one minute!" Max called down. "Good luck explaining why you were pointing guns at kids."

"You are deluded!" Niemand snapped.

"*You* are, if you think you can escape now," Max shot back. "I built Vulturon. I can turn it off and pull it loose. But I'll only agree to do that if you agree to let us inside."

"Max, they're here!" Alex cried.

"*This is security*—" Mr. Robles announced, as the boat pulled alongside them.

At the sound of Robles's voice, Niemand stiffened.

"Your choice, dude," Max said.

"All right!" Niemand snapped, sweat gathering on his forehead. "Do it, then—and hurry!"

Alex scrambled up next to Max, who dug his fingers into the guts of Vulturon and pressed the collapsible switch. Instantly the drone stopped buzzing and folded inward. With a quick heave, he and Alex lifted the drone out of the hatch.

"You go first," Alex said, holding tight to Vulturon.

As Max climbed down into the sub, Alex turned. Rudolph was standing in the boat now, glowering at her, whispering into Robles's ear. *"On behalf of the SS Sibelius,"* Robles said, *"and in accordance with international maritime law—"*

Alex lifted Vulturon high over her head. Then, with all her strength, she tossed it directly at Rudolph. With a scream of surprise, he lost his balance, slipped, and fell into the water again.

"Nice catch," Alex said, as she scrambled into the sub and shut the hatch behind her.

20

"TELL me why I shouldn't kill you now."

Niemand sipped from a steaming mug of coffee. He was pacing back and forth in a small, oak-lined study crammed with bookshelves and an antique globe. Through a porthole, the sea was a murky olive green, and the only sound was the hum of the submarine engine and faint tinny music from the next room. Niemand had already changed out of his wet clothes into a black silk T-shirt, black pants, and narrow black boots, with a black-and-orange silk scarf around his neck.

"Of course you won't kill us," Max said. "Because you didn't when you had the chance."

Niemand's body twitched. Coffee spilled from his cup and landed on the carpet with an audible *ssssss*.

Alex elbowed Max. "My cousin can be very logical," she explained.

"Also," Max barreled on, "the SS *Sibelius* now has Rudolph. And in case he lies, well, they saw the name of your company on the sub. Additionally, you and Rudolph bought tickets, which means the ship has your record on file. So two missing children will look bad. But two dead ones will look worse."

"Yeah," Alex said, her expression brightening. "That."

Niemand swigged down the scalding coffee and walked to the porthole. Outside, the slippery shape of an eel floated by. "Do you have any idea what you have stumbled into?" he said.

"A submarine," Max said.

Niemand spun around. "You offer sarcasm?"

"I will never understand that," Max said.

Alex felt her muscles tense. "He didn't mean it that way."

Squatting next to Max, Niemand leaned in so close that he could count the pimples on his face. "Tell me, what is your personal dream, lad?" he demanded.

Max gulped. He looked uncertainly at Alex. "To understand sarcasm?"

"Bigger!" Niemand stood, turned, and pounded the top of a wooden bookshelf. "Your *life's* dream! Tell me!"

"He's nuts," Alex whispered into Max's ear. "Keep him happy."

Max nodded. "OK . . . my dream . . . um, to keep my family from being evicted. Also to save my mom's life."

"Oh?" Niemand's face softened.

"My aunt is very sick," Alex explained. "My uncle had to take her away for treatment. That's why I came to take care of Max."

"Ah." Niemand nodded, his forehead furrowed. "So your attempt to sell the chest was . . ."

"To raise money," Alex replied. "To pay bills. We didn't realize the significance of the chest. My aunt is Jules Verne's great-great-granddaughter, so we figured we'd just found some of his random stuff. Until we read the note. Then I realized we had a shot at something bigger."

"Really . . ." Niemand pulled a handkerchief from his pocket and daubed his face. For a long time, he stared at a wall bookcase, as if trying to decide something. Then he turned back to them. "This explains a lot."

"It does?" Max said.

Niemand pressed a button on a remote, and a white screen descended from the ceiling. Slowly the lights in the room dimmed, until it was darker than the glow of the sea outside the window.

"You know, I have dreams too," Niemand said.

"Have either of you ever seen this?"

The first slide was a giant image of a newspaper article dated 1886, with the headline "Deranged Nephew Shoots French Author Verne!" Under the headline was a line drawing of a neatly dressed, bearded guy cowering in fear as a drooling, shabby-looking young man takes a shot at him.

"The gentleman we see is Jules Verne," Niemand said. "The assailant is Verne's nephew, who shot him but only managed to injure his foot, which was maimed forever."

"Why?" Max asked.

"Why indeed?" Niemand said. "Verne was a quiet, distinguished man. He wrote and traveled. And traveled. And traveled. He would sail for months at a time, several times a year. Poof—he would vanish for an entire summer with no written record. His family relationships began to fray—and quite badly, as we see. What was so important about those trips? What was his nephew's motive for attempting murder? Had he discovered something that Verne was hiding? What could he have been hiding?"

"Maybe the nephew was just insane," Alex said.

"Many thought so," Niemand replied. "But in fact, Verne had enemies. One of them was my own Niemand ancestor. He was a visionary man decades ahead of his time. He dreamed of enclosing entire civilizations in bubbles—with perfect weather, farms, businesses, homes. We could have life on other planets! Surely, my ancestor thought, Verne would be the perfect partner."

"Right—Verne wrote about an underwater city!" Alex said.

"Precisely," Niemand said. "And this is what Niemand Enterprises is all about. That dream. When the earth is a smoldering wreck—when climate change has made it uninhabitable—we will all need places to live!"

As he picked up the remote again, the image on the screen changed. "Now . . . do either of you recognize this?"

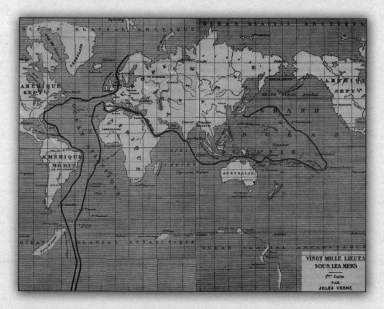

Alex leaned forward. "It's the voyage taken by the *Nautilus*, the submarine in *Twenty Thousand Leagues Under the Sea*."

"Brava," Niemand said. "This map was found among the artifacts recovered from the *Titanic* in 1912. It belonged to Verne's editor, a Frenchman named Pierre-Jules Hetzel, who framed and stored it in a watertight container. After Hetzel died, people remarked about what an unusual fuss had been taken to prevent damage to a simple map. So it was quietly auctioned off in New York in 1913, where it was bought at a bargain price by a wealthy collector . . ." He smiled. ". . . named Niemand."

"You don't look that old," Max said.

"*Roland* Niemand," Niemand said, "my great-great-grandfather. He had developed an interest in Verne, for reasons I soon discovered. Inside the frame, he had found hidden notes from Verne to Hetzel. Nonsense rhymes, silly sentences—perhaps plans for a children's book. It was only years later that I, Spencer Niemand, discovered a message. It described the chest in detail and hinted at a manuscript that would reveal the location of a great fortune. All my life I have been searching for this."

"You have a copy of that message too?" Alex said.

"Don't get too excited," Max said. "It's not the entire manuscript of *The Lost Treasures*—"

"Max!" Alex said.

Max sighed. "It's not a secret. He has the note."

"Smart boy," Niemand said, kneeling between the two. "Very smart. You remind me of myself when I was young. Well then, now that we're stuck with each other, I have an idea. You want to find the entire book of *The Lost Treasures*. So do I. How about creating something historic? Finally, for the first time in generations, the uniting of the Verne and Niemand families in a common cause!"

Alex leaped up from her seat. "You want us to work for *you*?"

"*With* me," Niemand said, looking from Alex to Max. "I can help you realize your dream. I have the resources to find the treasure, you have the motivation. Help me, and I'll make sure all your bills are paid and your mother gets the finest treatment from the best doctors in the world."

"But you're a liar and a violent, nasty guy," Max said. "Why should we believe you?"

Niemand laughed. "You'll see, I have a lighter side." He stood, turned off the slide presentation, and walked briskly to the door. "This is a great opportunity for all of us, young man. You want to save your mother, I seek to save the world. I shall notify my crew, and they will take you on a tour of the *Conch*. You will be very impressed. You'll see things are not as simple as they may seem."

"There is no way on earth we would ever help you," Alex said.

Halfway out the door, Niemand turned. "'No way' is not an option, young lady. I'm afraid you are deeply into 'no choice.'"

21

"**WHAT** did that slimy, ferret-headed toff tell you?" bellowed a bearded, broad-shouldered man as he bounded into the study. He wore jeans and a ripped forest-green polo shirt, and his hair was pulled back into a thick gray ponytail.

"You're the guy I saw pulling in the ladder," Max said.

"Honestly, I've seen rats scuttle when Niemand walks down the street!" the man went on. "He scares Halloween clear into Christmas. You outsmarted the little piker, you did. Good for his ego. Bring him down a notch. Now then, you didn't let him frighten you, did you? Because if he did, I'll be sure to pull out that silver stripe on his head and plant roses in his scalp. Just for our amusement."

Alex and Max stared, slack-jawed.

"I can't believe you just said that," Alex said.

The man slapped his own forehead and then extended his hand. "Forgive my bad manners. I'm Basile, the captain. In my position, I can say whatever I want. I've known Stinky for a long time."

"S-S-Stinky?" Max said.

"Sorry, my accent too thick?" Basile said. "I'm a Londoner, you know. Most people think Australia. Yes, Stinky Niemand. Stink. Key. He was my college roommate. Until he flunked out."

From the hallway, Niemand poked his head in and said, "Basile, you know I did not flunk out. I took a semester off. And if you continue to spread falsehoods and call me names, I shall fire you."

"Yes, sir, indeed, sir," Basile said with an exaggerated bow.

As Niemand ushered in three other people, Basile turned to Alex and Max and inserted his fingers into his mouth as if barfing.

The three other crew members eyed Alex and Max curiously. They were all wearing black uniforms with a silver swoosh across the front and an NE logo on the left breast.

"Are you smelling ham?" Alex murmured to Max. "Ham is confusion, right?"

"Yes, but it's canceled out by the smell of dark chocolate."

"What's that?"

"Relief. Because there's someone on this planet who isn't afraid of Niemand."

" . . . And these are the rest of my international team of geniuses," Niemand said. "Sophia is from Nigeria and speaks six languages. She is our chief engineer."

A deeply dark-skinned young woman with high cheekbones grinned and gave a tiny curtsy. "Welcome."

"André is German and the best mechanic in the Western Hemisphere. He keeps the *Conch* shipshape," Niemand continued, gesturing toward a gloomy-looking, rail-thin man with a shaved head and snake tattoos that ran up all sides of his neck. He didn't say a word, staring at Max with green eyes that seemed to glow from within.

The green was so bright, so unnatural, that Max had to turn away.

"And Pandora is our resident cartographer and navigator," Niemand went on, "fresh from university in Brazil."

Pandora had olive skin and dark, smiling eyes. She

glanced uncomfortably toward the mechanic. "Pleased to meet you. Forgive André. He doesn't speak much."

"Hrrtz," André seemed to say.

"Good then, I shall get back to my post," Basile announced. "Alex, Max, promise to stop by when you're finished with the tour?"

"I'll be sure they do," Niemand said.

"Or what—you'll bite their noses off?" Basile retorted with a blustery laugh.

As Niemand and Basile walked away, arguing, Sophia led everyone else out of the study. They emerged into a corridor wide enough to fit four people shoulder to shoulder. The walls were a white-gray metal with a brushed texture. Max expected the hallway to go straight, but it curved to the left as they walked.

"Most submarines are cylindrical—sort of a fish shape with all the inner spaces crammed and piled atop one another," Sophia said. "The *Conch* is unique. Mr. Niemand wanted a design inspired by the *Nautilus* that Jules Verne described in *Twenty Thousand Leagues Under the Sea*. At the center of the sub, I have created the massive circular space we are in. Like a great disk. Come."

Max followed her down the curving corridor, lined with doors on both sides. Sophia pushed open a door on the left to reveal a room with a perfectly made bed, a slanted desk, and posters of forest landscapes. "These are my living quarters," she said. "All our rooms are on the inside of the circle, so no windows, but still very pleasant. The most interesting rooms are on the right—along the perimeter of the circle."

The first was a game room lined with beanbag chairs and a futon. Metal shelves were stacked with board games and puzzles. Strewn about on tables were at least three iPads, four laptops, a Wii console, and Super Nintendo. In the center of the space was a brand-new foosball game. "Can this be my bedroom, please?" Max said.

But Alex was already peeking into the next room. "Whoa. Max, look!"

Max followed her into an entertainment center with a humongous flat-screen TV, plush sofas, a popcorn machine, and a glass cabinet stocked with candy bars. "The TV is seventy-five inches," Sophia said, "and because we cannot get Wi-Fi, we have collected three thousand movies and TV shows for viewing."

Pandora then took over the tour and guided them around the gym, the hospital, and finally the map room, which was loaded with stacks of paper charts. The maps' bright colors made the sea bottom look like an exotic landscape of smoking volcanos and vast mountain ranges. Next André showed them the engine room, the guts of the ship. It was the largest space of all, extending past the circular area and deep into the dark cylindrical guts of the sub. A massive camshaft turned with a deep and steady groan, its motion turning gears above and below.

"Fnnf," André said, gesturing toward an electronic board that extended nearly floor to ceiling with levers, switches, and gauges. "Und grssstn."

Neither Max nor Alex bothered to ask. But Max was relieved whenever the mechanic looked away. The green eyes bothered him. They reminded Max of a snake.

"Sometimes we need quiet," Pandora said, pushing open another door, "so we have a well-stocked library. Over one hundred thousand volumes here."

The smell of wood and leather wafted out through the door, and Max stared into a room lined with dark oak shelves and plush, red-leather armchairs. Books were crammed onto every shelf, and each desk contained an e-reader. "Amazing," Max said. "I like this almost as much as the game room."

"Yup, nerd paradise," Alex remarked.

"Here we have the fitting room and diving chamber," Sophia said as they entered with a *swoosh* of the doors. "Although *diving* is not the right word."

Four thick, massive suits, like the kind the astronauts wore on the moon, stood against the far wall like sleeping zombies. "When we explore the ocean floor, we don these special pressure suits," Sophia continued. "We enter a sealed chamber that exchanges air for water before we step out into the ocean."

"And last but not least, the captain's wheelhouse," Pandora said, throwing open another door.

"*Vin-che-e-e-e-e-r-a-a-a-a-h!*" The scream was so loud, Max nearly fell back.

Pandora darted inside. Basile was sitting on a stool, rocking back and forth, in front of a steering wheel and a periscope. He was wearing thick headphones, which Pandora yanked off his head.

"What, what?" Basile cried out, spinning around. "Oh. There you are. Do you like opera? Puccini? Come. Be truthful."

"No," Alex said.

"Very well, I shall sing it nonstop until you tell me where we are going." He got up from his seat and ushered the others out of the room. "Shoo, scat, the tour is over! Time for work!"

"Thanks, guys! That was awe— " Max shouted as the doors shut abruptly behind him.

Basile turned back into the room. Max gazed around. The walls were crammed with gauges and maps and switches and levers. In the center, where Basile sat, was a stool with a steering wheel and a periscope. A radar map showed a blinking white dot, and a massive pair of rectangular windows showed a panorama of the sea like a fish tank. On one side of the window was a big glass square attached to a small key dangling from a chain. Inside the square was a big red button labeled EMERGENCY DC.

Max liked this room. He wanted to know what all of it meant.

Humming a tune, Basile walked over to a small desk. He opened a drawer, pulled out the leather-bound Jules Verne booklet, and handed it to Alex.

"Like it or not, you're one of the family now, aren't you?" he said. "Now read this to me, and tell me where we are going next. Or Stinky is liable to have a fit and kill us all."

"Actually, we don't know. It's in some kind of code."

Basile grabbed a pair of glasses from a table. "Ha! With three great brains, we should be able to figure this out, easy peasy lemon squeezy! Go on . . ."

Alex placed the book down on the desk and opened it.

Upon reaching the great unruined chamber at the prime locations of the fifteenth, third, and second to the Pole Star and eleventh, seventeenth, and fourteenth to the sunrise, be guided by the camptodactyl of the king.

Basile's smile disappeared. "Greek to me. Actually, more like Martian."

"We figured we'd concentrate on the numbers, which we assumed were coordinates," Max said, "but it turned out to be in Niger."

He dug from his pocket for the napkin where he'd written it out.

$$15°3'2''N \ 11°17'14''E$$

"Not likely we'd reach there in the *Conch*," Basile squinted. "Prime location or not."

"Wait!" Max said with a gasp. "What you said— that's it!"

Basile's glasses slipped down his nose. "I don't follow . . ."

"The note doesn't say prime location," Max continued. "It says prime locations. Plural."

"But it's only one set of coordinates," Alex said,

"which means one location."

"Maybe," Max said. "But what if this is a kind of code? Why does he use the word *prime*? If I say the word *prime*, what do you think of right away?"

"Prime meats," Basile said.

"Prime numbers?" Alex offered.

"Alex for the win," Max said. "A prime is a number you can't divide anything into—except itself and one."

He began scribbling on the other side of the napkin:

$$2 \ 3 \ 5 \ 7 \ 11 \ 13 \ 17 \ 19 \ 23 \ 29$$
$$31 \ 37 \ 41 \ 43 \ 47 \ 53 \ 59 \ 61$$

Basile hooted a laugh. "Just spat that out from memory, did you?"

"I'm smart," Max said.

"And modest," Alex added. "But there's a problem, cuz. Look at the coordinates. The first digit is fifteen. That's not prime. You can divide it by five and by three."

"Okay," Max said, "so this is where we look at the word *locations*. Maybe Verne is not talking about GPS locations."

"What else could he mean, lad?" Basile asked.

"Think of cardinal and ordinal numbers," Max said. "Cardinal is one, two, three, four, and so on. Ordinal is first, second, third, fourth. Cardinal is a number. Ordinal is a place—a location!"

"So Verne might not mean fifteen, but fifteen*th*?" Alex said.

"Fifteenth *what*?" Basile asked. "My head is about to explode."

Max blanched. "Are you being sarcastic?"

"Yes, he is," Alex said. "Go on."

"I'm thinking that fifteen means *fifteenth prime number*," Max said. "The coordinates are prime locations—each one tells us which prime number to use! So fifteen means the *fifteenth prime number*, three means the *third prime number*, two means the *second prime number*."

Alex looked at Max's list of primes again. "The fifteenth prime number is . . . wait, let me count . . . forty-seven?"

"I got it! It's like a game! We just count along these numbers you wrote!" Basile said, putting his stubby fingers on the list. "The third prime is . . . five. And the second is . . . three."

Under his first set of coordinates, Max carefully wrote out the second:

15°3′2″N 11°17′14″E
47°5′3″N 31°59′43″E

"How are we going to find this without Wi-Fi?" Alex asked.

"You little bunnies don't know life without electronics, do you?" Basile reached into a deep, wooden map cabinet, pulled out a huge paper map, and laid it on a drafting table. "This is the northern Atlantic," he said, slapping a plastic T square on the map. "Let's match north . . . and east . . ."

He slid the instrument along the paper, found a spot, and then marked it with a pen. "About equal distance from the Azores, Kap Farvel in Greenland, and Cape Race in Newfoundland," Basile said. "Used to be a long line of furious volcanoes running up the center of the ocean in this area. With the Newfoundland Basin on one side and the Northeast Atlantic Basin on the other. There may have been land masses here ages ago."

"But now it's in the middle of the ocean," Max said.

Basile clapped him on the back so hard that Max nearly fell over. "So, my boy, are we!"

22

AFTER the seventh movie, Max got tired of entertainment.

After an unfortunate collision with André, who still hadn't forgiven him, Max stopped racing Alex around the *Conch*.

By the third day at sea, he had hurt his thumbs from too much *Legend of Zelda*, gotten sick from overeating energy bars, and made drawings of a hundred thirty-two different fish he'd seen out the window. Everyone had become a little crabby. Niemand stayed in his suite, coming out every few hours to yell at Basile for not going fast enough. And Alex had begun her novel. Which meant writing the first page and then deleting it about a million times.

For Max, the best part was just hanging with Basile in the wheelhouse, a sketchbook on his lap. The room looked out through two curved rectangular windows. It was quiet, except for Basile's horrible singing.

"You're the only one who doesn't make fun of me," Basile finally said.

"I tune it out," Max replied with a shrug. "I like just watching the fish. It keeps the smell of sweaty feet away."

"Ach, sorry, I suppose I should do some laundry," Basile said.

"It's not you," Max said. "When I feel smothered, I smell sweaty feet."

Basile swiveled on his stool to face Max. "You're an odd one, aren't you?"

"Yes," Max said. "My mom could tell you everything about me in forty-three seconds. I can't."

"You miss her, eh, lad?" Basile said softly, standing from his stool.

Max nodded. He disliked the way the conversation was going. It was headed in the skunk direction. So he opened up his sketchbook and flipped to a blank page.

"A gifted artist too!" Basile moved toward one of the large windows. "Come close! Ha! Look! Want a fancy writing implement? How about one of those?"

Max walked over and peered through. Rising up

from the seafloor was a long, white object, made of coral but thin as a string. It was fringed up and down with delicate coral threads like a ring of feathers, and it tapered to a narrow tip.

"The slender sea pen, aka *Stylatula elongata*—we don't have one of those in our museum." Basile pulled back the throttle. As the *Conch* slowed, he gestured to a Plexiglas-enclosed cabinet against the wall, about waist-high. Inside were specimens of brilliant-colored coral, salvaged antique-ship specimens, and fossils. "As you see, it is a small but select display. Let's add to it. Ever been in a Newtsuit? Come."

Without waiting for an answer, Basile left the room and entered the narrow hallway. Max followed him to a tiny room where four armored suits stood against a wall. They were made completely of metal, with a series of joints up and down the legs, arms, and torso. At the top was a huge spherical helmet with a round glass window and oxygen tanks hung over both shoulders. "Wait, you want me to put this thing on?" Max said. "I've never dived. Well, I snorkeled once. But not scuba—"

"With an atmospheric diving suit, one only needs to know how to breathe," Basile said. He grunted with the effort as he pulled one off its hooks. "It will feel extremely heavy when you put it on. The earliest versions were a thousand pounds, but this one is forged aluminum alloy. Developed by a fellow named Nuytten, hence 'Newtsuit.' May not fit you too well, but it'll work."

Max stepped back. The suit looked like it weighed a thousand pounds. "Can I just watch you do it? I'll stay and listen to opera."

Basile lay the suit on the ground and unlatched the helmet. "After you," he said with a grin.

Once Max was in the ocean, the suit didn't feel nearly so heavy. But his feet could not touch the bottom of the boot section, and he felt like he was sitting on a horse with no stirrups. He was only able to move by rocking left and right and thrusting his legs forward in a walking motion.

But it didn't matter. Max felt amazing in the suit. Snug and warm. He could have just stood there, planted in that exact space, for days.

A red-striped fish kissed his helmet not with its lips but with two thick, white whiskers on its chin. It disappeared among the tubes of a silver-red scrim of coral that seemed to explode from the seafloor like long trumpets. He saw flat silver-white fish that looked like floating dinner plates, a school of nearly transparent swimmers that moved like a sheet of gauze. As he took a lumbering step forward, the sand below him came to life, forming the fanned shape of a stingray and vanishing into the distance like a great white bird.

In the massive helmet he could hear only his own breathing, deep and rhythmic—with occasional screams of joy and discovery from Basile through a radio transmitter. As the old man collected specimens, he blurted out names that Max tried to memorize—*goatfish . . . organpipe coral . . . triggerfish . . .*

The suit's arms ended in grasping hooks, which Max was able to manipulate with a squeeze mechanism. Soon he was stooping to pick up shells and strange stones from the sea bottom.

"What do you think?" came Basile's voice as he lumbered toward Max, a chunk of white coral in one of his hooks and a sea pen in the other.

Max could see his own grin reflected in the eye panel. *"Two words,"* he shouted. *"Awe. Some!"*

"Ha! That's the spirit. We'll make a sea dog out of you yet—"

Basile's voice was cut off by the rasping bark of Niemand, radioing to them from inside the sub. "Playtime is over, boys! Have we forgotten that we have work to do?"

"Yes, sir, of course, sir, may I shine your shoes, sir," Basile drawled.

Max could see him wink through the thick Plexiglas.

Silently they returned to the port side of the *Conch*, where Basile opened the diving hatch. As they stepped in, the old captain hit a large red button. The door slid closed, and the pumps emptied the seawater. Max's suit grew heavier and heavier until he was afraid he'd fall over. At the sound of an all-clear horn, Basile opened another hatch and helped Max walk to the diving room, where they removed the suits.

"Sea fan—*Isis hippuris*," Basile said softly, indicating the chunk of yellow coral he'd brought in, which looked like a thousand surgical gloves fused together. "Contains a steroid that may cure cancer."

Max's heart began fluttering. "Seriously?"

Basile smiled. "Just a theory. My old chum Stinky may have some cockamamie idea about bubble cities, but I'm interested in more practical things. And I get to use the resources of Niemand Enterprises—"

Niemand peered into the room. "The boy is neither interested in nor welcome to know about our company's projects, Basile! And we are not in the business of stopping and sightseeing!"

"Ah, go back into the cage and finish eating your broken glass," Basile said.

As Niemand stormed away, Basile placed the piece of

yellow coral into Max's palm. "Be sure to keep this safe, lad. For good luck."

The next morning Max awakened to the sound of loud voices and thumping footsteps. He sat up as Alex burst into his room. "Do you hear that?" she said.

"What is it?" Max asked.

"Something I haven't heard in a couple of days," Alex replied. "Excitement. Something's up. Come on!"

By the time they got to the wheelhouse, Pandora, André, Sophia, and Niemand were all gathered around Basile in front of the viewing windows. André was trying to focus a search light on the area ahead. His bright green eyes scanned the sea bottom. "Lrwzbl . . ." he murmured.

"We're here," Pandora said.

"*Here* as in, where the coordinates told us to go?" Alex said.

"Really?" Max blurted out. "Where's the treasure? Can you see it?"

Pandora smiled. "There's very low visibility. The ocean floor is wildly uneven. This is a major continental fault line. If this were above water we'd see mountains, mesas, plateaus. Unfortunately the currents are strong. They're pulling up all kinds of muck from below."

Basile was cutting the throttle to slow the thrust, but

soon Max could see shadows playing on the surface, rising up toward them . . .

"What the——?" Basile muttered as an alarm sounded. *"Hold on!"*

The sub jolted. Max stumbled to the ground and grabbed onto a stool for balance. Scrambling back to his feet, he stood by André and looked into the viewing window. Alex was standing there, her jaw wide open.

The *Conch* had juddered to a complete stop. Directly outside the window, Max saw one great, sculpted eye, only inches away.

Niemand ran out of the room and returned a moment later. "I just saw what was out of the starboard-side window," he said. "It is an arm."

The others stared, uncomprehending.

"My friends, we are stuck," he said, "between the head and the raised arm of a giant statue."

23

"**THROW** it in reverse!"

"Secure the anchor!"

"Kill the engine!"

"Mind your business!"

Everyone was shouting. Max could barely think straight. He kept his eyes fixed on the scene outside the window. This was it. The exact location Verne had hidden from the public for all of these years.

Now that the sub was still, the seaweed and muck were settling down. Barnacles had crusted the eye of the statue. Max had the eerie feeling that the eye might turn and look at him. For the time being, it seemed to be gazing sadly over a scene of complete devastation.

Not far from the *Conch*, a massive gate arched

overhead. Or what was left of it. Two columns, ridged and as thick as oak trees, rose up from the sea bottom. At least ten people could pass between them, shoulder to shoulder. If Max squinted he felt like he could see them. In robes and sandals. Heading into a glorious city that . . .

Wasn't.

The columns were battered and slanting. Whatever lay across the top of the gate had long since fallen into rubble. In the dark thickness, all Max could see of the city were husks of buildings. They lined both sides of what must have been a grand avenue.

Everything in sight was draped with seaweed and pimpled with shells and barnacles.

"Max, come on, they're letting us explore," came Alex's voice.

Max turned with a start. "What?"

"Get on your suit!" Alex was grinning, pulling him away from the window. "Basile, Pandora, and Sophia are staying behind to dislodge the *Conch* from the statue. But you, me, André, and Niemand are going."

"Niemand and Old Green Eyes?" Max groaned. "Why do we get the bad guys?"

"Because the others can't stand them? I don't know—just get your suit on!" Alex was shaking with excitement. "Max, Jules Verne wrote about this in *Twenty Thousand*

Leagues. Captain Nemo brought him to a great ancient city in ruins. In the book, he claimed it was Atlantis."

"But Atlantis is just a legend," Max said.

"Just *come!*"

By the time they got to the fitting chamber, André and Niemand were already fastening their helmets. Max laid out his and Alex's suits and quickly taught her how to slide in and stand up.

"Testing . . . one two three!" came Niemand's voice through the suit-to-suit intercom. "Everybody hear me? Say 'Roger.'"

"Roger," said Max.

"Roger," said Alex.

"Rnchs," said André.

"We will have to jump down to the seafloor," Niemand said. "Stay close. These intercoms have a range of maybe thirty yards. Do we remember what the note said?"

"'Upon reaching the great unruined chamber at the prime locations of'—blah blah blah, we know that part," Alex said, "'be guided by the camptodactyl of the king.'"

"That's our mystery. We have only two hours to solve it before oxygen runs out," Niemand said. "We've come this far. Be quick and keep your eyes out for clues. When we figure this out, our reward will be enormous. This, my friends, will be the start of a new world! The wealth that will go directly to fuel the greatest experiment in human history. The Niemand Era!"

"Half," Max said.

Inside the helmet, Niemand's eyes moved toward Max. "Pardon?"

"Half of it will fuel the Tilt family," Max said. "Right?"

But Niemand had already hit the red button that controlled the entry/exit mechanism. Seawater began rushing into the chamber. Even in the suit it was deafening. Soon the side hatch slid open, and all four of them jumped into the world below.

Max floated down, landing in a kind of slo-mo cloud of mud, seaweed, and scurrying fish. Alex landed beside him along with the other two.

Slowly they made their way to the gate.

Max's footsteps sank as he forced the Newtsuit legs forward. It took all his strength to pull each step out of the goopy ocean floor. But as he approached the columns, the ground became firmer.

"There's some kind of stone under this," Alex said. "An ancient road."

Max was more interested in the strange ruins on either side of the gate. A low, jagged ridge, like the remains of a giant stone fence, curved away from the gate into the darkness on either side. It must have been extremely tall, because its pieces were strewn all over in great piles. Each piece was flat, and though in different broken shapes, they were the same thickness, maybe six inches. Max leaned down and lifted one with his grappling hook.

It was smooth and slightly curved. "Alex, have you seen this?"

"Yup, stone. There's stone all over the place!" Alex shot back.

"This isn't stone. It's more like . . . I don't know . . . plastic!"

"Put that down, Max—Bert and Ernie are way ahead of us."

Max dropped the shard and followed Alex through the grand entrance gate. Niemand and André were just lumps of gray along the road ahead, but neither Max nor Alex felt like going very fast. They swiveled their heads, gaping at the remains of buildings, wide boulevards, statues. It had the feeling of a great ancient city. "Do you see anything that says Atlantis?"

"This could be Lemuria," Max said. "That's another legendary city."

Alex pointed to a structure about Max's height, which was covered with sea growth and unrecognizable. "Look, ye ancient mailbox of the gods," Alex said.

They clomped slowly past the ruins of a big museum-like structure with wide steps and seven great, sculpted columns, two of which were now stumps. The building's roof had collapsed, and what remained was so encrusted with sea detritus it looked like a wrecked ship. Eels slithered out of windows, and a school of fish burst from the front door as if the recess bell had just rung. Farther down the street, the fallen walls of a giant house revealed magnificent metal cogwheels that once must have generated great power. A tangle of wires and tubes jutted upward from within, like the guts of a slaughtered animal.

"This is really weird, Max . . ." Alex said. "It looks like a power plant."

"In the ancient kingdom of Knossos on the Greek island of Crete, they had running water and flush toilets," Max said. "So, who knows?"

As they passed narrow stone posts, Max cleared away the seaweed to find carved words in a language he didn't understand. "Street signs," Alex said.

Niemand's voice crackled through the Newtsuit intercom. "What are you . . . far behind . . . come . . .!"

He was getting out of range, but it was clear he wanted Max to hurry up. As Max rushed forward, his foot landed on a patch of sand that exploded like a bomb. He jumped back, gasping.

A long, sleek body took shape in the grains of sand and rose up on triangular wings. "Watch out, Alex!" Max called.

The creature nearly clipped Alex in the helmet before disappearing into the subterranean darkness. "What was that thing?" she cried out. "A pterodactyl?"

"A ray," Max said.

As they trudged forward, Alex stayed close to Max. At the end of the block, the street opened into a vast clearing that must have been a great plaza. It circled an area maybe half the size of a football field. Max imagined ancient families in robes strolling after a meal, but now it was a wasteland of coral, hummocks, and glops of seaweed. Fish slithered around lazily, looking bored, as if Max and Alex weren't there.

Tall pedestals were equally spaced around the plaza. Most of them were attached to the feet and ankles of statues. "Max, we're looking for a king, right? That's what the message said."

"Right."

"What if one of these statues was the king? How will we know?"

Max thought hard. "No. He wasn't outside like this. He was in a chamber."

"Right, 'the great unruined chamber . . .'" Alex said.

"Max, if Jules Verne found this city, he would have seen pretty much what we're seeing now, right?"

"Except a hundred years ago," Max said.

"Would it have been that much different?"

"I don't know. I'm guessing most of the damage happened when the place sank. Which would have been maybe thousands of years ago."

"So let's say not much has happened here since Jules Verne saw it," Alex said. "Look around. Is there anything 'unruined'?"

They continued walking around the plaza. Niemand and André were skulking around some toppled wall. Max gave them a wave, but they were both looking upward at a huge, luminescent, flat fish that sailed overhead.

The fish dove behind the circle of crumbled buildings. It disappeared just behind the plaza, over the top of another roof that was completely intact.

"Okay," Max said. "Do you see what I see? Right over there, in the middle of all these broken old buildings?"

Alex smiled. "Looks unruined to me. Let's lose Niemand."

Together she and Max bounded through an alley, out of sight of the two men. They emerged into a street behind the plaza. It was not quite as wide as the great boulevard they'd entered on, and was even more clogged with ruins. In one pile Max thought he could see a bone jutting out. He felt his stomach turn and kept his eyes on the intact building.

Alex was already entering through the archway in front. Max followed her into a small entry room. Inside, protected from the currents, the walls seemed sturdy and mostly untouched. Through patches of sea growth Max could see the glowing colors of some intricate tile work. In the center was a broad stone altar or table.

Beyond that was another room, deeper in, that glowed with eerie green light.

He and Alex moved slowly toward it. They entered a grand, vaulted chamber made of a smooth marble festooned with green fronds, crustaceans, and rot. Max looked up to see a pair of great open rectangles in the roof. He figured they were probably glass windows at one time, but now they were holes overhung with spindly strands that waved in the water current like witches' arms.

At the center of the room was an enormous statue of a seated figure on its own pedestal. Max and Alex set to work clearing off the seaweed that was draped over it.

Slowly they uncovered the sculpture of a man on a

stiff seat. His gaze was intense, wise, kind, powerful—and so real it looked like he could come to life. But rather than a toga or robe, he was dressed in what looked like a scientist's lab coat, with sculpted pens and measuring instruments in his chest pocket.

"Doesn't look like a king to me," Alex said.

"Or ancient," Max said.

"Maybe Verne brought it here for some reason, and then left it. This thing is about his vintage."

"He would not have been able to fit this into a submarine," Max said. "This statue must be part of this world."

"So they were just fashion forward," Alex remarked. "Or something."

Max leaned in to the pedestal to read the plaque. He couldn't understand the words. But at the bottom was something completely unmistakable.

Max backed away. The blood was rushing from his face. He thought about all the strange things they'd seen—the structures that resembled mailboxes, power plants, street signs . . .

"Alex, this is not what we thought it was," Max said. "It cannot be an ancient city built on an island that sank. Like Atlantis."

"What else could it be?" Alex said.

"It was built here," Max said. "Underwater."

Alex laughed. "By frogs?"

"No," Max said. "By people."

He gestured to the bottom of the plaque, and Alex leaned close to read what had been carved at the bottom:

1863

24

"**THIS** is impossible," Alex said. "Maybe it's 1863 BC."

"There was no *C* to be *B*," Max pointed out.

"Say what?"

"BC means 'Before Christ,' but how could you know you were before Christ, if Christ hadn't been born yet?" Max said. "It's not logical."

"There's got to be an explanation," Alex said. "Maybe they were originally on land . . . and the land sank in 1863."

"Then we would have heard about it. It would be in the history books. Like the fall of Rome. The volcano at Pompeii. Columbus. The American Revolution." Max looked around, thinking. "Alex, Niemand has been talking about this crazy plan. Niemand Cities. People living in self-contained bubbles. It's his obsession."

"Max, no! That's not what this is," Alex said. "Bubble cities are sci-fi. We don't even have those in the twenty-first century."

"What if there was one, in 1863?" Max said. "And Verne discovered it. In his book, he *called* it Atlantis. But that was a cover-up, to make it sound mystical for his readers. Imagine if he tried to claim it really existed back then. No one would have believed him. That's the whole point of *The Lost Treasures*. He left that to us, to discover the truth. Now."

"Why?" Alex asked.

"Niemand's ancestors hated Verne," Max said. "I think Verne discovered something they really wanted. And they went after him. They converted his nephew—"

"His nephew shot him!" Alex said. "If the bad guys wanted Verne's secret, why would they kill him?"

"He wasn't shooting to kill—he wounded Verne in the foot," Max said. "Alex, listen to me. Just outside the gate, I found tons of broken material. The pieces were flat, like chunks of a wall. They didn't feel like stone. More like some human-made substance. Like plastic. This was a city under a dome!"

Alex let out a crazy burst of laughter. She looked up at the statue. "And this guy . . . with his pocket protector? Who is he?"

"I don't know," Max said. "The architect? The head scientist? The president?"

But Alex was walking toward the figure slowly. "Max, look at his hand."

With her hook she reached up about eye level and brushed off seaweed from the statue's hands, which were resting on a stone armrest.

Max walked closer to the left hand. All the fingers lay flat on the armrest, except for the pinkie. The knuckle was bent upward like a tent. "The sculptor kind of messed up on the pinkie," Max said.

"No, he didn't," Alex said. "Think. The note from Verne. 'Upon reaching the great unruined chamber . . . be guided by the camptodactyl of the king . . .' Max, back when I translated this, I looked up that word."

Max nodded vigorously. "It has to do with finger, right? Because of *dactyl*."

"How do you know that?" Alex said.

"I have a model of a pterodactyl. *Ptero* means 'wing' and *dactyl* means 'finger.'"

"And *campto*," Alex said, "means 'bent.'"

Max walked toward the statue. "Be guided by the bent finger . . ."

He turned toward Alex. Even through the thick glass

of her helmet, he could tell she was grinning.

She reached up toward the statue's hand, manipulated the hook open at the end of the Newtsuit arm, and grasped the crooked pinkie. With a solid click, the finger moved. It was pointing upward now, like someone daintily sipping from a cup of tea.

"What now?" Max said.

Beneath them the floor began to rumble. Clumps of seaweed began floating downward, dislodged from above.

From the corner of his eye, Max could see Niemand and André stepping into the room behind them. "What the devil—?" Niemand said.

Before they could turn to answer, Max felt himself losing his balance. The ground beneath them shifted. He leaned forward at the waist, trying as hard as he could in this bulky suit to look down.

André bounced toward them in his Newtsuit, moving with powerful leaps. He managed to grab one of Alex's arms and one of Max's, by trapping each between one of his own arms and his suit. Falling backward, he pulled them from the statue—until all three were floating free.

They landed on the seafloor. Max pushed down with his arms, thrust himself into a standing position, and turned toward the statue. The platform he and Alex had been standing on had slid away, just in front of the seated figure. The king.

What remained was a giant black hole.

Four massive helmets peered down into the abyss. The light from the holes overhead cast an eerie greenish glow into an underground chamber about eight feet square.

And in the center was an enormous wooden box.

A treasure chest.

25

"**WE** did it," Max said. "*We did it*!"

He didn't care about the shortness of his legs. He began dancing inside the suit. He saw his parents' faces in his mind, their looks of utter astonishment. He would buy them a new house. He would buy Smriti and her family a new house. He would buy Alex a house next to theirs. He would fly in the best doctors in the world for Mom . . .

Alex was grinning too. She tried to hug him, but in these bulky suits it was more like bumping torsos.

"Let's not get overexcited," Niemand said. "We haven't opened it yet."

André stepped into the hole and allowed himself to float down to the chest. He unraveled the rope from his shoulders and wrapped it around the chest side to side and back to front. Then he tossed the other end of the rope upward and said, "Chhrff!"

"You heard him—*lift*!" Niemand barked. He wrapped his end of the rope around the base of his arm hook, tying it into a secure knot. Max and Alex did the same farther down the length of the rope—and they all began to pull back, like a tug-of-war.

The chest was stuck tight to the bottom. It took ten pulls before André managed to dislodge it. It tilted upward, then rose end first. André dug his hooks underneath and gave it a boost.

Max yanked as hard as he could. The water's buoyancy helped. In minutes the chest was up onto the chamber floor. It was made of some superhard material, dented and covered with sea growth, but not broken through. "Dear Poseidon, what is this chest made of?" Niemand murmured.

Max was smelling mint. He almost never smelled mint. "I am extremely excited," he said.

"Eeeee!" Alex squealed. Even in the thick Newtsuit, Max could see her face bouncing. He knew that meant she was dancing.

"Can you tell how heavy it is?" Max asked.

"Of course not," Niemand snapped. "We're

underwater. We'll get it back to the *Conch* and open it. Now! Now!"

Alex gestured down into the pit. "What about André?"

"Right," Niemand said. "Of course."

He untied the rope from the chest and tossed it down to his crew member, who wrapped it around his own waist. André bent his knees and jumped upward, while Max, Alex, and Niemand pulled. When André was safely out of the pit, he stood and raised his arm to high-five Niemand.

But Niemand ignored him. "Hurry. The oxygen is low. You take one handle, and I'll get the other. I think we can walk this thing back."

Max looked at the oxygen gauge inside his mask. It read 33%.

Alex pulled him along. But she and Max quickly fell behind the two men. "Can't you go any faster?" Alex said.

"My feet don't reach down to the shoe part!" Max said.

As they slowly trudged back through the center of the ruined city, Max watched his gauge:

29% . . . 23% . . . 17% . . . 9% . . .

As they got to the columned entrance, the gauge was lit

red. The number 5% flashed brightly. Max was trying desperately not to breathe. Not to waste the oxygen.

Just beyond the columns, the upper body of a massive heroic statue lay on its side. But the *Conch* was no longer wedged between the cheek and the arm. Basile, Pandora, and Sophia had managed to free it. Now the sub sat on the seafloor, its guide lights flashing and its hull just slightly dented. The door to the diving bay was open and waiting.

Niemand and André were way ahead of Max and Alex. "You guys! Slow down!" Alex cried out.

But the two men were hoisting the chest up into the bay. They both leaped up and stood on either side of it. Max could see Niemand banging his hook against the red button. Slowly the door began to shut.

Niemand gave a little wave with his hook, then turned his back.

"Wait!" Max shouted.

"They can't be doing this," Alex said. She pulled ahead of Max, heading toward the sub in big leaps.

The scene in the bay was a blur. Max could see Alex reaching her arm out . . . jamming it into the closing door. *"Be careful!"* he screamed.

The door would crush her. It would rip open her Newtsuit.

As he moved faster, the sand roiled up from below him. For a moment he saw nothing. The oxygen gauge flipped from 4% to 3%. A bright light emerged from the murk, and it took a few seconds before Max realized what it was.

The *Conch*'s door was open. Alex was in the hatchway. Next to her, Niemand had his hand on the red button.

No, not Niemand. Max was close enough to see a different face through the helmet. A familiar pair of piercing green eyes flitted toward him.

Niemand had not opened the door. It was André.

"You saved our lives," Alex said, as she and Max walked into André's workroom.

"Arrrgll," André said, his face turning red.

"He says Niemand shut the door by mistake," Pandora said. "His oxygen had run out, and he panicked."

Basile spat out a curse. "Not likely. The bloke's soul is dead. I'll bet his body uses no oxygen."

The chest was sitting in the middle of the room. With a series of hooks and chisels, Basile and André had scraped away seaweed and barnacles from its surface. In the harsh fluorescent light, the chest glowed a dull gray green. A pile of tools lay on the floor—screwdrivers, chisels, a drill, and a hammer.

Sophia was examining the surface through a magnifying glass. "This appears to be some sort of polymer," she said. "But with extraordinary strength."

"I hope not too strong," Basile said, lifting a small hammer. "We have to open this baby."

He pounded the latch until the lock broke. Eagerly he, André, Sophia, and Pandora took turns trying to pry it open with chisels. *"Krampf!"* André finally yelled.

"Yup, shut tight," Basile said, grabbing a sledgehammer from the wall. "Stand aside, will you?"

But Niemand was entering the room behind him, smelling of cologne and wearing a crisp black shirt and a purple silk jacket. "I see someone has forgotten to follow directions. I asked you to wait."

"Blimey, what took you so long to get ready?" Basile asked. "Shaving the hair off your knuckles?"

"Hand that to me, Basile," Niemand growled.

Basile laughed. "Excuse me?"

Niemand removed his jacket and folded it over the back of a chair. "Do you need a written invitation? The sledgehammer, please. You may be a man-buffalo, but you lack technique. It's all in the wrists and the angle."

Niemand took the hammer and raised it high, bringing it down hard on the chest. It connected with a *bang,* then bounced away, nearly taking off André's head in its flight.

"*My hands!*" Niemand cried out.

"Good work, Thor." With a sigh, Basile picked up a circular handsaw and stood astride the chest. It buzzed to life, and Basile brought it down onto the center of the chest. Sparks flew as he penetrated the surface. The acrid smell of burning plastic and metal filled the room.

When Basile was done, he'd made a rough circle about the size of a head.

Max, Alex, Pandora, André, Niemand, and Basile all gathered around the chest. No one seemed to want to make the first move. Max's heart pounded as if he'd swallowed the sledgehammer.

Niemand was the first to thrust his hands in. His face went immediately pale. "What on earth . . . ?"

Max couldn't help himself. He wedged his own arm next to Niemand's and felt along the bottom. It was slimy and cold. But there was absolutely nothing there.

No. Not nothing. His fingers closed around a flat metal box. He pulled it out. It was brownish green and rectangular and just fit through the hole.

No one said a word as Max felt around the side of the box and pressed a tiny button. The box sprung open, and Max held it out for all to see.

"A book?" Niemand said. "Another blasted *book*?"

"For years you've been trying to find a book," Basile said.

"A book that led to a *treasure*, Basile," Niemand said. "I'm ready for the treasure now."

Max let the box drop and opened the book. "It's French," he said, handing it to Alex. "You read it."

Alex swallowed. All eyes stared at her, and she took a deep breath.

"I'll do my best."

26

THE LOST TREASURES

—PART TWO—

Dearest reader, if you have found this, I envy your intelligence and bravery. I share your horror over the vast destruction here. For the land of Ikaria was the hope of the world, the refuge of geniuses. Here, under a giant crystal shell, lived a modern place of peace and learning. Trees bursting with fruit, crops of infinite yield, controlled sunlight and darkness.

Whence did these people come?

We will never know. But I believe we were the first to find them.

The captain of the submarine had heard a rumor of this

place. From sailors. Men who had been ridiculed for their claims. But he was a man obsessed, searching for years. I took this to be scientific excitement, but I was wrong.

I should have suspected darker aims. At first he would not even tell me his name, saying only, "I am no one." Taking this for a joke, I dubbed him Captain No One, and he happily answered to this ever afterward.

And now, Captain No One and I were at a city like no other. Flabbergasted. Lo! People appeared from behind buildings. They ran through wide boulevards, they clung to the carapace to see us—men, women, and children of all heights and hues.

We saw the flash of artillery through the submarine window and felt the ship rock violently. And then another. "Barbarians!" cried the captain. "They dare attack us!"

"They appear human, captain," I said. "I believe they are frightened by us."

I made welcoming gestures, expressions of friendship through that window. I urged the captain to send some sign of peace.

"Destroy them," were the words of this man who wanted to be called No One.

I protested vigorously. What we could learn from these people! But nothing could stop him. And no words can describe my horror at the release of the depth charge.

With a flash of fire, the carapace was breached. A hole shattered the thick material, jagged and mean as a lightning bolt.

An explosion turned the sea to red. Our vessel spun away with the force, and it was luck that we were not dashed against coral.

I shall never forget our return to examine the wreckage. The carnage was astonishing. There were no survivors. All on board the submarine wept, save the man whose heart was granite.

As we donned our diving gear to explore, I vowed to learn the techniques of this advanced civilization, so that their work would not be in vain. What they had discovered beggared belief. Were they of another world? Another time? Why did they live in hiding?

Watching the captain, I realized that he had become obsessed with Ikaria's secrets long ago. He had been anticipating this very moment. The destruction of Ikaria was no act of revenge, but part of a plan. He ordered his crew to salvage what they could of the scientific records. Anyone smuggling so much as a stone would be shot.

It was in the great chamber that I happened upon a treasure so vast I needed to sit to regain composure. It was as if this extraordinary race had found some strange alchemy to convert seaweed to gold and jewels.

Now the crew, heretofore working together peacefully, became fractured. Two crew members were shot for their greed. Three more were forced to take the treasure back to the ship.

I fear I test your patience, dear reader. For where, you wonder, is this fortune?

Here must I take the opportunity to explain the odd nature of my greatest work, *The Lost Treasures*.

The book was written all at once by yours truly. Word of its existence was passed to my dear friend Hetzel. But I fear that the followers and family of my nemesis will waste no time trying to find it.

So, my dear reader, it is in pieces. Pieces that I have taken, over my later years, to the various sites of my adventures. For these places, tucked away in remote corners of the world, contain unfathomable secrets.

Part One, as you know, has been given to my son to keep safely hidden in the family. If you are reading this, then you have been guided by it.

Here, in your hands, is Part Two.

Upon leaving Ikaria, my enemy directed our ship, our treasure, and me to the village closest to the ring of ice on the eastern shore of the great land that least matches its own name. Upon entering the cove of the cook's competition, look for the bump on the elephant's forehead.

JV

27

"THAT'S it?" Niemand asked as Alex finished reading.

"I don't understand . . ." Pandora said.

Basile let out a giant belly laugh. "Haw! Elephant's forehead! The chap had a sense of humor."

"Do you have any idea what it costs to run this submarine?" Niemand barked. "And why have I done this—for a wild-goose chase leading to a nonsense note?"

"It's not nonsense, it's a code," Max said. "It's his way of keeping this a secret."

"From some crackpot submarine captain who's been dead for a century?" Niemand said. "Verne doesn't even name the fellow."

"It doesn't matter," Max said, spreading the book on a table. "We can do this."

"It's the Max method," Alex said. "Break the problem down into smaller components. Works every time."

Pandora, André, Sophia, and Basile gathered around the table. Niemand stood silently against the wall, examining his fingernails.

"Start from where it gets weird," Max said.

Sophia read, "'The village closest to the ring of ice—'"

"Stop there," Max said.

"Ring of ice . . ." Basile said. "Sounds like something up in the Arctic."

Pandora's eyes went wide. "A ring is a circle—he's talking about the Arctic Circle!"

Max nodded. "Good. So he means 'the village closest to the Arctic Circle'—"

"'On the eastern shore of the great land that least matches its own name,'" Alex read.

"Sweden! Because nothing there is sweet?" Basile blurted out. "Denmark, because there are no dens?"

"Kranj," André mumbled.

"André's right!" Sophia said. "Greenland!"

"That's what he said?" Alex asked.

Basile grabbed a map of the Atlantic Ocean and pointed to a massive island north of Canada. "Greenland. It's great in size, and it's mostly ice—so not very green."

Pandora ran her finger up Greenland's east coast,

stopping at a line of latitude. "This is between the sixty-sixth and sixty-seventh parallel. Where the Arctic Circle starts."

Her fingertip was just beside a small village, exactly where the Arctic Circle intersected the land. "Piuli Point . . ."

"*Hop to it, everyone!*" Basile thundered.

"It's about time," Niemand said.

As the other crew members dispersed, Alex pulled Max into the hallway. "We never got to the part about the bump on the elephant's forehead," Max whispered.

"Are there elephants in Greenland?" Alex asked.

"No," Max said.

Alex sighed deeply. "One step at a time . . ."

As the *Conch* broke the water's surface, Max shielded his eyes. The Greenland shore was an attack of whiteness—a towering ice cliff that filled the window from left to right. It rose from the water like a twisting curtain of great vertical prisms, growing larger as the sub came closer. The sun reflected pinpoints of white, green, and blue off the surfaces, which blinked and juddered as the *Conch* bounced off blocks of ice in the water.

"Up here, there are many words to describe ice," Basile said. "The little flat stuff is pancake ice—when it's like an island unto itself, it's an ice floe. Pudding ice, if it's mushy and mixed with snow. We avoid pack ice, which is all clumped together and could block our path. Icebergs are your heavy monsters mostly below the surface. That sorry-looking thing full of ridges? Old ice. And we're traveling through a path in a nice stretch of stream ice. When it gets really cold, sometimes the chunks of ice rub against each other, and the frequencies make a noise like singing."

"Opera ice?" Max said.

"Groaners," Basile replied. "Anyway, we could have approached underwater and avoided all of this, but I thought you might like to see it, eh?"

"Max, look—little penguins!" Alex said.

To their right, a battalion of small black-and-white birds had crowded onto a big, flat ice floe, fluffing their wings and staring at the *Conch*. "Actually they're puffins," Max said. "Much smaller than penguins. Penguins only live in the Southern Hemisphere."

They waddled, dove, preened, and argued as if the *Conch* weren't there. "That's my kind of life," Basile said. "Take the periscope. You'll see our destination. And not a moment too soon. We'll need to pick up some fuel while we're docked."

Alex looked into the periscope and moved it around.

"I see a cluster of buildings . . ."

"Keep your eye out for elephants," Max said.

"Eh, wha—?"

Basile was interrupted by a low rumble, like thunder. To their right, a section of the cliff moved. It separated from the wall and began sliding down, as if the wall of a giant skyscraper had suddenly come loose. Even as it was falling into the water, it sent up a wild, gigantic spray, sending out a wake that made the *Conch* rock sharply.

"Hooo-ha!" Basile cried out. "First time this old man has ever seen the calving of an ice shelf."

Max watched the ice topple into the water in an explosion of foam. It was the size of a small town, sinking and rising in slow motion, shedding waves of water each time it surfaced.

He was speechless.

"Happens mostly in the summer, when the sun weakens the ice," Basile explained. "Nowadays it's been happening more and more, though, as the northern ice mass diminishes—"

"We do not need a lecture on climate change!" Niemand's voice bellowed from behind them.

Alex and Max turned. Niemand stood in the doorway, leaning against the jamb. His usually neatly combed hair was flying out in all directions, and it looked like the silver streak had become wider. A salt-and-peppery beard stubble had spread across his face, and his eyes were slitted and red.

"Somebody needs his beauty sleep," Basile said.

Niemand strode across the room and brought his face to within inches of Basile's. "Perhaps you have forgotten who signs the paychecks here. The ride has become awfully unstable. Is there any reason we're not underwater—the way a submarine has been constructed to travel?"

"I wanted the kids to see the show!" Basile said. "And if you don't like it, put on a suit and swim."

Niemand narrowed his eyes. "My patience for you runs thin, Basile."

Basile's laugh seemed small and forced. "Come now, Stinky, we've been talking like this for years—"

"The dorm room is not a workplace," Niemand said. "I demand respect. Do not tempt me to find another captain among the seaworthy Greenlanders."

"Yes, sir, of course, sir," Basile said with a wry grin.

Turning on his tasseled slippers, Niemand strutted back into the hallway.

"I take it back," Basile murmured. "He doesn't need sleep. He needs a psychiatrist."

28

MAX hadn't been this cold since Dugan Dempsey poured ice down the back of his shirt last February.

Stepping up out of the *Conch*'s hatch, he couldn't stop shivering. They were anchored in the cove of Piuli Point. Two of the village's dockworkers had brought small motorboats out to greet them. Niemand, Basile, and Pandora were on one. Alex, André, and Sophia had climbed into another. Max was the last to board.

Standing on the submarine deck, he felt his teeth chatter. A round-face, smiling man reached up from the second boat, handing Max a blanket. "I'm Qisuk. Welcome aboard." He was wearing jeans, a flannel shirt, and a baseball cap.

Max felt like he needed three down coats. "I'm

M-M-M—" he said, before finally giving up.

He took a seat next to Alex and across from André and Sophia. As the boat puttered toward shore, the *Conch* retreated into the distance. Looking behind him, Max could see a set of low buildings. Wisps of smoke rose from their roofs into an icy white-blue sky.

"Your first time in Piuli Point?" Qisuk asked.

"Yes," Alex said.

"Are you coming to see the meteorites?" he continued.

"The what?" Alex said.

Qisuk smiled. "For a little place we have an awesome gems and minerals museum. For generations the Inuit have collected meteorites. Some of the densest material on earth. A dog-sized fragment can weigh three tons. Meteorites were considered sacred to the early settlers of Piuli Point."

"Does *P-P-Piuli* mean 'm-m-meteorite'?" Max asked.

Qisuk laughed. "It's the way our ancestors pronounced the last name of the American explorer, Robert Peary."

"The first guy to reach the North Pole?" Alex asked.

"The first white explorer, yes," Qisuk said. "Well, unless you ask the descendants of Frederick Cook. Cook said he got there first. Although in truth, the Inuit had most likely been there many times over the centuries. Probably by accident. I mean, who would *want* to be stuck up there?"

"In a f-f-few decades, with climate change, it'll be all w-w-water anyway," Max said.

"Your lips are purple, my friend," Qisuk said. "My sister owns the clothing store on the dock. Let's get you some warm new togs that fit. And a cup of hot chocolate." He winked. "We'll put it on the bill to Niemand Enterprises. It's not often we have a submarine visiting us, up here in the boondocks."

He guided them to the dock and lashed the boat tight. Max's legs shook as Qisuk helped him out. As they headed for the shop, Max looked out to sea at the *Conch*. Its periscope, windows, and antennae were floating like a giant alien crocodile.

"Take the stairs down one flight," Qisuk said, "and tell them to outfit you Greenland style."

As Alex descended, Max pulled out his phone. They may have been way on top of the world, but he had roaming cell service. He sent a quick text to his dad—*everything ok. you hang in there!*—and headed downstairs.

A half hour later, he was wearing a brand-new flannel shirt, a wool sweater, lined oilskin pants, thick boots, and a down coat with a fur-edged hood. As he emerged from the lower level, he saw Alex outfitted exactly the same. "We match!" he said brightly.

Qisuk was at the cash register, in an argument with Niemand about prices.

Alex grabbed on to Max's hand. "The others are still being fitted. Come."

They rushed out of the store. The sun was already brushing its bottom against the horizon, and the clouds above were a mesh of bright reds, oranges, and yellows. Alex darted down the snow-covered street. They ducked into a small parking lot near a food market, which contained as many snowmobiles as cars.

"We brought Stinky and his gang into our confidence, because we had to get here," Alex said. "But from now on, with the rest of that message, it's just you and me. And we need to move fast. Because the sun is setting." Reaching into the deep pockets of her down coat, she brought out two flashlights and handed one to Max.

"At this time of the year, in this place, the sun sets all night long," Max replied. "We're near the North Pole."

"Good point," Alex said. She reached into her inner pocket and pulled out the Verne booklet. "Anyway, the next clue is 'Upon entering the cove of the cook's competition, look for the bump on the elephant's forehead.' Breaking it down, I'd say we rely on the only word that makes sense."

"The?" Max said.

"Cove!" Alex led Max out of the parking lot. They followed the road that led from the shop down to the water. Stores on either side were closing for the evening, and shopkeepers smiled and waved through their windows. "Do they know who we are?" Max asked.

"I think they're just being friendly," Alex replied.

At the end of the road they made a right onto the path that curved along the dock. They were alone now, and the air was eerily silent except for the lapping of water onto the shore. Alex peered at a sign that said Piuli Cove. "Bummer. I was hoping that said Cook's Competition," she said with a sigh.

"Are there any other coves here?" Max asked. "Maybe Verne is talking about some kind of food competition? Which implies some kind of restaurant—?"

Alex spun to face him. "What if he didn't mean a restaurant? When is a cook not a cook?"

"I hate riddles," Max said.

"When it's a last name, Max! Remember what Qisuk said?"

Max nodded. "The other explorer, right? The guy who said he got to the North Pole before Peary . . ."

"His name was Cook! So 'Cook's competition'—that was Peary."

"And Peary is Piuli!" Max said. "So the cove of Cook's competition is . . . here!"

"Exactly," Alex said, sneaking a look at the mysterious passage. "Now . . . 'look for the bump on the elephant's head.'"

Max glanced around. "Elephants live in hot climates. Unless they're traveling in a circus, I guess. Or in a zoo."

"I don't see a zoo," Alex said. "Do you?"

Max glanced up the hill toward the small village. The scent of fireplaces gave the air a crisp, cozy feeling. Beyond the settlement, the houses gave way to fields of snow. He glanced to the right and left, along the seacoast. On either side of the cove, the earth rose up to distant jagged rocky peaks that loomed high over the water. Some were dotted with caves, and others seemed like mountainous ice sculptures, pounded into strange shapes. Just beyond the ones to the south, Max remembered seeing the giant wall of the ice shelf. Piuli Point was a sheltered cove, a valley between giants.

Alex was already trudging down the dock, looking around for clues. But Max's eyes fixed on a high, windswept peak just beyond Piuli Point to the south.

"Alex . . ." His voice was sharp and brittle-sounding in the thin northern air. So he yelled her name as loud as he could.

She turned and came running. But he didn't turn to her. He didn't want to lose sight of what he had just seen.

Instead, he just pointed upward. Towering beside the sea, as if standing guard against marauders from the south, was a ridge that outlined the profile of an elephant.

29

IN about a quarter mile, the houses and shops gave way to snow-covered fields, where low-slung buildings of tin and wood dotted the landscape like resting cattle.

And then the road just ended. Trails of footsteps led away in all directions. Max and Alex stopped. Snow had begun to fall lightly. The path to the elephant-shaped ridge was maybe a half mile through pure snow. To their left, the Atlantic Ocean stretched to the horizon.

Alex glanced over her shoulder, back toward the village. "By now they must have noticed we're gone. They'll be coming. And we've left big, fat footsteps to guide them."

"Not if the snow covers them up," Max said.

They took off across the field. The snow sloughed

away from their boots like granulated sugar. Max stepped quickly. Walking in the snow was a piece of cake compared to slogging underwater in a Newtsuit.

Max's body was warm except for his nose. He could see beads of ice forming on the furry trim of his hood. He squinted against the setting sun. The icy elephant peak was a hulking mass of grayish-black shadow against the crimson sky. It seemed to undulate as they moved closer.

In the silence and sameness of the snow, Max had no sense of time. It could have been an hour before they reached the base of the peak, or maybe ten minutes.

Alex was breathing hard. "This . . ." she said, gesturing to an upward-sloping path swept clear by the wind, "looks like the trailhead up the mountain."

They both stopped to rest. The silence had given way to the violent crashing of waves. To their left, at the base of the elephant mountain, was a sloping hill that led to another cove. This cove hadn't been visible from Piuli Point, and it couldn't have been more different from that calm harbor. Blocks of ice choked the inlet, sending white chunks to the shore on the crests of mighty waves. They crashed with the noise of colliding boulders.

The wind hit Max's face like a thousand hornet stings. "Only one way to go," he said. "Up."

* * *

"Where are we now?" Alex shouted into the wind. *"Can you tell which body part of Dumbo we're on?"*

She was about twenty feet ahead of him, creeping sideways along a sheer vertical sheet of ice. The path up the peak had become narrow, the wind stronger. Alex was swinging her flashlight along the path's edges, and the going was slow.

Max had been trying to keep their bearings, but it wasn't easy without maps. And he hated calling the elephant Dumbo. "I think we're at the top of the elephant's leg!" he called out. "I see the trunk from here!"

"I hate this," Alex shouted. *"We need climbing gear! And . . . and an antiwind shield!"*

Max dug his boot into the path's icy gravel, inching closer to his cousin. "The higher you go on a mountain, the worse the wind," Max said.

"What?" Alex shouted.

As Max leaned forward, his foot slipped. He felt himself sliding downward, his heels scraping the ice.

Alex screamed his name as Max's back slammed against the wall. His feet jammed on a small ledge, stopping the slide, but the momentum made his upper body lurch forward. He flailed his arms, screaming.

As his left hand smacked back on the ice, he felt

fingers gripping his wrist. *"Gotcha!"* Alex said.

Max dug his heels in. He could feel his knees shake.

"Can you hold on?" Alex shouted.

"Y-Y-Y—"

"Don't look down!"

Max looked down. The cove stretched out in an imperfect U shape directly below, its waves battering the rocky shore.

"Stop screaming!" Alex cried out.

"I'm screaming?" Max said.

"Yes! I said I have you. Can you turn?"

Max wiggled his body around. Alex was leaning over the ridge path, holding on to the whitened stump of a dead tree that had once grown out of the mountainside. Max's gloves were thick, but he managed to dig his fingers into an exposed crag in the rock wall.

"You can do it, Max . . ." Alex said.

Slowly, taking deep breaths, Max hoisted himself back up to the path. As he stood, trying not to panic, he felt his breaths coming in deep, hysterical gulps. "Th-Th-Thank—" he stammered.

"Dude." Tears were running down Alex's cheeks. "I thought you were a goner."

"Me too."

"Don't worry. We are going to stand here until you're

feeling like a human again. Just . . . breathe, Max. Collect yourself."

Max closed his eyes. *Do not look down . . . do not look down . . .*

The wind whipped his face, but there was a hole in his glove now, and his fingers were feeling the cold. He thrust his hands into his pockets and said, "I'm good. Let's go on, before I get frostbite."

"Slowly . . ." Alex warned.

They inched along, feeling the ground carefully before planting their feet. Max glanced upward. They were approaching the top of the elephant now. From this vantage point, the area that looked like a bump on the elephant's head was clear to see—a deep rocky platform in front of a small cave.

The path switchbacked twice above them, growing slightly wider until Max and Alex could walk forward instead of sidling along. As they stepped in front of the cave, Max swallowed deeply, staring into the blackness.

"Hallelujah," Alex said.

"It's—dark in there," Max remarked.

Alex took a deep breath. "After what we just went through, Max, I am not scared of some little old cave."

Caaawwww!

A black-winged bird shot out from the shadows,

buzzing the top of Alex's head. She shrieked, diving into Max, who fell onto the platform. "I changed my mind."

"We have flashlights," Max said.

"I dropped mine while pulling you up," Alex said.

Max took out his flashlight. Arm in arm, he and Alex stepped inside. Out of the snow and wind, the sudden silence jarred them. Max's ears rang. His flashlight beam settled on a cragged, uneven wall maybe twenty feet away. The cave floor had been worn smooth, and the ceiling vaulted upward to a dome about three times Max's height. *"Echo!"* he shouted.

"Stop that, you'll disturb the bats," Alex said.

"I hate bats," Max replied.

"They speak highly of you," Alex said.

"That's not funny. That's so not funny." Max moved farther in. The walls were smooth and seemed to be sweating with some slimy material, and he ran his fingers along it. "Candle wax?"

"Or the fat from animal sacrifice," Alex remarked.

"That's disgusting."

"Seriously, Max, it looks like some kind of ritual was practiced here."

Max's eyes were riveted on a black hole in the wall, just above eye level. It was about three feet square, as if it had been chiseled out of the rock, and it went in pretty deep. "Maybe this was part of the ritual."

As they moved closer, the flashlight picked up a faint golden glint from deep within the hole. "Is there something in there?" Alex asked.

"Give me a boost," Max said.

He stood directly beneath the hole and lifted one foot. As Alex cupped her hands beneath his boot, Max tucked the flashlight into the hole, then pressed his palms down onto the inside of the hole for support.

The rocky surface dropped a fraction of an inch. "That's weird."

"What's weird?" Alex said.

She boosted him higher, and Max peered inside. His palms rested on a square section of rock that was now pushed down. "It looks like someone cut a section of this rock into a square," Max said. "And when I touched it, it moved downward into the surface. Like some kind of button."

"This place is giving me the creeps," Alex said.

Max grabbed the flashlight and shone it inward. The hole was about two feet deep. Against the back was a tennis-ball-size chunk of some rocky substance that gave off pinpoints of reflected light. Max reached deeper and closed his fingers around it. It had the uneven roundness of a rock, but the sharpness of metal.

"Got it," he said, pulling it toward him. "This thing is incredibly heavy."

He braced his elbows on the slightly depressed square section of rock.

It moved again. Deeper down.

With a click, a section of the wall below thrust out directly into Max's chest. He and Alex fell backward, sprawling onto the ground. The heavy little rock thumped to the ground, and the flashlight clattered away from them.

Max scrambled to grab the light. It was pointing directly at the rock.

Close up, the thing was even stranger looking—solid black and studded with metallic shards. As he scooped it up, he saw something attached to the back of it, a rope that was yellowed with age and partially gnawed through. "It looked like they wanted to keep this in place, and I broke the security mechanism. Which was a rope."

"I guess it's valuable," Alex said.

Max heard a distant rumble outside. "What was that?"

"Thunder?" Alex said. "I don't know. Come over here, Max. Look at this wall!"

Max swung the flashlight around. A small square in the wall had popped open like the drawer in a filing cabinet. That's what had knocked them over. With a gulp, Max reached inside and pulled out a thick pile of folded cloth. It smelled of mildew, and it cracked as he unfolded it.

Inside was a small leather-bound volume. A rusted metal key slipped off the top of it and fell to the ground.

Max stooped to pick it up. It was clunky, heavy, and old-fashioned. "What's this to?"

"Maybe the note explains," Alex said.

Max shone the light over her shoulder as she opened the little book. The text was French. Max's heart raced as Alex began to read:

"'*The Lost Treasures*, Part Three,'" she said. "Weird. There's something written across the top of the page in all caps. He never writes in all caps."

"What's it say?"

Alex continued: "'WARNING! BEFORE CONTINUING TO READ FURTHER, TAKE NOTE: DO NOT UNDER ANY CIRCUMSTANCES REMOVE METEORITE FROM ITS PLACE.'"

"Meteorite?" Max said.

Alex scratched her head. "*Météore*. I'm pretty sure that's what the word means."

"If he didn't want us to remove it, why did he put it there in the first place?" Max asked.

"Unless someone else did," Alex said. "Max, you

pressed down on some kind of mechanism that opened the drawer, right?"

Max nodded. "Yup. Twice."

"You didn't put enough weight on it the first time," Alex said. "Verne must have meant for you to read the note first."

"Okay, so we took the meteorite, big deal," Max said. "We can put it back."

Another boom resounded, this one louder and closer than the other.

Max felt his blood running as cold as the air outside. He spun around and shone his flashlight on the dense, heavy, metal-studded rock.

And its broken tether.

"Or maybe," he said with a gulp, "we can't."

30

SPENCER Niemand hated climbing. It taxed the knees and weakened the spirit.

Stairs, he thought, should be seen and not taken. And if God had meant for humans to live among hills, he would have made them goats.

Never in his life did he expect to be trudging up Mount Wretched in Nowhere, Greenland, against the driving snow. In the company of Basile the Insult Oaf.

Necessity, however, was the mother of torture.

No human being in his or her right mind would choose to endure this. Certainly no children would, unless they had a good reason. Which is why Niemand had taken it so seriously when he'd seen the two little thieves sneaking off this way.

"A bit of a chill, eh?" Basile cried out.

"Chill? I'll be lucky if I survive this with any facial skin left!" Niemand shouted.

"Then it would be an improvement!" Basile said.

He did not have the energy to respond. Basile would pay for this later.

The going was molasses slow. Basile, to his credit, was an expert climber. He had scaled the seven highest peaks on seven continents. He had a coil of rope around his shoulders and a pickax tucked into his ample waist. He knew how to navigate. And he knew how to use a flashlight.

"Watch your step here!" the big man called out, focusing his light on one section of the narrow path, just ahead. *"Oh, dear. Oh, blast it . . . !"*

Niemand nearly collided with the cheeky beast of a man, who had decided to stop short. "What is it, Basile?"

"Looks like one of them may have gone over!" In the beam of his flashlight, the footsteps veered abruptly over the edge.

"You say this as if it's a bad thing," Niemand said.

Basile turned. Ice had gathered on his brows, lashes, and beard, and the venom in his glance made him look like Santa's secret devil. "This weather must make you feel toasty warm," he said, "because your heart is at absolute zero."

"Yes, where it is enjoying a nice cup of tea with your brain." Thunder boomed in the distance, and Niemand felt the ground shake. "Now stop the chatter and get us up there."

Basile thrust his pickax into a crag in the stone cliff face. "Hold onto this as you pass," he said.

After clearing the narrow, partially collapsed section of path, they found that the upward climb leveled a bit. The path widened slightly. Basile picked up the pace—and not a moment too soon, as another deep rumble shook the earth.

This one was closer. It brought both men to their knees. A sound came to them in the wind, the likes of which Niemand had never heard. It was not an explosion exactly, but a distant stuttering roar, like an avalanche.

"*Hurry!*" Niemand shouted.

"*We're almost there!*" Basile replied.

Niemand looked up. Not far above them, maybe another twenty yards, was the mouth of the cave. Footsteps led into it—that was clear. What wasn't clear was whether they belonged to one person or two.

He had to admit, he was grateful that at least one of them was alive.

He did have a soft spot for children.

31

"MAX, *where are you?"* Alex's voice shouted into the darkness.

The third boom had knocked Max off his feet and jarred the flashlight from his hand. He felt around for it and came up with only a battery. *"The flashlight's broken!"* he called out.

Alex's hand grasped his arm. She pulled him toward the cave entrance, where there was more light. "I moved it," Max said. "The meteorite. It had some kind of cable attached—and I broke it! Jules Verne said not to do it, and I did—and look what happened!"

"So the meteorite was attached to explosives?" Alex said. "Who would do something like that?"

From the distance came a low, extended rumble. "I

don't know," Max said. "But I don't want to stay here. We have the book. Let's get back to town and read it. Come on."

As they scrabbled to their feet, Max spotted the outline of the meteorite on the ground. He scooped it up and stuck it in the pocket of his coat, which made the coat sag practically to his knees.

Alex was already back out on the entrance ledge. The wind had kicked up another notch. It pummeled Max's face. He had to close his eyes against it. *"How are we going to do this without a flashlight?"*

"Very, very carefully!" Alex shouted. *"There's still some sunlight."*

As they stepped toward the path, Max heard a strange, distant hissing noise. It grew steadily louder as they walked. One moment it seemed to be coming from behind them, another moment from below.

"What is that?" Alex cried out.

"I don't kn— "

Before the word left his mouth, the hiss became an unmistakable roar. Far below them, the sea surged from the south. It was clogged with stacks of ice, jagged blocks of ice. The floes fought and tumbled and smashed each other to pieces, as if they were racing to the bay. A sound welled upward like a shrieking choir as blocks of ice scraped against one another. Waves pummeled the shore. Shattered ice plumed into the sky and landed in a brittle clatter like spilled bones.

From their vantage point, Max could see the front of the swell heading toward the peaceful cove of Piuli Point. *"Alex, we can't do this!"* Max said. *"Maybe we should stay in the cave until this passes!"*

Alex took a deep, indecisive breath. Her feet were glued to the path, her eyes fixed on the destruction below.

And that was when Max saw the shadows moving beneath her, coming slowly up the path. The hair on the back of his neck felt like needles of ice. *"Alex!"*

He grabbed her arm. She lost her balance, stumbling toward the edge of the path, but Max held tight. *"Max, what are you doing?"* she cried out.

A voice called up from below in the semidarkness. The sound of it chilled Max more than the weather.

"Is this the party?" said Spencer Niemand. *"I brought the ice."*

"What are you doing here?" Max shouted. *"How did you find us?"*

Niemand smiled. "A little puffin told us."

If it weren't for Basile's flashlight, Max was sure he'd be dead.

The big guy was very patient about turning to illu-minate the edges of the path as the four of them hiked downward.

The wind was still stiff and punishing. But the thun-dering explosions had stopped, and the raging water was beginning to slow. Packs of ice were forming, melding together, splitting off. They floated into the bay in new formations, turning, smacking against moored boats. Max had seen at least three of those boats capsize.

"You have made some idiotic calls, Stinky!" Basile said. *"But climbing down this path right now? That bloody well tops them all."*

"Just do your job!" Niemand insisted. *"And remember, you're responsible for three other souls!"*

"Two if you're counting souls!" Basile shot back. *"Two plus twenty-three if you're counting egos. Now be careful here. This is the place where someone slipped."*

"Me!" Max shouted.

"Right. Everyone grab on to the pickax for support."

Max heard a metallic chink as Basile dug the pickax into a rock fissure.

Basile went first, then Niemand. Max clung tightly to the ax handle, using it to support his weight as he leaped across the bad section. He nearly came down on a small chunk of ice that must have been blown up onto the path from the turmoil below.

He felt Basile's arms grab hold of him from behind, to keep him from falling.

"Are you all right, lad?" Basile asked.

"Y-Y-Yes," Max replied. "Thanks."

"*Everyone be careful of the ice!*" the big man announced, kicking the chunk off the ledge. "*The closer we get to the bottom, the more of these we'll see. They're being blown up here by the wind!*"

Alex was the last to get over the rough spot. As they all moved forward, she shouted, "*What do I do with the ax?*"

"*Sorry?*" Basile shouted over his shoulder. "*I can't hear in this blasted wind!*"

"*The pickax!*" Alex shouted back.

"*Leave it!*" Basile bellowed. "*I don't think we'll need it from here.*"

"*Nonsense!*" Niemand snapped. "*We can use it back on the* Conch*!*"

Basile stopped and turned around. "*What?*"

"*We'll need it on the* Conch*!*" Niemand repeated. "*I say we get it!*"

"*Look down there, for heaven's sake—there will be no* Conch *if it gets clobbered by one of those bergs!*"

As Basile stepped backward, his foot came down on another loose ice chunk.

Max saw the big man's body teeter. He watched

Basile's left hand trying to grasp on to the rock wall. He heard him shout *"Bloody ice!"* followed by a sharp skidding noise as the ice chunk shot away from under his foot.

And then came the scream—deep, raw, animal-like— as Basile fell off the ledge and into the teeming white mass below.

32

MAX'S stomach lurched up into his throat. Behind him, Alex was screaming. Even Niemand seemed shocked.

He had to turn away. This was impossible. Not Basile.

He heard no special splash, no last cry of terror. The sea below was a chaos of foam and spindrift, a wash of white into which the big, blustery guy had simply disappeared. Like a rock or a meteorite. Like a shrug of nature.

And that was the biggest horror of all.

Max felt his back smack up against the rock wall. As he began to sob, Alex took his hand, and he let her. Neither wanted to let go, so they stayed there, battered by the wind, for what felt like a year.

It wasn't until they heard the blast of a distant siren that Max opened his eyes. He could see that a fire had broken out in the village of Piuli Point. The dock was flooded, and boats were floating in the streets.

Max looked down the path. Spencer Niemand was making his way slowly. He was using his own flashlight. "Why didn't he tell us he had one of those?"

"He wanted Basile to do all the work," Alex said.

Max took a deep breath. The shock of Basile's death was hardening inside him. It was transforming into a rage that filled his nostrils with the smell of cat pee until his entire brain felt toxic. Silently, slowly, they made their way down the path. The wind sprayed splinters of ice against Max's face. It battered his ears. But none of that was as painful as the image that kept repeating itself over and over in his brain—Basile being swallowed up in whiteness.

He felt numb. At least twice he tripped on the path. By the time they got to the bottom, he could not feel his toes.

"We got here by snowmobile!" Niemand shouted. *"Follow me!"*

For a moment, looking around, Max was convinced they'd come down the wrong path. The area here looked nothing like it had when they'd started. Where there had been a long slope down to a rocky shore, now a swell of seawater churned and spat. Ice-choked and thick, the surf raced upward against gravity, then pulled back with a hollow roar.

Max, Alex, and Niemand stayed close to the base of the peak, trudging slowly back the way they had come. The numbness in his toes made Max's steps clumsy and uneven.

As the elephant ridge curved sharply inland, the ground angled uphill. They followed the curve, heading for the field they'd crossed a couple of hours ago. Here the terrain became more familiar, the wind weaker.

Now the sun's crown was just visible above the horizon. In its dull glow, a snowmobile waited on the crest of the hill. Niemand wiped off some of the snow that had piled on it, and he beckoned them to get in.

His face seemed brittle and gray, and Max had a great urge to spit in it. The idea of riding in the same vehicle with Niemand made his stomach turn. But his toes were frigid and his cheeks felt like they were cracking. Under the circumstances, getting as far away as fast as possible seemed like a great idea.

He strapped himself in next to Alex. It would be a tight squeeze with three people, and she scooted over to make room for Niemand. "I hope you're happy with yourselves," Niemand said through chattering teeth. "We will need to hire a new captain, and if you think that's easy in this godforsaken wilderness—"

Alex had had enough. "Your friend just died, Niemand. Before your eyes. Before ours. He did it trying to keep us safe. And all you can think about is what an inconvenience it is for you!"

Niemand was walking around behind them now. Max heard a click and a creak as he opened a small storage area in the rear of the snowmobile. "I grieve in my own way," Niemand said. "And in case you're worried, I promise I shall grieve for you equally."

"You won't have the chance," Alex said. "You'll go way before we do, and I will be the first to dance on your grave."

"Oh?" came Niemand's voice. "Don't be so sure."

Max felt something drop down over his head from above.

A rope, thick and stiff, pressed tight against his and Alex's chests. Before they could react, it pinned them against the back of the seat. With their thick coats and gloves, Max and Alex could barely move. "Cozy?" Niemand asked.

"What are you doing?" Alex demanded.

Ignoring her, Niemand kept wrapping the rope. He circled it around each of them individually. He tied it down to various places on the snowmobile. Each turn held them tighter in place.

"This is nuts!" Alex yelled, struggling against the binding. "Are you afraid we'll jump off on the way back? We have nowhere to go! Don't do this. I thought you didn't hurt children."

"I smell fish I smell fish I smell fish . . ." Max murmured.

"Of course you do." Niemand's breaths made frigid puffs as he leaned against the side of the snowmobile. "You have been very useful to me. You should be proud of yourselves."

He reached into Max's pocket, quickly yanking out the meteorite. "Do you have anything else for me?"

"No," Alex said.

"You want to live, don't you?"

Alex glared at him. "Left jacket pocket."

Niemand reached in and pulled out a small leather-bound volume. He opened it and smiled. "French is such a daunting language," he said, quickly pocketing it with one hand and holding the meteorite high with the other.

He stared at the dangling, broken fuse. "Well, doesn't

this just get curiouser and curiouser . . . ?"

"Okay, you have what you need," Alex said. "Happy? Now unwrap us, and let's get back."

Niemand perched on the edge of the snowmobile, reached in, and flicked the ignition switch. The engine roared to life. "When the coasts flood, and people flock to a bold network of my underwater cities," he said, "your names will grace street signs and office buildings. I will forever be grateful that you helped me get to Ikaria. I intend to learn much from their ingenious prototype." He held up the book from Alex. "I intend to learn much from this too. And profit very well by it."

The rope was digging into Max's skin, cutting off circulation. "This hurts."

"Trust me, in a moment you will no longer feel pain," Niemand said, standing up. "Oh, by the way, have I told you what *niemand* means in German?"

Alex and Max stared back, agape.

"It means 'no one,'" he continued.

Max thought back to Jules Verne's diary. *When I asked even of his name, he said, "I am no one." Taking this for a joke, I dubbed him Captain No One, and he happily answered to this ever afterward.*

"You're Nemo . . ." Alex said, her eyes wide and her

voice a hollow rasp. "You're the insane captain in *Twenty Thousand Leagues Under the Sea* . . ."

"Smart girl. *Nemo* indeed means 'no one' also. But I am not he. Just as you are not Jules Verne." Niemand barked a laugh. "I am a descendant. Like you, I am committed to carrying on a great man's work. And finding *your* great man's treasures. For which, I'm afraid, I no longer need your help."

Max stared straight ahead. The front of the vehicle was pointed directly toward the violent, crashing surf. "*Fi-i-i-i-ishhhh.*"

"Here's what I will tell people," Niemand said. "I will describe how Basile and I found you ruffian hoodlums desecrating a holy site, attempting to steal a valuable meteorite. Perhaps the gods themselves unleashed the violent calving of ice shelves that caused all this damage. When we valiantly tried to bring you back, you tossed poor Basile to his death. Then, as I beat my chest in grief over my comrade, you cruelly stole my snowmobile. And as we all know, children and motor vehicles are a volatile and often tragic mix . . ."

Max wasn't hearing the words. He was lurching to both sides. Alex was cursing and screaming. *"You don't kill kids!"* she screamed.

"I do have a soft spot, my dear." Niemand leaned into the vehicle and put his hand on the gearshift. "So I will not watch."

Niemand flipped the lever to Drive. And he walked away.

33

NIEMAND had lied. He couldn't help but steal a look.

He followed the vehicle with his eyes until it vanished into a rude, billowing cloud of ice and vapor.

The screams of the children did tug at his heart. But two lives were nothing compared to the lives of many. And children needed to know their place. Right now, their place was certainly not to stand in the way of progress.

Not that there was no sacrifice on his part.

Niemand turned away from the wind and sighed. He had agreed to this brutal hike in the first place, and now he would have to walk the entire distance back to the village alone in this ungodly cold. Certainly there would be no rescue vehicles coming for him. The streets of Piuli

Point were flooding, and buildings were on fire, so who would even notice his absence?

Still, though shaded by sadness, this event had given him fresh energy.

He would hire a new captain from the Inuit, after they'd tidied up the damage to the town, of course. For which he would donate a generous portion of funds, asking nothing in exchange, save perhaps an ocean-view suite in their finest hotel. Certainly Piuli Point could provide that.

He would give Sophia the book to translate and decode upon his return. Verne was a crafty old coot. There might be many, many more steps on this journey.

Niemand held up the meteorite he'd found on the boy. He recognized the cord hanging from the back. It looked very much like a fuse. Which, when broken, would ignite explosives. And some explosives, he knew, lasted a very long time in the cold.

It appeared someone was trying to make mischief— to actually cause an ice shelf to calve. It would be the only explanation for the catastrophe that followed. But what ogre of a human being would do such a thing? What cruel, sadistic maniac?

For sure the culprit was not Verne.

Niemand laughed at the sheer audacity. "My dear

Nemo," he murmured, staring at the dense stone. "Is this your idea? Was this part of some larger plan? Would that you were alive to tell me." He patted the book that he had taken from the girl. "Perhaps I shall find out. I am, as always, all ears."

As he picked up the pace, Niemand put the meteorite back into his pocket. He glanced up to the heavens and smiled at No One.

No one smiled back.

34

MAX saw nothing. Felt nothing.

The ice whipped his face until he bled. He knew he was screaming. He knew Alex was screaming. He heard their voices, but he felt separate from his battered body. As if he were floating overhead. Floating in a sea of fish and skunk and sweaty feet.

He remembered the snowmobile jouncing against ice. In his mind, he saw it lifting into the air like a space-ship . . . spinning . . . its once rigid sides now smashed in. The ropes that had been tied so tightly to their sides no longer held. They had some give. He felt Alex fighting in the seat beside him . . . both of them fighting until the rope jolted upward, nearly taking off his nose. And then they were lifted away from the seat, floating free, not knowing up from down. He remembered seeing the snowmobile being swallowed up in the icy river below them. The pain knocked the air from his lungs and the thoughts from his brain.

Until now.

"Max!"

Alex was calling his name, and he felt cold fingers close around his arm. His eyes blinked a thousand times until he saw Alex in the water. He had landed on the flat top of a floating sheet of ice. Alex was swimming, floating, trying to keep her head above water beside him, struggling to hold on. Her lips were blue, her eyes white as paper.

Max reached down to his cousin. Her forehead was bleeding, her lips quivering, but she had the strength to grab his outstretched hand and hold tight. He feared sliding into the water, but the ice's rough surface provided enough friction so he wouldn't slip. With more strength than he thought he possessed, he yanked her out of the water. She tumbled onto the frigid platform next to him, nearly falling clear off the other edge, which was only three feet away.

"A-a-ah—are—ah—" Max was trying to speak, but his mouth was stiff and unmoving. *Are you okay?* was all he wanted to say, but instead he silently collapsed next to her, exhausted and cold and aching all over.

"M-M-Max?" She was slapping his face now. "Max, stay awake!"

Each slap was a stab of pain. He felt blood rushing to his face.

"Max, hang on!" she was shouting. "I s-s-see lights, Max! We're moving f-f-fast! We're moving away from the mess! Do you hear me, Max? *D-D-Do you hear me?*"

Max blinked. He could see Alex's face looming over him. Her skin was a ghostly blue-white shade. "L-L-Lights?" he murmured.

Her face broke into a desperate grin. "Look! To your left!"

Max didn't have a chance to look. Because the iceberg struck something hard and solid, jolting both of them. He felt himself sliding . . . rolling . . .

Alex grabbed his arm before he could fall into the black water.

"Wha . . . what . . . was that?" Max asked. He felt himself sitting up. Blinking.

Alex was turned away from him now, and he struggled to turn his body. Facing them were two giant glass eyes, staring up from the water.

And a bent antenna.

"The *Conch*, Max!" Alex said. "Do you see it?"

Max nodded numbly. It was the *Conch*. No question. The platform was tilted and bent, the hatch still shut tight.

As he struggled to face the moored submarine, his body ached and his teeth chattered. "How . . . how did it survive the explosions . . . the flood . . . ?"

"Dentedly," Alex said. "It's a sub. It has sides of steel."

They both looked around at the chaos. The current was thundering past them like a raging freight train. Behind them where the cove met the sea, the harbor's edges were curved inward like a horseshoe. The shape sheltered the area—somewhat. Still the cove was clogged with ice. The water was high, the shore flooded. Only about half of the boats remained upright, and they were rocking violently. One small boat was puttering slowly in toward the shore, with one person at the motor and another standing with a metal pole, pushing the ice away. The boat was framed by the flames that rose from buildings on shore. Lights swirled and sirens blared as fire fighters and first responders rushed to the scene.

Alex held tight to the *Conch*'s metal footholds to keep them still. She cast a glance to Max. "Come on. Let's break in."

Max shook his head violently. The *Conch* meant Niemand. *No no no.* "I can't go b-b-back in there."

"We'll never make it back to shore, Max!" Alex shot back.

"What if he's in there?" Max shouted. *"Waiting for us!"*

Alex held his arm firmly. "We took the express snow-mobile to the water, Max, and then rode here on a flood. Do you really think Niemand would have made it back to town on foot and then gotten out here in that time?"

Max took a deep breath. The math made sense. And he was feeling so cold.

He nodded.

Alex used the foothold to boost herself to the platform. She reached down to help Max up. He clenched his teeth against the pain of three zillion bruises. Together they knelt on either side of the hatch. Opening it meant turning a solid metal ring. They both grabbed on to it.

But it began moving. Slowly. By itself.

Alex sprang back. Max grabbed on to the round railing to stop himself from falling into the water.

The ring made a creaking noise as it traveled a full circle. Then a click. The door swung open on its hinge.

"Max . . . ?" Alex said.

"Fish fish fish," Max said.

From the center, the shadow of a figure began to emerge.

35

"**GREAT** suffering cephalopods . . ." came a hoarse, scratchy voice.

Two swollen eyes peered out from a face mangled by fresh scars and crisscrossed by rivulets of blood and seawater.

"*B-B-Basile?*" Alex said. "But you're . . ."

"Dead!" Max added.

The face nodded. "Well then, I must be in heaven. Because I've been visited by two angels."

Alex let out a shriek of joy.

There he was. Alive. Battered, but alive.

Dark chocolate . . . ham . . . Max never smelled them both together. Relief. Confusion.

It didn't seem possible. They had seen him go over the

cliff. This was a miracle, and Max felt like he wanted to cry because this whole mission needed miracles to happen.

"I can't believe—how—but you—" Alex reached down and threw her arms about the old captain.

"Gently," Basile said, his face twisted with pain. "I'm not half the man I used to be. Come. It's awful nippy out there. I managed to turn on the lights and heat."

Alex and Max followed Basile down the ladder and into the sub. The big man was moving slowly, grunting with each step. Max could hear a steady beeping from inside the control room, and fluorescent lights illuminated the sub's interior.

Basile was hunched over badly. As he stepped aside from the ladder to let them down, his left leg dragged beneath him. The floor of the sub was smeared with blood. "Would one of you be so kind as to help me return to the medical room?"

Max linked arms with him. "You're losing a lot of blood."

"It's only . . ." Basile winced as they started walking.

"A flesh wound?" Max said.

"Exactly," Basile replied. "Go slowly, lad."

"How can you be here?" Alex said. "We saw you fall!"

"Believe I hit the side of the peak on the way down," Basile said. "Rather well padded with snow, I suppose.

Broke my fall. Nearly broke my back. Slid the rest of the way. Don't quite remember what happened afterward . . . woke up on the deck of a fishing boat. I imagine they would have preferred a net of herring. Great seamen, those chaps. Managed to keep us afloat until we got to the harbor. Then the keel split on the port side. One of the patrol boats was stuck in the cove, and they saw us. Bloody fellows wanted to take me to shore. But I made quite a noise. Insisted I had medicines and first aid on the *Conch*. Honestly, I did not want to see Stinky again. Afraid I would rip him apart and be thrown in jail. I think they allowed me to board just to shut me up—although I imagine they'll be back once the commotion dies down." The map of blood and hair shifted on his face as he managed a smile. "Then I heard you two squirrels up top."

As they neared the medical room, Alex stopped to hug him. "It's a miracle!"

"It's physics," Max said.

"Don't get too emotional, young fellow," Basile said with a weak laugh. "Now, I'm dying to know how *you* managed to get here!"

As Alex quickly summarized what had happened, Basile's face grew redder. Even before she finished, he was muttering curses under his breath.

At the door of the medical room, he turned toward both of them. "I shall never forgive that man. As long as I am alive, I will seek to bring him to justice for what he did to you. Now, if you'll excuse me, I need to freshen up. Then we'll review our options."

As he collapsed into a chair in the corner of the room, blood dripped steadily onto the floor at his feet. "I think one of us should stay and help you," Alex said.

But Basile's head had lolled back into the seat, and he was fast asleep.

"He needed stitches," Alex said as she entered the command room.

Max looked up from the instrument panel. His cousin's face was grim and a little teary. "Yuck."

"I know. There was surgical thread. Basile insisted on doing it himself. I tried to help, but . . ." Alex turned away. "He's strong, Max. But those injuries were bad. His eyes are moving funny. The bruise on the left side of his head is swelling."

"*Nonsense!*" boomed Basile's voice from behind them. "I'm feeling fresh and dewy and good as new!"

Alex spun around. "You were supposed to rest, Basile."

"Miles to go before I sleep!" Basile entered the room

using crutches. His left leg was wrapped in a crude-looking cast. His beard was mostly cut away, and bandages decorated most of his face. An enormous, blood-soaked gauze square covered his head. As he hobbled toward his navigator's stool, Max hopped off. "Thanks, laddie, for keeping that warm."

"I was curious about how you start the engines," Max said.

Basile let out a snort as he sat. "Ah, the mystery of the ignition. We've all been trying to figure that out."

"You don't know?" Alex said.

"Astonishing, eh?" Basile said. "Niemand is the one who starts the sub. Every time. Makes us look away as he enters the code. The blasted fool doesn't trust anyone else to do it. He thinks someone will try to steal the sub!"

Alex exhaled. "He's with us even when he's not with us."

Max focused on the steering column's ignition panel.

"Seven panels, twenty-six possible letters for each," he murmured. "That's about two billion possibilities."

"Well then, it'll take a bit of work to crack it," Basile said.

"Like, years," Max said.

"It's a password, lad," Basile said. "There's a jolly good chance we're guessing words, not random letters."

"Exactly!" Alex said. "Try using GREED and INHUMAN and HORRIBLE and MURDERER. If those don't work, maybe we can figure out how to hot-wire this thing. Just get us out of here. Back to New York where we can pick up our car, go back to Ohio, and start all over again."

"*What?*" Max said. "We can't just give up, Alex. Niemand has the clue to the next location. We have to get it back."

"We can't," Alex said. "Because he doesn't have it."

"He does!" Max said. "He took it from your jacket pocket, remember? It had the leather cover. He opened it up. He checked to see that it was French and everything."

"He doesn't read French, Max," Alex replied. "If he did, he would have noticed it was the book we got in Ikaria—*that's* the one I had in my jacket pocket."

"Wait—then who has the one we found in the elephant's forehead?" Max asked.

"I put it in my jeans pocket," Alex said. "I fooled him."

"*Haw!*" Basile bellowed. "Ouch, that hurt. Brava

to you, Alex. So we go forward—not back! That's the spirit!"

Alex fished the soggy leather-bound book from her jeans. "Except that it's pretty much useless now, Basile. It went with us in the water."

Max's heart sank. He couldn't believe his eyes. All of this for nothing. They would be going home now, empty-handed. Even Alex could go home to Canada. Max would be going home to . . . what?

Alex was trying to open the book, but the pages were stuck together, so she just tossed it onto an instrument table. Max sat on the floor of the sub and began rocking back and forth. "Fish fish fish . . ."

"Max," Alex said gently.

"It's my fault . . ." He thought about Vulturon's trip into the kitchen. He had scared Mom. It was probably the zillionth time he'd done something wrong. He never did things right. He didn't know how to interact with anyone. He couldn't read people's faces. He said all the wrong things. Too many things. Too few. He gave Mom and Dad stress. Stress led to sickness. And now he was going to be kicked out of his own house. He would have to explain what happened. That would give her more stress. "It's my fault!" he repeated.

"Hey, cousin, we did the best that we could," Alex said. "It was a great try. Jules Verne would have wanted us to do this."

Alex's hand was on his shoulder, and he pushed it off. Now the words from that first booklet were scrolling in his mind. The words he had locked in his memory. The words that had made him lose his senses and agree to this crazy, ridiculous, idiotic plan.

"'*The Lost Treasures: A Memoir* by Jules Verne Part One Translated from the French by the Amazing Alexandra Verne,'" Max said, spitting the words out as fast as he could. Getting rid of them like they were so much garbage—

"Max, please—"

"*I hate them!*" Max shouted. "*I hate the words! 'Dear reader, if you have found this I am profoundly grateful for it means I trust that the world still exists that the aims of my nemesis have not borne fruit I write this in a pen—'*"

As he stopped short, the words continued in his mind. Alex and Basile were staring at him as if he'd grown another head.

Max grinned.

He looked at the leather booklet that Alex had thrown onto the table. "Open it," he said.

"Wait, *what*?" Alex said. "We can't, Max. The pages are stuck."

"Dry them," Max said. "Don't look at me like that, just dry them and open it!"

Alex darted out of the room and came back moments later with a hair dryer. She held up the booklet sideways so the edges of the pages faced her, then flicked the dryer to the High setting and let it roar.

In a minute the pages began to curl and buckle as the water evaporated. "I don't see how this is going to do any good, lad," Basile said softly.

"Can you open it now?" Max demanded.

Alex turned the dryer off, set it down, and carefully slipped her finger inside the booklet. With a soft crackle, the cover separated from the first page.

The paper was still wet. But the words were all there, deep and bold without even a blot.

"What the . . . ?" Alex said.

"The text . . ." Basile said.

"'I write this in a pen using ink based in iron,'" Max recited, "'in the hopes that it will last . . .'"

"Iron-based ink!" Basile said. "Crikey."

"Iron," Max said, "is not affected by water at all."

"*Eeeeeeee!*" Alex screamed, as Max took the booklet

and held open a full page of glorious, French, Jules Verne handwriting.

"The game is afoot!" Basile said.

"Max, you are a genius!" Alex blurted. "Can I hug you?"

"Hug this," Max said, handing her back the booklet. "Then translate it."

36

THE LOST TREASURES

— PART THREE —

Dearest reader, it is here in Greenland that I, Jules Verne, planned to leave my vast treasure. But here marked the beginning of the end of my fragile alliance with this captain of dark moods and deep intellect. I thought no act could be more hideous than the destruction of Ikaria. But here is where I learned the true scope of his plans. The depths of his delusions.

I am a man of science. Yet I stand in awe of the mystery of nature. The former exists to understand the latter. To break down the natural world into smaller parts for examination. Yet the combination of nature's parts can be put back together in new ways. They can create monsters of their own—substances of explosive energy. Death sticks whose force can vaporize a human being in seconds. This power makes a mockery of gunpowder and bullets. And this power is what my enemy seeks to use to ever-more-destructive aims.

Having seen the calving of an ice shelf by chance upon his voyages, he set his mind upon causing one such event himself. For his pleasure alone! For now, I have defused his demented plot. But someone will trip the meteorite, and I pray for the survival of all the gentle souls nearby. And then what? The development of ever-greater methods of destruction? The taming of the atom itself, a goal which my nemesis has professed to seek?

I fear he is drunken with the success of his plunder of the Ikarian secrets! In his lifetime, he believes, he will master the building of an underwater civilization. It is then that he will set in motion his plan of devastation. And when the cities empty, then into his triumphal kingdom will flock his chosen people—chosen by their willingness to accept him as master.

Reader, if you have made it this far, I can only imagine your astonishment. But it is crucial that you know what happened. That you see the depravity of the demented genius who calls himself

No One. It is here that I decided upon his final fate. May God forgive me. May you forgive me.

Take this note. Secure this cave. Proceed, as I did, to the northeast, stopping at the port of Tourbillon D'Eau.

JV

37

"**TOURBILLON** D'Eau . . ." Basile said, running his finger up and down the map of the Greenland coast. "Not seeing it. What in the blazes does the name mean?"

"*D'Eau* means 'of water,'" Alex said. "*Tourbillon* is like 'turbulence.' If that helps."

Max woke up with a start. He hadn't even realized he'd fallen asleep. But he was on the floor of the control room covered with a blanket. He struggled to his feet, but every muscle in his body ached. "Owww. I feel like I'm a hundred years old."

"You don't look a day over ninety-eight, Mr. Van Winkle," Basile said. "Good morning."

Max rubbed his eyes. The sky outside the *Conch*

window was a deep blue. "It's morning?"

Morning.

It was a seven-letter word.

"Why did you let me sleep?" Max cried, racing to the ignition panel.

He typed MORNING into the squares, but nothing happened.

"You were dead to the world, lad," Basile said. "We all caught a few winks."

"But . . . Niemand . . ." Max said.

"Niemand is busy on the shore, trying to convince some poor sap to be his new captain," Basile said. "Don't forget, lad, he thinks we're dead."

"Niemand *is a seven-letter word!*" Max shouted.

"We tried that," Basile said. "We tried quite a few."

Max began pacing. Everything felt bad. Last night when they'd survived and met Basile, everything felt good. When they'd opened the book and seen the text, everything felt good. But now his mind was running yesterday's events like a horror movie. He saw the avalanche and the snowmobile and the ice floe. He thought about how close to death they had come. He saw the grin on Niemand's face. And the way he had walked away from the snowmobile.

A smell like a warm blanket welled up around him. "Ozone," he said.

"Beg pardon?" Basile said.

Max began pacing. "That weird smell . . . before it rains . . . and after."

"What does that mean to you, Max?" Alex asked.

"I want to get out of here now!"

"Okay, it means impatience. I get it. And I don't blame you." Alex took him by the shoulders and looked him in the eye. He tried to meet her glance, but it was hard. "Max, listen to me. I translated the note. Turns out Niemand was telling us the truth about Nemo. Way back in the eighteen hundreds, Nemo was plotting to set off a series of explosions up and down the Greenland coast. The Antarctic coast too. He wanted to create climate change all by himself and force people into underwater cities. Sound familiar?"

"We left home to help my mom," Max said. "Yesterday we almost died. What if we had? *How would she ever know?*"

"Max, I need you to listen," Alex said. "Focus. We know where we're going. It's a place called Tourbillon D'Eau. A port. We're trying to locate it on a map. The point is, we need to start up the *Conch*. Can you focus on figuring out that password?"

Basile peered through the periscope. "There are motorboats in the cove. Checking things out. Making sure people didn't get stranded. Or worse. They don't know we're here, but they know we're missing."

"Ozone," Max said. "Ozone ozone ozone."

"That's five letters, laddie," Basile said with a smile.

Max turned to him. The big guy was sitting at a tilted angle. The bandage on his head was so completely soaked with blood that it was nearly black. "You need to change that bandage," Max said.

Basile nodded. He stood slowly from the chair and grabbed the crutch. "Very good, then. Carry on. I have faith in you, Maxwell."

"Maximilian," Max said.

As he hobbled away, Alex whispered, "I'm worried about him."

Max felt an odd sense of relief. "When you started that sentence, I thought you were going to say you were worried about me."

Alex smiled. "I don't worry about you anymore, cousin. You are the greatest."

She kissed him on the forehead, and he let her. As she walked away, he wiped it off. But it didn't feel too bad, honestly.

"If you need me, holler," Alex said. "I can hear you in the infirmary."

"Roger," Max said.

He spun back to the pad and typed in HOSPITAL and then BANDAGE.

Too random.

"Familiar words . . ." Max muttered. He swiveled the chair and hollered down the hallway: *"Basile, what are the names of some of Niemand's family members? Or pets? What does he like?"*

"His parents were Oliver and Octavia, but he didn't like them!" Basile called back. *"He only likes himself. And money. Jewels. For a month in college he had a ferret named Lucifer before it got away."*

HIMSELF

SPENCER

OCTAVIA

LUCIFER

JEWELRY

DIAMOND

EMERALD

"Come on . . ." Max murmured. None of the words was working.

He needed more help. Basile had to know more. He got up and tromped down to the medical room.

From inside came a deep, anguished scream. Max slowed his pace. At the edge of the door, he leaned in to look.

Basile was lying on his back on a padded table. Alex had placed a metal basin on the floor under his head. She was rinsing off his wound with water poured from a beaker. As the pinkish-red blood splashed into the basin, Max could see a track of sutures holding together a deep blackish scar.

Nausea welled up, and he had to turn away.

"Come in, Max," Alex said.

Max stayed where he was. He forced himself to speak, even though he wanted to throw up. "I . . . nothing's working. With the password."

For a moment no one answered. Then he heard Basile's voice, sounding weary and thin. "Stinky loves to talk about Nemo. Captain No One. I think the chap reads *Twenty Thousand Leagues Under the Sea* once a year. Blathers on about it all the time until we're sick of it."

"*Nautilus!* The submarine name!" Alex blurted out. "No, wait. That's eight letters."

"What about the characters?" Basile added. "There's Ned Land. The impulsive harpooner. Also Conseil! He's my favorite, the trusty manservant."

"Harpoon . . . Ned Land . . . Conseil . . . they all have seven," Alex said. "Also Aronnax, the hero!"

Max spun away and returned to the control room. His put the words in one by one.

HARPOON

NEDLAND

CONSEIL

ARONNAX

From outside came the sound of a siren. Max quickly peered through the periscope, turning it around until he saw a boat approaching the *Conch*. It was moving slowly, as two men with metal poles shoved aside blocks of ice. There were three others on board, two of them wearing official-looking uniforms and caps, the other dressed completely in black. One of the uniformed men was pointing directly toward the *Conch*, gesturing for the others to look. Max realized it was because of the periscope. The guy had seen it move.

Max zoomed in. They were all standing now, moving around, talking, gesturing. As they motored closer, Max finally got a look at their faces. Qisuk was one of them, and he was holding a megaphone. The man dressed in black was wearing a floppy canvas hat and sunglasses. As he raised a set of binoculars to his eyes, he removed the hat. And Max saw a shock of silver down the middle of his thick black hair.

Niemand.

Max's hands tightened around the periscope handle. The boat was pulling alongside them, and he could hear fists banging on the *Conch*'s hull. Now Qisuk's voice rang out through the megaphone, loud enough so Max could hear it in the *Conch*. *"Hello! Anybody in there? Request permission to board!"*

Pulling away from the periscope, Max turned and shouted into the hallway. "Alex! Basile! They're coming! The dock people—with Niemand!"

He heard a clattering of footsteps in the hallway, and Alex raced in. "Are you sure?"

"Yes. I saw him," Max said. "And Qisuk. They're patrolling. We have to get out of here! We have to escape!"

Alex stared hopelessly at the ignition keyboard. "The passwords—none of the passwords worked?"

"We see the lights! Whoever you are, squatters are not permitted on board, and any damages will be recovered by Niemand Enterprises!"

"Fish fish fish fish . . ." Max muttered. He held on to the instrument panel and breathed as deeply as he could. Only one seven-letter word was in his mind now, and it was *failure*.

"Max, we have to think," Alex said. "We need to escape before they get here."

Behind them, Basile was hobbling silently into the

control room. Above them, the hatch wheel creaked as it began to turn. *"Open up, right now!"* Niemand shouted from above them.

"Well, well, if it isn't Stinky," Basile muttered. "Let me get my hands on that man . . ."

Before either of them could stop him, Basile was forcing his way up the ladder to the hatch, using both his arms and one foot. At the top, he pressed a button marked OPEN, which electronically turned the hatch's ring.

When it clicked, he pushed the door open.

Immediately Niemand's voice resounded. *"This is private prop—"*

But at the sight of Basile, Niemand's words choked in his throat. His face was white as a sail. "I am s-s-seeing a ghost . . ." he murmured.

"You are seeing your worst nightmare," Basile replied.

He grabbed Niemand by the collar of his silky black shirt and pulled his face to within an inch of his own. A silver chain hung down, and a strange, small, blunt plaster object swung out into the air. "Good God," Basile said, "is that . . . a pinkie?"

"What do you want, Basile?" Niemand squealed. *"A raise? A title? You name it, it's yours!"*

"The password, you murderous, bloodless sack of sewage in a human body," Basile growled.

"I—I don't understand—"

Basile closed his other hand around Niemand's neck. "The password to the ignition, Stinky, or your life."

Niemand's eyes were bugged out, his mouth flapping open and shut. "KISSUMS."

Basile tightened his grip. *"Do not mock me!"*

"I swear, Basile, it's K-I-S-S-U-M-S! It's the name of my pinkie!"

Max was already typing the letters into the keyboard.

KISSUMS

A deep *fffooooom* shook the *Conch*. Around the control room, the gauges came to life.

"Take me with you, Basile!" Niemand said. "There is a place for you in the new order! I have the next set of instructions. They're being translated right now! Please, old roommate, think of our friendship!"

"Good luck with the instructions," Basile said. "I think dear Sophia is in for a bit of a surprise. And here's what I think of you, Kissums, and our friendship."

He let loose a massive glop of spit that landed directly between Niemand's eyes. Then he lifted his old roommate by the shirt and tossed him into the frigid bay.

38

"LAAASPERAAAAANZA!"

Basile's singing was so loud and awful that Max had to cover his ears. But he didn't really care. He didn't mind the opera music either that blared through tinny speakers.

That's because Alex was dancing, and Max himself was spinning round and round as fast as he could. "Bye-bye, Stinky," he sang, "bye-bye, Stinky . . ."

When Alex grabbed his arm, he nearly fell over with dizziness. "Max, stop. Look."

Hunched in his seat, Basile was coughing like crazy. His body was heaving, his face had turned purple, and the red ooze on his head bandage was blooming.

"Basile . . . ?" Alex said.

Basile clutched his stomach and began taking choppy, deep breaths. Max couldn't tell if he was laughing or choking. "Crikey! Remind me never again to try a high C on the high seas. *Haw!* See what I did there?"

"Just a sec." Alex raced out of the control room and returned moments later with a basin, a beaker of water, and a fresh bandage.

Basile was already looking through the periscope, breathing deeply. As Alex gently began removing the old bandage from his head, Max flicked off the music.

"Ah, that does feel better," Basile said. "You children are too good to me."

"You scared us," Alex said.

"You're not the first person who's said that about my singing," Basile replied. A laugh bubbled in his throat. "But blast it, I sing when I'm happy. And the thought of Stinky's face when he saw me . . . *haaaaw*!"

"Hold still, Basile . . ." Alex said. She cut the last piece of adhesive and gently taped down the edges of Basile's new bandage. "I feel bad for the others. Pandora, Sophia, and André. What's going to happen to them? Can you run the *Conch* alone, Basile?"

"Those three will fend well for themselves wherever they are," Basile said. "And I intend to train you to help me run this thing."

The *Conch* jolted, and Basile nearly fell off his seat. "Blasted bergs are so sneaky!" he cried out.

Out the window, Max watched the shape of an iceberg float slowly past. The edges looked strangely feathery in the depths, sending up streams of tiny bubbles. Fish slithered in and out of the iceberg's crags like visiting tourists. A narrow fish turned toward the window, stared, blew up to three times its size like a balloon, and then swam away.

"Blowfish," Basile said.

"Scared me," Max remarked.

"At least we're away from the worst of the ice—and Niemand," Alex said softly. "Things will feel better when we're farther away."

"It's going to be a long time," Max said, "till things feel better."

Two hours later, the water was a muddy gray green. The icebergs were gone, and the fish were crowding the window. On the sonar map, the *Conch* was well north of Piuli Point and moving slowly. "Anything yet, mates?" he called out. "We are running low on fuel, and we'll need to dock somewhere."

Max and Alex sat on the control room floor, surrounded by geographic maps, satellite images, and topographic maps of all sizes and magnifications. They had dragged in everything they'd found in the map room—including a cache of historical maps dating to the nineteen hundreds.

Max wiped his brow. The sub was getting warm. "Nothing," he said. "I don't see Tourbillon D'Eau on any of the maps."

"Me neither," Alex said. "I've looked at every single port on the east coast. Also the west, for good measure. I even checked out some old maps, figuring the port might have changed its name. But nada."

A sudden grinding noise interrupted her sentence. The *Conch* shuddered, and the engine started to whine. Both Alex and Max ran to Basile. "What happened?"

Basile was leaning forward at an odd angle, blinking his eyes rapidly. "Ach, must be a sand bar! Sorry. Didn't see it. Hang on."

Max could feel the sub begin to rise. Alex was staring closely into Basile's face. "Your eyes are moving, Basile. Like, one is going different places than the other."

"Really?" Basile said. "Need sleep, I suppose. Surprise, surprise."

As he leaned forward to look through the periscope, the *Conch* jolted hard. It began shaking. Juddering. Tilting to one side as if something were pulling it.

"What's happening?" Alex asked.

Basile was furiously checking gauges and LED screens. "What the blazes—it's the hatch! Something's stuck on it. It's dragging us."

Max grabbed the periscope and maneuvered it to look back over the top of the sub. The water was thick and muddy, but there was definitely a big, thick mass on the hatch. "Can't tell what it is. Big, though. Maybe a glob of seaweed."

"Or a car, or a large farm animal, some sort of modern detritus that some idiot human being dumped into the sea," Basile said. "But I'm afraid if we do not get it off, it will damage the ship. So that shall be your first task as my crew. I will attempt to rise to the surface, so we don't flood our happy little home. You may want to get some sort of tool to poke the thing off."

Alex and Max ran out of the control room. As Alex went for the hatch, Max ducked into the power room, grabbed a crowbar, and raced after her. "Can I go first?" he said.

"We can fit together," Alex said.

They grabbed opposite sides of the ladder and climbed up. Holding the crowbar in his left hand, Max held on to the hatch lever with his right. *"Basile, are we above water yet?"* he shouted.

"Yes!" came the answer. *"Go ahead!"*

Max flipped the electronic Open lever. The hatch engine whined, then shut off with a click.

"It's stuck," Alex said.

"Push!" Basile shouted back from the control room. *"Press the safety latch and push!"*

On the underside of the hatch was a lever marked EMERGENCY. Alex put her shoulder on it and put all her weight behind it. "Get off, you big old piece of sea garbage!" she shouted.

When it didn't budge, Max wedged himself next to her. Now they both pounded it with their shoulders. "It's a heavy sucker," Max said.

"On three," Alex said. "One . . . two . . . *three*!"

They slammed upward as hard as they could. Max could feel the hatch jerk open. With his left hand, he quickly shoved the crowbar into the slit. He swung it left and right to dislodge whatever was there. *"I don't think it's seaweed!"* he shouted. *"It's rubbery. Dense. Like an old truck tire!"*

"Charming," Basile called out.

Max thrust one more time. This time, the crowbar stuck tight. He tried to pull it back, but it resisted.

"What the—?" Max gave it another pull.

Whatever was outside the hatch yanked the crowbar clear out of his hand and into the darkness above.

"Aaaaaaghhh!" Max nearly fell back off the ladder.

Alex grabbed his arm. "Max, what hap—?"

The word caught in her throat. The hatch's lid was lifting, the opening growing wider. By itself. Something gray and gelatinous undulated on the other side. It swelled and moved, until a giant white mass filled the round hatch.

A mammoth, unblinking eye.

39

"BASILE!" Alex screamed.

Max's knees locked. A long, gray finger-like object, thick with slime, oozed its way downward through the opening. Its tip touched Max's arm. It was cold and rough.

"Get down, Max—get down!" Alex was pulling on him, but something else was pulling harder.

The gray finger was plunging downward, stretching and twisting.

No. It was not a finger but a tube—a hose, a thick, endless tentacle, alive and moving fast. Its surface was festooned with rough-edged suction cups that scraped Max as the tentacle twined around his torso, pinning his right arm to his side. Max screamed as it continued down into the sub, sliding around his waist and his legs.

The tentacle's thickness crowded the ladder, pulsing, pushing against Alex until she could hold on no longer. *"Max!"* she shrieked as she fell. *"Basile!"*

Max tried to free himself. He punched the tentacle with his free arm, but that did nothing. Above him, the top of the tentacle was attached to a gelatinous gray mass that undulated in the hatch. Its skin slid and crackled as if it were rolling, and Max no longer saw an eye but instead two sharp pincerlike objects that together resembled a giant bird's beak.

As Max felt himself rising slowly upward, the beak opened. It bulged downward, its surrounding skin straining against the hatch.

"No-o-o-o!" Max screamed.

"Alex, give this to him!" Basile was shouting now. *"Max, pay attention! It is a giant squid, and that is its mouth. You must do as I say. Look down! Take the weapon from Alex!"*

Max struggled to breathe. His left hand now was jammed against the ceiling, and he pressed into it with all his strength to stop his upward movement. Inches above him, through the open beak, he could see into the fleshy mouth of a giant beast. Alex was climbing the ladder as fast as she could now. She was thrusting the hilt of a machete toward him.

"I can't . . . I can't let go . . ." Max said, not daring to reach downward.

Another tentacle squeezed through the hatch. It surged right past Max and headed down toward Alex. She screamed, dropping the machete before letting go of the ladder and falling to the floor. The tip of the tentacle dropped onto her face, bounced, and then began slithering under her back.

"*Stop!*" Alex yelled. She tried to get onto her feet, but the tentacle forced her back to the floor, wrapping itself around her in a slow spiral.

Basile had run back to the power room, and now he was returning. He struggled with the pain, his teeth gnashing and a crutch tucked under one arm. In his other hand he held an ax.

With a guttural roar, Basile swung the ax at the appendage that held Alex. Its long, slimy column reached from the hatch to the floor and provided a perfect target. The blade split it in two, the top part skirting upward in a violent spray of milky liquid. Alex rolled away, pushing the ripped flesh off her body and springing to her feet.

Max felt the beast's grip around his body slacken.

"*Let go of the ceiling while it's in shock, lad!*" Basile bellowed, scooping the machete off the ground and holding it up toward him. "*And then shove this into its mouth!*"

Max pulled his left hand away from the ceiling. He reached down and gripped tight to the machete's hilt. The weapon was heavy, and he felt weak. But the beast was regaining its strength, squeezing him harder, yanking him closer. Its beak was open wide.

Max drew back his arms and thrust the machete upward. Its blade disappeared into the blackness of the creature's mouth, which shut with a tight *snap*.

The force yanked the weapon out of Max's hand. The machete was stuck in the squid's mouth like a toothpick, but the blade had sliced off the beak's tip. A plume of white goop surged toward Max's face, and he turned away.

As the tentacle loosened around him, Max slid downward. He thumped to the floor of the *Conch*. The monster must have opened its mouth again, because the machete clattered beside him.

He, Basile, and Alex all lunged for it.

But the tentacle got there first. It wrapped around the weapon and pulled it upward toward the hatch.

Max leaped. He grabbed on to the hilt and pulled as hard as he could. The blade twisted. Max could see it penetrate the beast's skin. With all his strength, he maneuvered the blade so it sliced cleanly through the beast's fleshy appendage. The severed part of the tentacle jerked upward, dangling on a fleshy flap.

As the beast withdrew, the skin holding the tentacle ripped, and the appendage hurtled downward. Max jumped out of the way, tensing for another attack.

But the creature was gone.

Max waited for a moment, then slumped against the ladder. Basile was doubled over, his teeth gritted in pain. "Are you all right?" Max asked.

"Max, look up!" Alex screamed.

A gaggle of quavering tentacles squeezed through the opening, like a nest of snakes. They slithered down, curling around the ladder, sliding along the ceiling, dropping straight to the floor. As Max backed away, he looked up, terrified. The monster hadn't retreated. It had repositioned! *"How many tentacles are there?"* Max cried out.

"T-T-Ten!" Basile said. *"Eight for swimming and two for holding prey and passing it to the mouth!"*

Now the squid's entire upper body was twisting through the narrow opening like some grotesque monster toothpaste. Once through, it instantly expanded to twice its girth. Finally its beak and eyes reemerged, and with a dull *shhhlurp*, the whole monstrous thing dropped to the floor in front of them. *"Stand back!"* Basile said.

Max didn't even see him throw the ax. But he saw the flash of steel as it hurtled forward, embedding itself directly in the beast's eyeball.

The squid let out no yell, no sound at all. Instead, its head dropped to the floor, and its tentacles rose into the air—looking to Max, miraculously, like it was surrendering.

Max quickly turned to check on Basile, but the old man's eyes were wide. "Be careful, lad!"

As Max spun back around, an acrid liquid hit him in the eye. In an instant he realized the tentacles had risen not to surrender but to expose a kind of blowhole. The force of the spray knocked him back, and he slammed against the wall. Tears sprang into his eyes, and he tried to wipe them clean with his sleeve.

As he blinked, he could see that his shirt and arms were covered in black. Alex was doubled over next to him, screaming, her face and hair a matted mass of black gunk.

"It's ink!" Basile shouted. "It won't harm you!"

The old captain was heading down the hallway and into the control room, trying to distance himself from the squid. But a tentacle rose up and then plunged down and wrapped around Basile's legs. He flailed his arms, dropping the crutch and grabbing on to the control room's doorjamb. The squid lifted him and slapped him back down.

"Whatever you do, do not let it damage the controls!" Basile screamed.

Blinking the ink out of his eyes, Max staggered to the machete and raised it again.

From the hallway floor, two tentacles shot up directly toward him. One of them knocked the weapon from his hand. Together the tentacles thrust around both sides of Max, trapping him. *"No!"* he shouted.

"Let go of me!" Basile shouted from the control room.

No no no no no no no no no, Max's brain screamed.

"Leave them alone!" Alex's voice echoed.

She raced into the engine room, dripping with black liquid. Moments later she emerged with a lit blowtorch. She thrust it at one of the tentacles that held Max. It singed the skin, sending up a puff of greenish-gray smoke. The tentacle recoiled and went limp, hitting the floor. As the other one loosened, Max jumped away.

A sickening smell of fish—real, burned fish—permeated the air. Alex was moving slowly toward the control room now. She thrust the torch forward like a sword against the skin of the tentacle that held Basile. With each hit, the beast's skin retreated like a wave, uncoiling from the old captain. The squid was pulling away from Alex's attack, shrinking back toward the ladder.

As soon as the path was clear, Max ran behind Alex

into the control room. Basile was still on the floor, writhing and moaning in agony.

The sight made Max angry. The squid was at the base of the ladder now, a huddled mass of quivering flesh, spotted with black where Alex had burned it. Severed tentacles littered the floor around it. Max could see the ax, still jutting from the eye. He couldn't stop himself. He ran for the ax and yanked it out with a sickening *thh-hhurpp*. The squid's flesh flinched, and one of its intact tentacles reached toward Max.

"Max, what are you doing?" Alex shouted.

He leaped back, preparing to swing the ax again. But the tentacle changed direction in midair. Its tip pointed upward, then back to the ladder. It smacked against the rungs and began twining up toward the hatch. Another tentacle joined it, and a third. The squid's upper body was tilting now, sliding toward the ladder as the tentacles pulled on it.

Alex lunged again, letting the flame singe the beast's flesh, but Basile managed to call out a hoarse, "No!"

Alex and Max turned. The captain was struggling to his feet, one hand pressed against the wall. "It's trying to get away!" he said. "Let it go and shut the hatch. There are more coming!"

"More?" Alex said.

Basile gestured to a distant black mass out the control room window. As it came closer, Max could see the flash of eyes, the jetlike thrust of tentacles, the trailing clouds of black. "They travel in packs!" Basile said. "We have to get out of here before they overwhelm us. *Shut the hatch!*"

The squid oozed up the ladder, tentacles first and then body. Its thick flesh contracted as it squeezed itself through the hatch. Alex prodded it with the torch, and Max followed carefully behind, tightly gripping the slimy ladder.

When the domed top of its head disappeared, Max pulled the hatch shut and locked it. Alex fell back against the hallway wall, shutting her eyes. "Thank God it's over."

"We're good to go, Basile!" Max shouted.

He dropped to the floor. He kicked aside a section of tentacle that was already starting to shrivel and curl into a ball.

In the control room, Basile threw the steering wheel to the right. The *Conch* was shuddering now. Alex and Max ran in and stood beside him.

Through the window, the water was a dark, menacing gray. In it, Max saw dozens of oval eyes and snapping orange beaks. A giant tentacle smacked itself directly on the window, its suction cups spreading wide and holding fast.

"They're attacking!" Max said.

Basile broke into a coughing jag that nearly toppled him from the seat. "Fire . . . the depths . . ." he croaked.

"What?" Alex said.

"The depth charges!" Basile said, gesturing to the wall near where Max was standing, just to the left of the window. "Fire the depths!"

Max turned. He was eye to eye with the red button labeled EMERGENCY DC under a larger square of protective glass. A chain hung from the glass with a key.

DC. Depth charges.

"Now, lad! Now!" Basile yelled.

Max inserted the key into a hole at the side of the glass square. When it popped open, he jammed his hand down on the red button.

An ear-splitting siren sounded. The *Conch* jolted violently, and Max lost his footing.

But he held on long enough to see what looked like a torpedo slice through their cloud of attackers before exploding with a distant boom.

40

THE squid were gone.

The water was a slate gray. Basile sat at the controls, blinking and looking like he was about to keel over.

And Max and Alex were back to searching for the location Jules Verne had given them.

"She rides quicker now . . ." Basile said absently. "The *Conch*, that is. We're a little lighter without the depths. That's a good thing . . . mostly . . ."

Max looked up from the maps and gave Alex a concerned look.

"Are you sure you're okay, Basile?" Alex said.

"Fresh as the bay I was dorn," Basile declared. "Well, not really. After today's shenanigans, you can bet I won't be eating calamari anytime soon."

"You said 'bay I was dorn,'" Max said.

"Did I?" Basile replied.

"Maybe we should stop somewhere," Alex said. "Get you to a real hospital."

Basile laughed. "This isn't New York City, lass. Puffins outnumber humans here. And they don't take my health insurance. But . . . erm, we do need to hit land soon. For fueling reasons."

"How low are we?" Max asked.

"A couple more hours at the most," Basile replied. "I'd planned to buy some diesel from those nice chaps at Piuli Point. But you know how that went. So keep your eyes out for civilization. Have you really not found the place?"

"No Tourbillon D'Eau anywhere," Alex said. "There's got to be some kind of mistake."

"Or maybe it's a code," Max said. "Should we rearrange the letters?"

"Why would a town in Greenland have a bloody French name to begin with?" Basile let out a big yawn and began rubbing his eyes. "The Danes and the Inuit are the only ones interested in the place."

Alex nodded. "The French hate the cold. The ones who liked it went to Canada."

"What the—" Basile said, moving the steering wheel

to the right. "Why in heaven's name is she pulling to starboard?"

Max went to the periscope and peered through. "I don't see any squids."

"Has this ever happened before?" Alex asked.

"It could be a strange riptide," Basile said. "Or we're caught on some infernal cable. What else do you see, lad?"

Max made the periscope rise above the surface. He scanned the horizon. An island lay ahead of them in the distance slightly to the left. Between the sub and the island, the sea was choppy, but Max's eyes were drawn to what looked like a distant black circle on the horizon directly ahead, in the middle of the water. "I think I see an oil slick."

Basile cocked his head. "This isn't anywhere near the tanker routes. What does it look like?"

"Big and round," Max said. "Really dark. Kind of like a black hole."

"Let me see, if you would." The old man pushed Max aside and glanced through the scope, blinking hard. In a moment his smile vanished, and he looked up again at the sonar map. "That's not an oil slick. It *is* a black hole."

"What?" Max said.

"The nautical equivalent." Basile began flicking

switches and looking at gauges. "This is a maelstrom, lad. A whirlpool."

"Is it dangerous?" Max asked.

"You're bloody correct, it is!" Basile said. "These things pull in great ships. You know what this is, my chickens? Punishment! Neptune does not like us for associating with Stinky!"

He yanked the steering wheel to the right and blinked his eyes furiously, trying to focus on a sonar chart. "I bloody well wish I knew which direction to go."

"You don't?" Max said.

"I have never been in one of these, my boy."

Alex's fingers rose to her mouth. "Tourbillon D'Eau . . ." She scooped a dictionary off the floor and flipped through it. "I don't believe this . . ."

Basile and Max both stared at her as she ran her fingers along one of the pages.

"*D'Eau* means 'of water' and *tourbillon* means 'turbulent'—but I never looked up the phrase, the two words together!" Alex said. "'Maelstrom'—that's what *tourbillon d'eau* means! Jules Verne wasn't giving us the name of a village. He was warning us about this!"

"*Now* you tell me, lassie!" Basile said.

"Are we in it already?" Alex said. "Are we going to die?"

Max began walking in circles. He fought back the smell of fish. "Something isn't right . . ." he murmured. "Something isn't right about the clue . . ."

The *Conch* was slowing, the engines churning loudly. "Trying to cut the engines, put her into reverse," Basile said, "but the current is wicked."

"The parts . . ." Max murmured. "Break it down into the parts . . ."

He closed his eyes and pictured the translation. *Proceed, as I did, to the northeast, stopping at the port of Tourbillon D'Eau . . .*

"Max, what are you saying?" Alex cried out. "What parts?"

Northeast . . .

Stopping . . .

The port of . . .

Max raced over to the periscope and looked through. To the island. The whirlpool.

"Left!" he blurted.

"Excuse me?" Basile said.

"Go to the left. Now."

"Why?" Alex said. "How do you know?"

"Verne said 'port of Tourbillon D'Eau,'" Max said. "He didn't mean a *port*, he meant the *port side*," Max said. "There's an island on the port side of the maelstrom. That's where he wants us to go!"

Basile peered through the scope. He let out a gust of breath. "I never thought I'd see the day when a twelve-year-old boy outnavigates a salt like me."

"Thirteen," Max said. "My fourteenth birthday is in—"

"Hold tight!" Basile said as he spun the steering wheel to port.

The *Conch* veered left. The engines moaned as Basile pulled back the throttle.

Max hung on to the instrument panel. His eyes darted up to the radar screen. The sub was a white blinking dot, making a sharp left-hand turn. He bent down and looked through the periscope. The sub was looping far to the left, swinging clear of the black hole. "You're doing it, Basile!" he shouted.

"Not yet, lad . . . I've got to access overdrive . . ."

The sub was vibrating. The specimens in Basile's museum cabinet were clattering against each other. Max could hear something crash to the floor in the medical room.

The old man had sweated through his head bandage. His eyes were bloodshot, and the knuckles of his fingers were white on the wheel. "Fire the depths," he said.

"What?" Alex blurted.

"Again! Fire all of them! They will reduce our weight! And the recoil will give us an extra jolt away from the maelstrom!"

Max turned and slammed his palm against the red emergency button.

With a dull, deep thump, two black charges hurtled forward like oversized bullets.

"Keep doing it!" Basile shouted.

Thooom.

Thooom.

Thooom.

Max slapped his hand down until nothing happened. He could feel the ship recoiling after each one, but now it was rolling, pitching from side to side . . .

And then, without warning, the engine went silent. The lights flickered.

The sub had lost power. Max slapped the controls until his hands hurt, screaming at the top of his lungs.

41

"SSSSH, Max," Alex said.

Max gulped down his screams. The only sounds in the control room were the beeping of gauges and the dull slap of the tail of a wandering fish on the left-side window.

"What happened?" Alex said.

"Did we make it?" Max asked.

Basile bowed his sweaty, bloodied head. "We made it," he said. "We're out of the current. For now, we're safe. Thanks to our intrepid young laddie here."

"Wait," Alex said. "That's . . . that's amazing! Max . . . Basile, you're awesome! You are the best captain in the—"

"Not so fast." Basile held up his hand. "We're also out of fuel, lassie."

Max swallowed hard. "So . . . what do we do?"

Basile looked up. He was working hard to keep his eyes steady now. With a sigh, he said, "We need to move fast. The sub is using auxiliary battery power for the interior electricity, but that won't last forever. In the diving chamber there are wet suits, goggles, and flippers. Also headlamps. These will be crucial."

"We have to *swim*?" Alex exclaimed.

Basile shrugged. "Aye, no other choice. The island is maybe half a kilometer away. The water will be frigid, but the suits should do the trick if you go fast."

"You mean, 'we,'" Max said.

"Right," Basile replied. "Of course. We. Chop-chop now. Don't shilly-shally."

Alex and Max helped Basile to the diving chamber. They pulled wet suits from a chest and quickly put them on. Basile reached into a supply chest and handed them each sealed bags. "Tuck these into your suits. The suits are waterproof, head to toe. You put the flippers on over your enclosed feet. Inside the bags you'll find matches, flint, even some dry paper and kindling. The island will be cold. Once there, you'll want to keep your suits on for the insulation, but a human being can only take so much exposure. Oh, and Max . . ."

"Hmm?" Max said.

"Tell me, do you still have that specimen I gave you?"

Max smiled and felt for the lump in his pants pocket. "Sea fan—*Isis hippuris*," he said. "I carry it wherever I go. You said it was medicinal."

"Very good," Basile said with a smile. "Precious stuff. Wouldn't want you to leave it behind."

Alex and Max took their bags and tucked them in. Basile grimaced as he pulled his suit over his injured leg. Alex helped him fit the hood gently and then his mask, snorkel, and headlamp. "Are you sure you can make it?" Alex said.

Basile smiled. "Haw! By the time you get to the shore, I'll have already prepared lunch."

He put the snorkel into his mouth and gave a thumbs-up.

Max and Alex donned their equipment. Basile pressed the button to open the chamber, and water cascaded in.

The old captain was the first to dive. As he disappeared into the dark water, he waved.

Max took Alex's hand. Together they thrust forward into the ocean, and they swam away from the *Conch* for the last time.

42

BLACKNESS.

Cold.

Time.

Pain.

Max's eyes blinked open into rainy darkness.

He was on a bed of rocks, wet and sticky. He had no memory of the last few minutes. Thunder boomed overhead. He braced for a flash of lightning, but there was none. No light except the faint orange glow of a smothered sun taken hostage by clouds.

Max stood, pulling the goggles from his eyes and letting them hang around his neck. Every muscle shrieked at him, commanding him to lie down. His body unfolded in waves of ripping, searing pain.

Still, he ran up and down the coast, shouting.

"Alex! Basile!"

They were gone. He staggered up into the scrubby woods behind the shore and called again, into the spindly branches and thickets. He looked back out to sea, wading into the frigid water, even though he could barely feel his feet.

"Alex! Basile!"

There was no echo in this place. The sound stopped two inches from your face and then was absorbed in the pouring rain.

Fish fish fishy skunk skunky fish skunk fish fish.

He paced, talking to himself. Talking was good. Talking worked. He counted the shells until his teeth were chattering so much he couldn't even think.

He wrapped his arms around himself as if that would keep him warm. Out to sea, his eyes located the black hole, the maelstrom—a distant, smudgy black blot.

Tourbillon D'Eau.

This was it. This was the island Jules Verne had led them to, the goal of their hunt. Somewhere—behind him? under him?—a massive treasure waited. Unless it didn't.

And none of that mattered.

Max slumped down onto the rocks. He felt his

thoughts darkening. One by one they were blotted out by a thick marker that was the color of squid ink, by the blackness of death. This had been a quest to find a fortune. The fortune was supposed to save a life.

The score so far? No lives saved, two lives lost.

And me. What about me?

He could jump into a pile of gold, and no one would ever, ever know he was here.

"I'm sorry, Mom," he murmured. "I'm sorry, Alex. I'm sorry, Basile. I'm sorry, me. I'm so, so sorry."

Throwing his head back, he let out a cry that welled up from his stomach and ripped the back of his throat. Overhead, as if in answer, a thick black shape on a tree branch unfurled its vulture wings and began flying upward, gliding black against the silver-gray sky.

Max felt a shiver and stood. *"Alex!"* he tried one more time. *"Basile!"*

No answer, of course, except for the splashing of water. He squinted carefully at the ripples, the shadows and swells. The wind battered his face and froze the tears on his cheeks, and even though he was in a wet suit, he knew he wouldn't survive too much longer. He would die here on the shore if he didn't find some warmth, some food. He wanted, more than anything, to sleep.

As he turned away, a tiny blot of blackness rose and

fell on the water to his right. Frozen and numb, he fought the urge to ignore it and lingered a second longer. It was a piece of flotsam that looked at first small and then massive. It hid and reappeared on the crest of a swell that was slowly bringing it to shore.

His fingers nearly numb, Max managed to remove the flippers from his feet, which were still enclosed in the waterproof material. As he ran across the shore, the shadow rode another wave that deposited the debris on the rocks.

It had arms and legs.

And flippers.

Max ran despite the near-total lack of feeling in his legs. He dropped to his knees and turned the body over onto its back.

Alex. Unmistakably Alex. Still in her wet suit. He ripped off her mask and snorkel.

She was not breathing. Her skin was cold.

No.

Max began pounding her chest. One . . . two . . . three . . .

He'd never done CPR. But he'd seen it a million times on shows. He'd read about it too. Watched videos. Memorized the facts.

One . . . two . . . three . . .

Sometimes people's lungs filled with water, so you made a vacuum and sucked the water out. Some people said that wasn't necessary. But some said it was. So he exhaled, emptying his lungs. Leaning forward, he grabbed Alex's lips in his hands. Then he put his lips on hers, trying to make a seal. He wasn't exactly sure how to make a vacuum seal with lips. So he pressed hard. That was probably good enough.

Her lips were as cold as steel. What next?

More compressions. Speed was important.

One . . . two . . . three . . .

Max sat back on the rocky shore, numb. He was breathing hard. This wasn't working. Because sometimes the facts weren't enough. Because you couldn't learn everything from a book or a TV show. Like building a drone, driving a sub, capturing a treasure, fighting a squid, escaping a cruise ship. Making a person breathe. You couldn't learn those by reading. *"Breathe!"* Max screamed. *"Breathe breathe breathe breathe breathe!"*

Even lifeless, Alex looked like she was about to talk. Alex always said good things. She was awesome. He had known that the first day he'd met her. She had convinced him he could leave the house, travel without his mom and dad, search for a treasure. She had given Max good advice. The best advice ever.

Sometimes you can't be ready to do the things you really need to do. You just do them. And that makes you ready.

That was what Alex had said. It was how she lived.

Max took a deep breath and leaned over her again.

One . . . two . . . three . . .

You . . . just . . . do them . . .

One . . . two . . . three . . .

One . . . two . . . three . . .

He felt the tears dripping down his cheeks as he pressed his lips against hers one more time and prepared to inhale.

Alex gasped and sat bolt upright. She twisted away and threw up water—once, twice, three times.

Max screamed, falling back onto the rocks.

"Max!" Alex said as she wiped her mouth on the sleeve of her wet suit. "I didn't know you cared."

43

SHE felt cold. But hugging her made him feel warm.

"You're—you're alive!" Max screamed. *"You're alive you're alive!"*

"But not ready to party . . . just yet." Alex blinked. She looked left and right, coughed, and then turned on her side and spat up more water. "We're here, right? The island at the port side of *tourbillon d'eau*?"

"Yes." Max hooked his arms under her shoulders and gently dragged her up the shore, away from the water that lapped over her legs. They rested on a couple of large rocks, not far from the ridge of pine trees that led deeper into the island. The rain had stopped, but the rock was still slippery.

"What are you smelling?" Alex asked.

"The good things," Max said. "But they're making me hungry."

Alex laughed. "I smell seaweed. Max, is Basile here?"

Max shook his head. "I haven't seen him. Maybe he's in the woods. He said he was going to make us lunch."

Alex didn't nod. Her face grew sadder. She looked out to sea and didn't speak for a long time. "He was really weak, Max," she said finally. "His leg wasn't working. I think he had a pretty serious concussion too."

"But he told us he was feeling strong," Max said.

"He was lying," Alex said. "He wanted us to swim to safety. He checked to see if you had your valuable specimen. He was saying things like he was sure he'd never see us again. He knew that you and I had a chance if we went together. If we'd fussed over him and tried to make sure he was safe, none of us might have made it."

Max looked out to sea. "He sacrificed himself."

"I think so. Yeah."

Her eyes were watery. She held Max close, but they didn't take their gaze from sea. It was just too hard to believe. Max hoped that somehow the big guy would suddenly surface with a great big "Haw!"

Finally Alex stood and turned to look into the woods. "We need to get warmer, Max. Start a fire maybe."

"Do you think someone will rescue us?" Max said.

Alex nodded. "We've seen settlements up in this area on maps. Which means supplies have to get here. Which means shipping."

She reached into her wet suit and pulled out the waterproof bag Basile had given her. Inside was a box of matches and some kindling made of specially treated wood. Together she and Max gathered the driest wood they could find, buried under great big deadfalls. They piled it on the rocky shore, just at the edge of the woods.

It took a long time to get the fire going. The wood let off a lot of thick smoke. But it felt good and smelled better than good. As the aroma seeped into their nostrils, Max and Alex huddled together for warmth.

"Are you tired?" Alex asked.

"No," said Max, before his eyes dropped shut.

Max didn't realize they'd both fallen asleep until the sun woke him up. He had to squint against the light, shielding his eyes with his arm. The storm had moved on, and the sun was low in the sky, peeking out from behind a scrim of fluffy clouds. "Alex, wake up."

"I was dreaming about summer vacation," she moaned. "I'm going back to sleep."

Max smiled.

She would be starving when she finally woke up.

They hadn't really eaten in twenty-four hours. The thought made him imagine a plate of eggs and bacon, and his mouth filled with saliva. If they were going to survive, they'd need to be like pioneers. Pick berries and catch fish from streams with their bare hands. He had read about how to do those things.

Max stood up and turned toward the island's interior.

Who knew? There might even be people here. A camp, maybe, or even a small settlement.

In the light, the place was less scary than it had seemed hours ago. They'd fallen asleep at the top of the shore, near a copse of dense bushes. Behind them, the ground rose into a thick growth of low, green-gray scrub brush, dotted with gnarled trees and a few pines.

On the positive side, his legs were no longer numb. On the negative side, some of the thorns had even cut through his wet suit.

He walked to the top of the hill, where the land leveled off. He was now at the edge of a thicker forest that led into the island's interior. Berries of all sizes dotted the bushes, and his mouth began to water again. Most of them looked like blueberries and raspberries. He had read about how to tell those apart from poison berries.

He pulled the goggles from around his neck and held them by the strap. They would have to be his bucket.

As he began picking berries, he tossed some in. And ate some.

There were no paths here, so Max made his own, taking a big stick and whacking away as much underbrush as he could. After a few feet, he looked back and felt a wave of panic. Everything looked the same. He knew that if he went any farther, he'd never find the way back.

He put down his berry-filled goggles, unzipped his wet suit, and felt a rush of freezing cold. Quickly he reached into his pants pocket and found a few slightly soggy receipts left over from the shop at Piuli Point. He could rip them into small pieces and use them as markers—jamming each piece into a tree along the way with a stick. Even small white markers stood out. This was a smart idea.

As Max walked, the tree cover grew thicker. His goggles filled with berries, and so did his stomach. He had no idea how much time had gone by, but by now he was pretty sure he wasn't going to find people.

At least he had enough for both him and Alex to eat.

As he turned to go back, he noticed a shift of light in the woods just ahead—the soft yellow glow of a clearing. His heart thumped. A clearing could mean an encampment.

He pinned his last paper marker to a tree, leaned the

walking stick against it, and balanced the goggle-pail on the stick.

Another minute wouldn't hurt.

Trudging through the brush, he stopped at the clearing's edge. It wasn't an encampment, but an almost perfectly round circular area at the top of a ridge. There wasn't much special about it. But looking beyond, he could see the sea winking at him through the tree cover. He had reached another shore.

He turned, deciding what to do. He could follow the markers back through the trees and brambles, or he could instead go down to the shore and follow it around, back the way he'd come. Either would bring him to Alex. He liked the shore idea better. Lots of rocks, but no thorns.

He began walking across the clearing toward the water. The ground was sunken, the soil gravelly and sparse. It was as if a house had been in the clearing and suddenly disappeared from sight. His foot clipped something hard, and he tripped, landing hard on his left hip.

Groaning with pain, he sat up. He kicked the rock that had tripped him.

But it wasn't a rock. It was a piece of metal, jagged and broken.

He looked around the clearing. There were other pieces of metal lying around, rusted and corroded. On all fours, he began digging around the piece at the center, the one that had tripped him. It was a part of something bigger, but what?

A crashed plane, maybe. In which case there might be food aboard. Cookies, peanuts, or pretzels. Or even the stuff you had to pay for.

His mouth began to water as he grabbed one of the loose shards of metal. It was about the size of a shovel. He began digging.

And digging.

The bigger piece of metal, the one that had tripped him, went deep. At its base, it widened into what looked like the metal frame of the plane. The deeper he got, the softer the soil was. He worried about Alex. She might be awake now. She would be wondering where he'd gone. But he was curious. Just a few inches more . . .

"Max? What are you doing?"

Max looked up with a start. Alex was standing on the rocky shore by the water, looking up at him.

"Alex!" he blurted. "Sorry. I was trying to get us something to eat—"

"I thought you were taken by wolves!" she said, trudging up to meet him.

"I found something! Come up here, this is so weird."

Alex's eyes widened when she saw Max's excavation.

She grabbed another small metallic shard, knelt by his side, and dug in.

They worked silently, concentrating, focusing all their strength. Neither of them knew how much time had gone by, but it felt like days. Every few minutes revealed something new—a wire like an antenna, a section of a rounded hull, the broken remains of a long pipe with broken pieces of glass.

"This looks like a telescope," Max said, holding the pipelike thing up to the sun.

Alex was digging furiously. *"Max, look at this!"* she cried out.

Her tool was uncovering a section of the hull that contained the rusted remains of white lettering. Max jumped in to help, digging like crazy, until they both had to stop to catch their breath.

They sat back, staring at the word that glinted against the golden rays of the low-slung sun:

NAUTILUS

"I don't believe this . . ." Max said. "So . . . a plane crashed here that was named after the *Nautilus*. What kind of coincidence is that?"

Alex shook her head slowly. "I don't think it's a plane, Max."

"What else could it be?" Max said.

"Jules Verne sent us here. He did that for a reason."

Max stared at the word. "You think this is the submarine from *Twenty Thousand Leagues Under the Sea*? But that's a work of fiction."

"Verne was here, Max," Alex said. "And so was the real Nemo. If Nemo existed in real life, then maybe the *Nautilus* did too. It was a real submarine. It had to be."

Max sat back, catching his breath. "But then what's it doing here, buried on dry land?"

Alex smiled. She held up her little digging utensil. "Cousin, there's only one way to find out."

44

WORKING with two broken pieces of metal wasn't exactly the best way to dig up a nineteenth-century submarine. But it kept Max warm.

He and Alex broke often to eat berries. Hundreds of berries. They gathered fish that washed up on the shore alive. Using their digging utensils to gut them was sloppy and disgusting at first, but it was all worth it when they were roasted over a fire.

The *Nautilus* was tilted to its side. Max and Alex dug until they were able to free the observation deck and the hatch.

Using broken pieces of metal as crowbars, they jimmied open the top. Foul, musty-smelling air rushed out. The interior was angled to the sun, and Max could see a ladder leading down into a holding area.

"It really does look like the *Conch*," Max said.

"Only older," Alex remarked.

He turned and began walking down the ladder.

"Are you sure you want to do this?" Alex said. "This isn't like you."

Max shrugged. "I'm not like me anymore."

The dark didn't scare him. Nothing scared him now. He'd come too far, risked too much. He crawled into the hole, clinging onto the ladder.

At this angle, it was like scaling monkey bars in the playground. The rungs were almost parallel to the earth. When it was safe, he leaped down into a corner of the sub. His foot jammed against a pile of debris, and he squatted to sort it out. Everything was lopsided.

A lamp. A jar of kerosene. A flint lighter. The lamp's metal was corroded, but the wick was still good. When he lit it, there was enough light to see the interior of the ship.

Alex was looking in from above. "Looks spooky."

Max squinted, looking around. Lying in a slanted heap on a slanted wall was a thick cord of well-preserved rope. He brought it to the hatch and tossed the end up to Alex. "Anchor this thing to the top rung of the ladder. I may need to hold on to it for balance. The sub was buried at a tilt. It's hard to stand up. Even for a Tilt."

"Will do," Alex said.

In the flickering flame, shadows danced across the hallways, disappearing in and out of rooms. Max braced himself as best he could, walking on walls as often as on floors. He swung his lamp into the control room, the diving chamber, the library. It was a lot like the *Conch*, but smaller. Decay and rot had destroyed or damaged nearly every table, every panel, every piece of equipment. All that was left unruined was the steering wheel and the husk of the captain's chair. Even the windows were nothing but holes.

"See anything?" Alex called down.

"It's a mess," Max said, moving methodically through the entire sub as he hung onto the rope. He stooped to pick up a plastic cup with an ancient-looking Coca-Cola logo. "Looks like other people may have been down here."

"What?" Alex said. "Do you think they took the treasure? Like people who looted the pyramids in Egypt?"

"Maybe," Max said. "Unless the treasure was never here in the first place. Verne is unpredictable. He might have left another note. Maybe *The Lost Treasures* had a Part Four."

Max could hear Alex's enthusiasm deflate. "Keep

looking. Keep your eye out for a leather booklet."

The more he looked, the deeper his heart sank. Any possible hiding place was rotted away, any secret corner was a hole or a rusted pile of metal.

As he climbed back out, Alex looked at him expectantly. But he shook his head. "No treasure. No note. At least not that I could find. Whoever was here cleaned it out."

"But—this place—who could have discovered it—?" Alex said.

"I don't know." Max sighed. "There are a lot of things we don't know. Like what is the sub doing here in the first place?"

The two sat quietly on the soil, and Alex leaned her head against Max's shoulder.

"We failed," Max said.

"Don't say that," Alex replied.

"It's a fact," Max said. "We came all this way. We nearly died. We actually caused someone to die. And we have nothing to show for it."

"Not *nothing*," Alex said. "We discovered the wreck of the real *Nautilus*. That will be worth something to a museum or a collector. So we'll have a treasure, kind of. Just not such a huge one."

Max nodded, desperately trying not to be swallowed

up by disappointment. "I guess you can write about it. Maybe you can get paid for that."

"Yup." Alex looked out to sea. "Now let's set a nice smoky fire and keep it going until someone sees us."

She slipped her hand into his, and they stood. Behind them, a rustling in the bush made Max spin around. An animal was running through the trees, a flash of fur and foot.

"What was that?" Max said.

"Dinner," Alex replied, running in the direction of the movement. "Come on, Max. Let's do something fun."

"Hunting is fun?" Max called out.

"Fish is great," Alex said, "but meat is better!"

She picked up a branch and broke it so that its end was pointed.

"That's your spear, Katniss Everdeen?" Max shouted.

"Ha! That was sarcastic, Max!" Alex said.

"For a reason!" Max said. "This is crazy!"

But Alex was off. "If you're not with me, you're against me. Come on!"

Max followed her into the woods. Hunters, he knew, were supposed to be quiet. They were supposed to stalk their prey by surprising it. But Alex was tromping through the woods like Sasquatch.

He stopped every few feet, taking a mental snapshot of where they were. Getting lost was not in the plan, and he was out of receipts.

When he could no longer hear her, he spun around. She was nowhere in sight. "Alex!" he cried out.

Nothing.

"Alex! Where are you?"

His voice echoed in the woods. He looked down and saw what he thought were footsteps. He followed them as best he could, shouting her name.

Until he finally heard her answer from behind a grove of trees. "Sssshhh, Max."

He nearly ran into her at the edge of an inland pool. It was about as long as a city block and teeming with fish. Alex was following along the edge, holding a long stick, eyeing a school of fat fish. Her arm was drawn back as if the stick were a spear.

"I thought you wanted meat," Max said.

"That critter was too fast," Alex replied softly. "But Katniss is going to nail one of these tasty babies."

Max folded his arms. "This I have to see."

Alex stopped. Her arms went slack. "Max?" she said. "Max, come here, you have to see this."

He ran to her side. She was no longer eyeing the fish. At her foot was something round and white partially buried in the soil. Along with what looked like part of a buried silver necklace.

Alex began digging around it. Max grabbed a stick himself and joined her. Slowly they uncovered something rounded and deep. With two eye holes. And a jaw.

A skull. And definitely human.

Max squatted next to it, dug his hands around the side, and pulled it out of the ground. The chain came with it. It broke with the force, sending a metal plate flying toward Alex, who picked it up.

It was small, about the size of a military dog tag, and as she turned it over, she wiped it clean of dirt.

Alex dropped to her knees. "Bingo . . ."

Max knelt next to her as she held out the chain, and he read the inscription.

NEMO

45

"**HE** died here," Alex said in a hushed voice, lifting the silver tag and turning it over in her hand. "Captain Nemo was here on this island with the *Nautilus*, and he died."

Max held his fingers to his forehead. "Why . . . ?"

"I don't know," Alex said. "This whole island scares me."

"Break it down into parts . . ." Max said, his eyes squeezed shut. "So Verne travels with him to explore the world in this crazy invention, the submarine. They find Ikaria, and Nemo destroys it, stealing their secrets and their treasure. He wants to make all of these underwater bubble kingdoms and become ruler of the seas. He figures he'll drive people into the domes by causing the seas to rise, which will flood the cities and cause panic. So he starts planting dynamite in remote places. At some point in the future, he's going to set them off. Ice sheets will break into the Arctic Ocean like crazy, and his plan will come true. Except for one thing."

"He's a total wack job," Alex said.

"Yup."

"Runs in the family," Alex said. "So Verne writes *The Lost Treasures* as a set of clues leading to the Ikarian fortune. He doesn't think anyone will believe it, so he leaves the first part with his son and tells him to keep it in the family. To be safe, he sends some clues to the only other person he trusts, his editor Hetzel. Verne spends the rest of his life revisiting the places he discovered with Nemo, leaving sections of *The Lost Treasures* along the way—so someone can see what Nemo has been planning and stop it from ever happening. And as a reward, they get the treasure."

Max sighed. "The fact is, Nemo's plan could never have happened. He would never have enough explosives. So the two guys have some kind of fight in Piuli Point, and they end up here."

Alex looked back toward the *Nautilus*. "So, what exactly happened on this island after Nemo and Verne got here?"

"Plans went wrong, I guess," Max said. "Nemo wigged out, Verne took action. Verne won. Score one for the good guys."

"Score zero for you and me though," Alex said. "And a big one for the person who struck it rich by looting Jules Verne's treasure."

At the edge of the pool, Max saw a crab scuttling out, moving sideways along the edge. His stomach groaned. "All this disappointment is making me hungry."

"Me too." Alex raised her pointed stick. Together they tiptoed around the pool, drawing closer to the scuttling crustacean. *"Hyeeahhh!"* Alex shouted, thrusting the stick down.

It missed the crab and plunged into the soft sand. Alex's stick broke in two. As the crab began digging a hole and vanishing inside, Max lunged for it. He thrust his hand into the wet sand, grasping for the creature.

But his hand jammed against something solid and cold.

"Yeow! What the—?" he cried out. "There's something in here."

"It broke my spear . . ." Alex said. "Is it the rest of Captain Nemo?"

Max began digging. He exposed a rusted piece of metal. "It's not a skeleton."

"We need our digging tools," Alex said, darting away into the woods.

"I didn't leave markers!" Max called out.

"I was in Girl Scouts!" Alex yelled back. *"I can track footprints!"*

She was back in minutes. They dug together around the metallic piece, which was long, heavy, and solid. At one point, it made a sharp right turn. A corner. *"What is this thing?"* Max cried out. "A car?"

They began digging harder, faster. They uncovered a rectangle of metal and began digging around it.

It wasn't a car. More like a box.

"Mint mint mint mint . . ." Max hummed.

"Stop that, Max, keep digging!" Alex said.

They cleared away all four sides. On the two shorter sides they found metallic handles, riveted to each side of the container. Alex was grinning. "Do you think . . . ?"

"Dig more first. Think later," Max said, closing his fingers around his handle. "Ready?"

"Heave . . . ho!" Alex said.

The thing was stuck solid. They dug down all the way to the bottom edge, but it wouldn't budge. They tried at least five times, finally collapsing in the soil.

"What do . . . we do . . . now?" Alex said, catching her breath.

"We could use that rope in the *Nautilus*," Max said. "Be right back!"

She flew back through the woods and returned a few minutes later with the thick rope Max had used for balance. "I'll knot the handle," she said. "You throw the other end over the thickest branch you see."

Max looked up into the canopy of a sturdy old fir tree. It had a branch extending over their heads like a goalpost. He tossed the rope over it and caught the end as it came down. "Ready!"

"Okay—pulll!" Alex urged, running to his side.

Using the branch as a fulcrum, she and Max yanked the rope downward as hard as they could. The container began to rise. It slanted upward, out of the muck, but it wouldn't go much farther. "I'll try to hold the rope steady!" Alex said. "You try to maneuver that thing out of the mud."

Max ran over, putting one hand on the chest handle, another on the rope. The chest was solid steel and felt like it weighed a zillion pounds. Pulling as hard as he could, he managed to angle most of it over the dry soil. "Let go!"

Alex released the rope, and the chest *whomped* downward, nearly half of it still in the mucky water. Holding the rope like a tug-of-war, they dug in hard and pulled. *"Heave . . . ho!"* Alex yelled.

As it slowly came clear, they fell to the ground and caught their breaths.

The chest was a mass of mud, slime, scuttling crabs, tiny fish, and a metal surface that peeked through in places. Max grabbed a thick fallen branch and got up to walk to the chest. Holding the branch with two hands, he slowly ran it over the surface of the chest like an awkward squeegee. The mud sloughed off slowly, and Alex joined him, wiping the side of the chest with the sleeve of her wet suit. The whole thing was awkward, but in a few minutes they managed to expose the surface.

Aside from the handles, it had no ornamentation at all—no tags, signs, decoration, initials, leather straps, locks, nothing.

Just one keyhole on the side.

Alex pulled out the key they had found in the elephant cave. "Niemand never got this either," she said.

Max felt his entire body quiver as Alex inserted the key. It slid in roughly. She turned it.

With a deep *scraaawwwwk*, the lid opened.

The entire Russian army could have attacked at that moment, the skies could have rained marshmallows, the trees could have transformed into kangaroos, and neither Max nor Alex would have noticed.

They were staring at a thick tapestry of woven fabric,

folded at the top of the chest, just under the lid. "R-R-Rugs?" Max said.

He dug his hands into the folds of the carpeting. Despite the tight fit of the lid, the tapestry was pocked with holes and covered with blackish-green mold. He pulled it out, only to reveal another one underneath, better preserved, but brittle and disintegrated.

"I don't believe this . . ." Alex moaned.

The tapestry split in two as Max lifted it out, the other half falling back into the chest. His stomach churned.

This was the treasure. Hand-woven tapestries.

"I guess . . . they were worth a fortune back then," Max said.

"I don't know whether to laugh or cry," Alex said. But tears were already flowing down her cheeks.

Max didn't know what to feel either, but he smelled cat pee. And that meant he was furious. He lifted the broken half of the tapestry over his head and threw it into the woods. Then he dug out the other half. He had planned to drop it into the water and stomp on it with both feet, when a glint from inside the container made him stop.

Alex was leaning forward now, her eyes as big as softballs. "Um, maybe you want to come here . . ." she said.

Max ran to her side and knelt by the side of the chest.

He had to hold on to the edge of the box. For support.

Because what he was seeing inside made him feel faint.

It was as if the sun, feeling lazy all day, had decided to put on a dance. Its light freckled the surface with reds, greens, blues, and gold. Rubies winked, sapphires glowed, diamonds flashed, and gold coins by the thousand kept them a civil distance from one another.

"Am . . . I . . . dreaming . . . ?" Alex said. She and Max dug their hands in, feeling the weight, playing with the luminescence. Alex pulled out a heavy chain of emeralds and threw them around her neck. She clasped a diamond bracelet on her wrist and placed a gold tiara on her head.

Not to be outdone, Max donned a tiara of his own. He quickly slid gold and silver rings on every finger, holding them up to the sunlight and laughing so loud he began to cry.

Instead he threw his head back and shouted to the sky: "Thank you! Thank you, Grandpa Jules!"

"Merciiiiiii!" Alex screamed.

They were both crying now. Max turned to his cousin and wrapped her in a hug. "I don't believe this I don't believe this I don't believe this I don't believe this . . ." Alex shouted.

Max let out a hoot and began dancing, shouting at the sky. "Yes yes yes yes yes yes!"

Alex took his hand and danced with him. "We're going to do this so right, Max! We'll get out of here with this loot, and you'll tell the world what happened!"

"We'll keep the house!" Max said.

"You'll buy a castle!"

"I'll get Mom the best care!"

"She'll live to be a hundred!"

He dug his hands in and tossed up a shower of gold coins. They rose high into the air, turning and winking among the canopies of the island trees, then came hurtling down to the earth.

"Ouch," a deep voice called from inside the woods.

Max and Alex jolted upright. The surrounding woods had grown darker, and for a moment they only saw the hint of movement. "Close it," Alex whispered to Max. "Close the chest!"

Before Max could move, an arm reached out of the shadows. It was holding out a gold coin.

"I believe you lost this," said Spencer Niemand, stepping into the light.

MAX was always picked last for baseball in gym class, but he threw a ninety-mile-an-hour sapphire that was a perfect strike to Niemand's left cheek.

The man flinched, muttering a curse. "Well, it's a good thing I arrived before you threw away all my inheritance."

"How did you get here?" Alex demanded. "We left you—"

"In that godforsaken icy backwater, freezing cold and with a glob of Basile's putrid saliva on my face?" Niemand said, stepping closer. "Yes, you did. I had to take three showers to rid myself of the smell of old-man breath."

"Basile was your age, and he was worth a thousand of you," Alex said. "He didn't make it. Did you know that? He died saving us, Niemand. Does that even matter to you? Does anything matter to you?"

"Everything I do matters greatly, but every noble cause has its lost soldiers, I'm afraid," Niemand said. "I shall have my people send a condolence note to his family. Though I must say, the people of Piuli Point treated me with more grace than my old chum ever did. Such a trusting group of people! No one locks anything. Everyone leaves keys in the ignition, you know. Even, say, a speedy, fully equipped cutter in the bay . . ."

"Qisuk's boat," Alex said. "You just stole it?"

"Borrowed," Niemand said. "On a long-term lease. We took off the moment the news broke that the remains of a submarine called the *Conch* had been found near a remote island beyond a rather notorious whirlpool."

"We?" Alex said.

From out of the woods behind him stepped André. His long, stringy hair hung about his face as he focused his green eyes at the open chest. "The others decided to stay in Greenland—permanently," Niemand said. "Let's just say there was a disagreement over whether the ends justified the means."

Max slammed the chest shut. "You can't have this."

"Oh, I believe I can," Niemand said with a little snort. "What you are guarding was taken from my family unjustly. And now it can finally be put to its best use—saving humankind from its own stupidity." He stooped to pluck the skull out of the ground and held it high. "Alas, poor Nemo! I knew him, Horatio!"

"Nrgmf?" André asked.

"It's a Shakespearean quote, you numbskull!" Niemand tossed the skull over his shoulder and stepped toward Alex and Max. "Who do you think you are? You commandeer *my* submarine, cause the death of *my* crew member, and find *my* treasure—which, by the way, was taken upon the murder of *my* great-great-grandfather many years ago by the likes of a French stockbroker turned second-rate science-fiction writer."

"Your great-great-grandfather wanted to destroy the world so he could become dictator of an undersea empire!" Max said.

"He wanted to save the world, and so do I," Niemand said through clenched teeth, his face tightening with anger, and his skin turning red. He turned and snapped his fingers toward his new second-in-command. "The faster we load this up, André, the bigger the percentage you'll receive!"

Max sat on the chest. As André approached, Max thrust himself off with his hands and kicked upward, landing a solid hit on André's chin. The scraggle-haired man fell backward, arms flailing.

Alex lunged for him, grabbing a hank of his greasy hair and running him smack into a tree.

"I didn't know you could do that!" Max said.

"Neither did I," Alex replied.

As Niemand reached into an inner pocket of his down coat, Alex flew toward him, head butting him in the stomach. He lost his balance, falling against a tree. Alex turned to where she had dropped her metal digging tool and scooped it up off the ground. Now André was racing toward her, hands outstretched. *"Alex, watch out!"* Max shouted.

Alex spun around, but not before André had pinned her arms to her sides in a bear hug. He lifted her off the ground and spun her in the air. She screamed and pounded on his head, but he let out a guttural roar and tossed her like a bale of hay.

Max saw her body fly over a thick copse and smack against a tree trunk. He heard her head thump and saw her limp body drop down to the forest floor.

"Alex!" he shrieked.

No. No. No no no no no. Max held on to the sides of

his head. He felt himself spinning.

"What is he saying?" Niemand demanded.

"Yrrj," André said.

"Something about fish?" Niemand said.

Max heard the words and spun faster. Was he talking? He didn't think he was talking. But spinning felt good, because it sometimes got rid of the smell, because maybe if he spun enough times, counterclockwise, he might be able to reverse time. He knew that was ridiculous. It was not factual at all. But facts weren't always everything. Miracles happened too. And maybe at the end of the spinning it might be the beginning of June again, and this time he would not let Vulturon scare his mom, and maybe that would be the thing that turned everything around, and Alex would be back in Canada and he would still be home now—

"Will you stop him!" Niemand screamed.

He felt André grab his arm. The spinning stopped, and Max was dizzy. But he could see Niemand glaring at him. The man's eyes were angry, but also confused. And maybe scared. Max had trouble telling those things apart sometimes. One thing he had no trouble telling was that Niemand was holding a gun. And it was pointed at Max. "Fish," Max said. "Fish Fishy McFishface."

"You are a child," Niemand said. "The strangest child I have ever seen, but a child nonetheless. And unless I have to, I am not inclined to shoot a defenseless innocent."

"Ha! Ha ha ha!" Max burst out laughing. "You think you're doing good. But you're not. That's a fact. You're a murderer! Look what you just did to my cousin!"

"André did that—" Niemand spluttered.

"And the snowmobile—"

"*Silence!*" Niemand barked. "Just step away from that chest."

"No," Max said.

Niemand pointed the gun at his face. "I imagine your sick mother would take it very hard if her precious little boy went missing forever. It might just kill her."

Max began to shake. The anger had risen up from his toes, flooded his body, and was now turning his vision red. "*Cat pee cat pee cat pee cat pee . . .*"

"Just put your hands in the air and back away," Niemand said evenly, "so we can get this over with and all go home."

The click of the cocked gun turned Max's anger to sheer terror. He put his hands in the air and sidled away slowly from the chest. Niemand gestured toward the metal shard that Max had been using to dig. "Is that your shovel?" he asked.

Max nodded.

"Primitive but effective," Niemand said. "Pick it up. Go ahead, *pick it up*!"

Max scooped the shovel off the ground and held it out to Niemand.

"I don't want it," Niemand said. "I want you to dig."

"Dig?" Max said.

"You heard me!" Niemand gestured behind him, to the place where he'd thrown the skull. "I want my ancestor's entire body. Every bone! And when you're done, when you've gotten the whole thing out, make the hole nice and comfy. Because you will be spending a lot of time in there." Niemand smiled.

Max blanched. His fingers went slack and the shovel dropped from his hands. "You said we would go home . . ."

"Yes, but I get to choose who is included in *we*." Niemand smiled. "Now dig."

"You wouldn't . . ."

"Make you dig your own grave?" Niemand said. "It's either that or make André do it for you. Your choice. On the count of three. One . . ."

Max bent to pick up the shovel but he couldn't feel it in his fingers. It was as if his entire body had shut down. No smells, no nothing. "Please, Mr. Niemand . . ."

"Two . . ."

Forcing his hand to clutch the metal shard, Max began to dig.

47

"THREE!"

Alex's voice shouted from the shadows. Niemand spun around. He fired a blind shot into the woods.

Max flinched. "Alex!"

"Three!" Alex said again, from a different place in the woods, further to the left.

"Shkch?" André asked.

"Find her, you nincompoop!" Niemand fired a shot into the air. *"Go!"*

André looked left, then right, then ran straight up the middle. From the woods directly behind Niemand, Alex leaped out of the shadows and onto his back, screaming, *"Three!"* She brought the end of her shovel down hard on his head.

His mouth dropped open, and the gun fell from his hands. Max jumped away from the chest and pulled the old tapestry from the ground. He flew toward Niemand, shoving the moldy rug into his face. As they tumbled to the forest floor, Max landed on top of him. For a moment Niemand was out cold, and Max managed to roll him into the rug so his limbs were pinned together.

In a moment, Niemand's body convulsed with a sneeze. He kicked and wriggled, coughing violently. *"As . . . As . . . Asthma!"* he shouted.

"Now you tell us," Alex said.

André emerged from the woods. Seeing the gun on the ground, he leaped for it.

But Alex got there first. She held it in her hands like a rotten fish. "I hate these things," she said. "Don't make me use it."

André stuck his hands in the air.

"As . . . achoo! . . . asthma!" Niemand spluttered.

"Is that true?" Max asked André. "Is he asthmatic?"

"Why are you asking him, Max?" Alex said. "We can't understand a word he says."

André held up a finger. Sheepishly he grabbed a stick and traced a word in the ground.

LIE

"Klmpf," he said, sneering at his boss.

"Whaaaat?" Niemand's body shook side to side. "You disloyal, mangle-tongued, green-eyed, snake-headed disgrace to humanity—"

André put his fingers in his ears, stuck out his tongue, and said, "Ppppttttt!"

"That I understood," Max said.

"Max," Alex said. "Do you think we're being rude? I think Stinky would like to take a tour of the *Nautilus*." She untied the *Nautilus*'s rope from the chest. Moving quickly, she wrapped it around Niemand's torso, trapping him tightly.

"Good idea, Alex," Max said, picking up the end of the rope that held Niemand. "Maybe André can help you drag him there."

"Wait—no! Don't you understand? The fate of the world is at stake. Only I can make humanity great again! None of what happens here is as important as Niemand Domes! Do you understand? Where will your families live when the oceans rise? Let me go! We can share this opportunity—OWW!" Max followed Alex and André as they dragged a writhing, carpet-wrapped Niemand through the woods. "This is cruel and unusual punishment! Entrapment! Assault and battery! You will hear from my lawyers! You will hear from my board of directors! You will spend the rest of your lives in court!"

When they reached the dug-out submarine, Max opened the hatch with his free hand. "Today only, admission free for two people."

"Smmtch?" André said.

"Now!" Alex and Max said at the same time.

André dumped his boss into the sub. Niemand's cry of pain wafted up from the musty dark. Max waved the gun, and André climbed in after him.

Max slammed the door shut, and Alex jammed her shovel between it and the railing, to keep it from being forced open.

"They'll figure a way to get out," Max said.

"I know. We just need to buy enough time to get away," Alex said. "Come on, let's move."

"Where?"

"They came on that cutter," Alex said. "Do you know how to drive it?"

"No," Max replied. "Do you?"

"No."

Max shrugged. "Well, I like learning new things . . ."

As he spoke, the deep *thrum* of whirring blades sounded in the distant sky. Max dropped the gun. He and Alex ran out of the clearing, through the woods, and out to the rocky beach.

Far overhead, a helicopter hovered, tilting left and

right as it scoured the island. The two cousins began screaming and waving their hands. *"Here!"* Max cried out. *"We're here!"*

Alex inserted her fingers into her mouth and let out an ear-splitting whistle.

"Who are they?" Max shouted.

As if in answer, the chopper tilted to the side. Qisuk was staring down at them through a pair of sunglasses.

"Hiiiii!" Max screamed, waving his hands.

"I guess," Alex said, "he came looking for his boat."

Max threw his head back and let out a howl of joy. "And wait till he sees the tip we give him!" he shouted, as the helicopter slowly began to descend.

EPILOGUE

"SO is it true that you managed to flag down a helicopter by sending smoke signals from a homemade raft?" a woman asked over the phone.

Here we go again, Max thought.

He leaned back in his new Barcalounger. It still smelled of fresh leather. It was noisy in the living room. It had been chaos for nearly two days. He pressed the Mute button on the remote for his new sixty-five-inch TV. By now he was used to the image of himself and Alex on the screen. Especially this one—the two of them waving from the deck of the SS *Nutterdam* as it pulled into a Norwegian port. Behind them was the treasure container with a big, red bow wrapped around it. In the next image, three armed guards stood at attention while Alex took the big bow and wrapped it around them. They were smiling.

Max never got tired of watching that.

But he did get tired of phone calls with the same dumb old questions. "Max? Are you still there?" the voice said.

"We were on the beach when we were rescued," Max explained as politely as he could. "There *was* a boat there, but that was a cutter that Spencer Niemand had stolen. We didn't use it. And there were no smoke signals, just lots of hand waving."

"One more thing: Is it true that Spencer Niemand has been detained in a house for the criminally insane, where he accuses his jailers of stealing a puppy from him named Kissums?"

"Absolutely false," Max said. "It's not a puppy. It's a pinkie finger."

The moment he hung up, the phone rang again. "This is Rob Markum from KHTY. We just received word from the *Enquirer* that your fortune is worth thirty million dollars. Can you confirm this?"

"No!" Max rolled his eyes. "It's worth thirty-one million, one hundred seventeen thousand, eight hundred twenty-two dollars and seventy-four cents. But that amount changes day to day based on the price of gold."

"So basically, the answer is 'Yeah'?"

"No!"

"Yeah?"

"Yeah . . . *No!*"

Max hung up. *"I can't believe this!"* he yelled.

Alex came running in from the kitchen with two huge bowls of ice cream. "Will we ever get tired of watching ourselves?"

"Probably tomorrow." Max looked over his shoulder through the slats of the half-drawn blinds. Three news vans were parked at the curb. Reporters were flagging down neighbors, taking photos, and speaking into cameras.

As Alex opened the front door to check the mail, cameras flashed. Smriti ran in from outside, rolling a small suitcase. "I can't believe we're going to Minneapolis and back in one day."

"That's why they invented private planes," Alex said, lugging in an entire USPS mail sack that had been left on the porch. "What's the latest report on your mom?"

"I spoke to Dad a couple of hours ago. Mom got her first results from the experimental treatment," Max said. "She's stable. Stable is good. We're flying in a specialist from Stanford later today."

"That's awesome!" Smriti said.

"Totally awesome," Alex said, opening the mail sack and digging in.

Smriti was agog at the enormous sack. "Is that mail just for today?"

Alex nodded. "People love us, I guess."

"Dad needed to rent a room in a hotel just for the flowers people are sending Mom," Max said.

"Oh! Oh!" Alex was ripping open a piece of mail. She let the envelope fall to the floor and read the note aloud: "'This is to inform Mr. George and Ms. Michele Tilt that the Savile Bank relinquishes any and all liens and claims on the property at 34 Spruce Street, upon the recently notarized and accepted full payment of mortgage'—in other words, the whole house is paid for to the last penny!"

"Woo-hoo!" Smriti shouted.

"Follow me into the Food Preparation Chamber, for the Ceremony of Fire!" Alex announced.

All three ran into the kitchen, where Alex held the eviction notice over the sink, lit a match, and watched the last of their debt go up in flames.

"OK, now I need some ice cream, too!" Smriti cried out, running to the freezer.

As she pulled it open, Max's phone rang again. "No,

there weren't any smoke signals!" he said, anticipating the same old press questions.

"Uh, this is dishthedirt.com," the voice said, "and we're investigating a report of a secret message found at the bottom of your world-famous treasure discovery. Would you care to comment?"

Max felt the blood rush from his face. He cast a glance into the study, where a leather-bound volume sat on a table where Alex had been working on it. They'd seen it the moment they'd finished emptying the chest in the presence of the Tilts' accountants. But Max was certain he and Alex had snuck it away without anyone noticing.

Neither of them had expected to find another part to *The Lost Treasures*. Not *after* the treasure was found. And neither of them could have imagined that this part would be worth much, much more.

Smriti and Alex were looking at him curiously. Max put the phone on Speaker and set it on the kitchen table. "Yup, thanks for asking, we did find a secret message!" Max replied. "Right at the bottom of the chest! Just sitting there!"

"What are you doing, Max?" Alex mouthed.

Smriti nearly dropped a quart of Ben & Jerry's Phish Food. "How do they know?" she whispered.

"Cool," the voice said. "So . . . could you tell us what it said?"

"Yup!" Max replied. "It said 'Redeem This at Your Nearest General Store by July 1890 for a Free Supply of Mustache Wax!'"

"Uh . . . wait . . . mustache . . . ?" said the voice at the other end.

"Have a nice day!" Max said and hung up the phone.

Alex flopped into the chair. "You scared me. I didn't know you knew how to lie."

"How could they have found out about the note?" Smriti said. "No one was there but us and the accountants."

Max shrugged. "It doesn't matter. They'll lose interest. All anyone wants to talk about is money."

At the ringing of the doorbell, Alex sprung up from the chair. "I'll get it! I think it's the new foosball table. Come on!"

Smriti set down the ice cream and ran after her, but Max remained in the kitchen. "I'll be right there!" he called after them.

As the two girls disappeared, Max headed the other way. Into the study.

He sat at the table, opened the leather-bound volume, and slid out the translation Alex had printed. He'd already read it a hundred times, but it never, ever got old.

THE LOST TREASURES

— PART FOUR —

Dearest reader, you cannot imagine the joy upon my face for knowing the joy that must be upon yours. For if you have reached this note, you are in possession of two valuable things: this remarkable fortune and the knowledge gained through the voyages to reach it. It is my fervent hope, dear reader, that the schemes of my nemesis No One have been dashed to the rocks of failure.

As you now possess the freedom for great excursions without financial pressure, I implore you to consider the bargain I propose.

I led you to this treasure not as an end, but as a means. It would pain me to know that you ignore this entreaty. For what I have described thus far was merely my beginning. What follows from my adventure with Nemo is a wonder greatly surpassing the glitter of earthly wealth. For wealth, as we know, does not travel with the possessor after death.

As it happens, death itself was the subject of my further adventure. Namely, the reversal thereof. There exists in human biology a vexing problem: cells within the body so vigorous, so alive with growth, that they devour all around them and destroy the very body they occupy.

This condition goes by the name of the greedy beast visible in the night constellations, Cancer the Crab.

Who knew that my tragic voyages with Nemo would bring into my possession one specimen (among thousands collected) that would lead to a discovery too powerful to expose to the world in my lifetime. A cure to that disease which knows no mercy.

For this, dear reader, one cannot begin without *Isis hippuris* . . .

Max read the last line again. Another time, a different set of circumstances, and he would have thought it was some kind of code.

But it wasn't. And that was a fact.

He reached into the desk drawer, pulled out an envelope, and carefully spilled the contents onto the table.

Sea fan, Basile had called it. *Isis hippuris.*

Max smiled.

Tomorrow morning, as soon as the noise and the chaos died down, they had to get back to work. Their adventure had barely begun.

THE ADVENTURE CONTINUES WITH

TAKE A SNEAK PEEK!

PROLOGUE

NO one ever paid attention to the man with the drooping eye. He moved swiftly through the London streets like a stale wind. Sometimes he mumbled, and sometimes he broke into a dance that resembled a fit of electrocution. He smelled oddly sweet and moldy, and his skin was like parched paper. These traits were fine for a book but not so much for a human.

So of course people avoided him. On a gray August morning when he stopped short on a crowded sidewalk, they walked politely around the man as if he didn't exist. They kept their eyes on their phones. They minded their own business.

Hearing a noise, the old man looked up. Even in the summer he felt cold, always cold, and he pulled his thin black raincoat tight around him. He'd lost the belt years ago, a great disadvantage on a damp, cloudy day. He trained his good eye on a neon orange-and-black jet emerging from the clouds. His sight was weak, but he could make out the name emblazoned on the tail.

TILT.

It was a strange name for a jet, to be sure. But that did not explain the old man's reaction.

"By the ghost of Gaston!" he squealed. Then he leaped into a complex little jig, his legs twirling and twiddling like rubber sticks. It would have been an impressive display, but as no one was watching, there was no one to be impressed.

Fishing a flip phone from his pocket, he tapped out a message. They're here.

The answer came back immediately. Yes, I noticed. Not modest, are they?

With a grin, the old man shoved the phone back into his pocket. As he shuffled quickly through the grim and growing crowd, he smiled. He was in a good mood now, so he muttered merry greetings.

But he got no replies.

No one ever paid attention to the man with the drooping eye.

1

A FEW DAYS EARLIER...

MAX hadn't planned on drifting off into space. Space found him.

To be more precise, what found him was a conveyance *into* space.

It was just sitting in a field behind his school. A lot of other things were sitting in the field too, like a dozen trailers, a roller coaster not quite fastened down, three wooden stages, stacks of metal risers and chairs, tools and tape, and a garish sign that said Midsoutheastern Ohio State Fair Coming in August.

Conveyance was a word that meant "a way of getting someplace." It was a better word than *vehicle* or *vessel*. That was a fact, and Max was fond of facts. His home-made drone Vulturon was a conveyance, but that had been crushed in the hatch of a submarine in the Atlantic Ocean.

This conveyance, the one in the field behind the gate, was, in fact, a balloon. A big hot-air balloon.

Now, outside of the land of Oz, it is not normal for a hot-air balloon to be sitting in a field all ready to go. It is even less normal for a balloon to beckon to a human being. But a day earlier, Max had looked out his bedroom window and seen it floating high above his house, trailing a banner to advertise the fair. In its basket were a man and woman in old-timey clothes, waving to the roofs below. In the center of the basket, a thick flame shot upward through a hole at the bottom of the balloon. The hot air was lighter than the cooler atmosphere, which caused the balloon to rise. That was another fact.

Max had nearly dropped his iPad in his rush to get to his window and wave back, but they hadn't seen him. Maybe they'd been looking at the roofs. Shingles were interesting, if you really took the time to read about them. But Max had had the weird feeling that the balloon itself had noticed him. It had seemed to turn toward him, dipping in the direction of his house. As if it were bowing.

Now, standing outside the field in the wee minutes before sunrise, Max decided to investigate. He didn't always take sunrise walks, but sometimes he had insomnia, and this seemed as good a thing to do as any. He didn't feel unsafe. He was, after all, thirteen and could take care of himself. And after he and his cousin Alex had found the treasure hidden by the famous author Jules Verne, everyone in Savile had become supernice to him. That included the Fearsome Foursome who used to make fun of him for being "on the spectrum," which wasn't a bad thing when you realized that rainbows were spectra and they were pretty much perfect. Also most people didn't know that spectra was the plural of spectrum, a fact that Max liked very much.

As he strolled closer to the field, he realized the gate was open.

It occurred to him that it shouldn't have been left open, and that someone had probably stumbled out of one of those trailers, forgotten to shut the gate, and was now fast asleep, facedown in a plate of scrambled eggs at the Nightowl Diner on Ash Street. But open gates, as far as Max was concerned, were meant to be walked through. Which he did.

He stepped around the platforms and metal beams and piles of this and that. "Hi, thanks for inviting me," he said as he approached the balloon basket. He knew this was silly because balloons do not really make invitations, but saying it made him smile because it sure felt that way. The basket was smaller than he'd expected. He could have just stepped over the edge into it, but there was a door with a latch, so he used that. Metal bars rose up from the sides of the basket to form a kind of frame that came together a foot or so over his head, making a small platform. In the center of the platform was a contraption that looked a little like a gun and a little like a miniature barbecue, pointed upward. This was called a *brazier*. Max wasn't sure how he knew that, but a steady diet of facts did that to you sometimes. Above that contraption was the balloon material, limp like a pile of blankets. It was made of a special kind of fabric, but Max couldn't remember what that was called.

He spotted a pair of gloves on the basket floor, which he put on. He reached up, grabbing a handhold at the base of the gun-like contraption. His index finger came to rest on a switch, so he snapped it down. It sparked.

That seemed pretty cool.

He tried it again and again—until finally a flame burst upward from the contraption. That caused him to pull his hand back with a start. It seemed like the flame should have burned the balloon material or melted it. But that didn't happen.

Instead, the fabric began to move, as if it were alive, waking from the night's sleep. It shifted around slowly, and then a little faster. The flowing pattern of the fabric's motion was so fascinating to watch that it took a while for Max to realize that the stuff was actually rising.

Max knew that it would continue to rise until it assumed the shape it had been sewn to, which in this case was a balloony sphere. But he did not want that to happen *at all*. He grabbed the handhold again but couldn't figure out how to turn it off. Whatever he was doing only seemed to make the flame stronger.

He considered running away. But it wouldn't be right for the balloon to float up and away from the state fair, to be lost in the atmosphere. That was like stealing.

Max pressed buttons, flicked levers, twisted, yanked, and turned anything he could. He concentrated so fiercely on the contraption above him, that he wasn't really noticing what the balloon itself was doing.

Rising.

The fabric reached its balloon shape faster than he expected. He felt the basket teeter, and he almost fell out. As he left the ground, he gripped the edge of the basket wall. The field below him began to recede. He could see the roof of his school. Fear of heights was called *acrophobia* and he didn't have that, but he did have unlimited-rising-into-space-with-no-way-to-control-it-phobia. And he was beginning to move fast.

"He-e-e-e-ey!" he shrieked. *"He-e-e-elp!"*

But even before the sound left his mouth, a door flew open in the side of a trailer, and a large barefoot man in a T-shirt and checked boxer shorts was racing outside, spitting out some very bad words.

"Throw up, dope!" the man shouted. At least that was what Max thought he said, until he repeated it and Max realized it was "Throw out the rope!"

Max hadn't even noticed the rope coiled in the corner of the basket. It was thick and heavy, but he managed to hoist it out over the edge. As the coil hurtled downward, the basket tipped again. Max clutched tight to the rope, his knuckles white.

The smell of fish rushed into his nostrils. For reasons no one knew, Max always smelled fish when he was afraid.

The end of the rope slapped against the ground, and the man in the T-shirt grabbed onto it. He was shouting something, but Max couldn't hear it. Now another man had joined him. That guy was shouting too. Max held tight to the rope as the guys pulled and pulled the other end. The basket was tipped almost horizontal now. On the positive side, that caused the flame to angle away from the hole in the bottom of the balloon, which helped keep it from rising. And the men were strong, pulling

Max and the balloon closer.

On the negative side, Max was about to fall.

He felt his feet sliding along the now-horizontal basket. He tried to hang tight to the rope, and at this distance he could hear the men clearly. They were saying, "Don't hold onto the rope!"

Now they were telling him.

Max let go. The basket juddered. But the sudden upward thrust of the edge caught him at the knees and he flipped upward.

And over.

Max screamed. As he dropped toward the ground, he caught a glimpse of the horizon, and it occurred to him it would be the last sunrise of his life.

2

"YOU did what?"

Smriti Patel's voice sounded different in the new kitchen. It was bigger than the old one. They were standing in the part that used to be a driveway, before the Tilts had bought the house next to theirs and torn it down. Now they had a beautiful garden, a humongous kitchen, and a glassed-in study for Mom that was protected by a Hulk action figure Max had made with his 3D printer. Also a bathtub shaped like a battleship, Sonos in every room, furniture from Italy, toilets from Japan, two Teslas, a private jet, and a framed portrait of the science-fiction writer Jules Verne hanging in their living room.

These are the kinds of things that happened when you found a secret buried treasure on an island off the coast of Greenland. Which Max and his cousin Alex did, due to finding a hidden note in their attic left by Verne, who was Max's great-great-great-grandfather. After his adventure, Max was ready to have a normal life without mortal danger and media attention. He didn't mean for his balloon escapade to happen. But Smriti was the first person who had actually noticed the bruises on his arm.

"I fell off a trampoline," Max said in answer to her question.

He and Smriti and their friend Evelyn Lopez were making cupcakes for Max's mom's birthday. Not long ago it had looked like she might not see the day. But doctors had found a way to make her cancer-free, so this was the most special birthday of all time, and it needed the most special chocolate cupcakes of all time.

Smriti was Max's best friend. She lived across the street. Evelyn was Max's partner in robotics class and was just about as addicted to facts. One fact about her was that she had a condition called scleroderma. It made her skin waxy and hard and forced her to use a wheelchair. Basically, all her organs were hardening and there was no cure, so things were either going to stay the same or get worse, but those were facts they both preferred not to think about. Evelyn had a great nose for things that weren't facts too, so Max was not surprised when she said in response to his trampoline comment, "I don't believe you."

"Yeah, that's a lie," Max said, taking a heavy bag of peanut M&Ms out of the cupboard. They'd already put cinnamon, white chocolate chips, and bananas into the cupcake mix, but it needed more. "But that's what I promised I would say. The state fair people didn't want me to admit what happened. They thought it would be bad for their reputation."

"So what's the truth?" Smriti said.

"I took a ride in a hot-air balloon."

They both gave him the LSS Look. Long, Silent, Stupefied. Max didn't understand that look, but he knew that people had ways of thinking that didn't exactly connect with his, which was OK. Sometimes they just drifted off into a confused silence and figured it out later, and Max was patient.

Dumping some M&Ms into the mix, he snuck a quick glance at the clock—6:37. Mom's book club buddies were scheduled to bring her to the house at seven o'clock for the surprise. The cupcakes would take twenty minutes to bake.

"Perfect," he said. "Let's do this."

Together, the three ladled the mix into cupcake tins. As Max shoved the tins inside the oven, a scream rang out from the doorway behind them: *"I cannot believe they did this to us!"*

It was his cousin Alex, that's all, but she had a habit of getting overexcited, and Max jumped. His wrist touched the oven edge, which was a couple of degrees short of a gazillion. *"Yeoow!"*

"Ohhhh, sorry!" she said. "Let's get that wrist under cold water."

She was holding her phone, so she set it near the sink and shoved Max's wrist under the cold water tap. Alex was eighteen, five years older than Max, with a luxuriant explosion of curly hair courtesy of her African-American mother and piercing green eyes from her French-Canadian dad. But right now, her face was a shade of deep crimson.

"Is he going to be OK?" Evelyn asked.

"We can always do a wrist transplant," Smriti said.

This, Max knew, was a joke. He could tell by the way the left side of Smriti's lip curled.

"Finish baking the cupcakes first, then surgery," Max said through gritted teeth. As Smriti shut the oven door, Evelyn wheeled herself closer and glanced curiously at Alex's phone screen. "You just complained that somebody did something to you. But all I see is an obituary."

Max leaned over and looked:

—BASILE WICKERSHAM GRIMSBY—

Beloved uncle, brother, colleague of many, Mr. Grimsby was a man of diverse talents: singer, cartographer, sea captain, marine biologist. He perished undersea after the malfunction of his submarine, while saving the lives of the two young American heirs to the Jules Verne fortune. Memorial service to be held Sunday, August 21, at the Alfred P. Twombley Funeral Parlor, London.

"Basile is the guy who saved our lives," Alex said. "When the submarine ran out of fuel, we could have been sucked into a whirlpool. But he made us all swim to safety. Max and I barely survived. He didn't. He sacrificed himself for us."

"His last name was *Grimsby*?" Max said. "He never told us that."

"Check out the date," Alex said. "August 21! Two days from now. Did we know? No! No invitation, no nothing. What's up with that?"

"You could send flowers," Smriti offered.

"Are you allowed to Skype into a funeral?" Max asked.

"You could just go," Evelyn said. "I mean, what good

is owning a jet if you don't use it?"

"Ding ding ding ding!" Max's dad chimed, which he always did when he wanted attention. He popped into the kitchen and announced: "Mom is on her way!"

Max cast a quick, panicked glance at the oven clock—6:44. "She can't," he said. "She's not supposed to be here till seven. The cupcakes won't be ready."

His dad shrugged. "Nothing we can do now. Her book club buddy just texted me. Guess their dinner ended early."

"They must have been discussing a lame book," Alex said.

Max opened his mouth to protest, but Alex, Dad, and Smriti were already rushing out of the kitchen. Evelyn rolled back toward the opposite side of the kitchen. "I'll join you guys in a minute. I think I need to take some meds."

But Max was focused on the stove. This sequence of events was all wrong. Mom was supposed to see the cupcakes when she opened the door. Smell them. That was the plan, and plans were supposed to work. Max was getting angry, which meant he smelled cat pee, and that wasn't too pleasant when it was mixed with chocolate.

"Max, are you OK?" asked Evelyn from behind him. *Give up the things you can't change*, Max told himself, which was something his therapist was always getting him to work on. *Breathe deep. Close your eyes.* "Fine," he said.

A few last-minute giggles erupted from the living room, followed by a flurry of *sssshhh*es. Max opened his eyes. He glanced toward the front of the house, then at the stove.

Before joining the others, he quickly flicked the oven temperature all the way up.

The living room lights were out. Everyone whispered nervously, hiding behind furniture. On the coffee table was a cookie-dough ice-cream cake with a sugar-photo of Mom, Dad, and Max. It was inscribed HAPPY BIRTHDAY, MICHELE! WE LOVE YOU!!! MAX, ALEX, & GEORGE. Streamers hung everywhere, along with collages of favorite family photos.

"I see them—quiet!"

At the urging of Max's dad, the room fell silent. Outside, a car engine grew louder, then stopped. Soft footsteps clomped up the front walk. A key was thrust into the lock, and the door slowly opened. Dad counted to three by holding up his fingers, then . . .

"Surprise!"